Praise for Anita Shreve's

The Stars Are Fire

"Long before Liane Moriarty was spinning her *Big Little Lies*, Shreve was spicing up domestic doings in beachfront settings with terrible husbands and third-act twists. She still is, as effectively as ever, this time with a narrative literally lit from within."   —*The New York Times Book Review*

"Like her sensational bestselling 1998 novel *The Pilot's Wife,* about a widow who discovers her pilot husband had a second family, *The Stars Are Fire* explores what happens in the secret spaces between married people.... Masterful ... lingers long after the last page is turned, like the smoke from a wildfire."   —*USA Today*

"Precise, evocative prose brings the story's vivid characters to life ... original and gripping."   —*People*

"Anita Shreve's books are reliably engrossing literary page-turners, never formulaic.... Shreve consistently creates complex characters and plots, often drawn from the historical record or from obscure headlines.... Then she tells their stories in unobtrusively elegant prose."
—*The Washington Post*

"This is a suspenseful and heartwarming story of not just overcoming but also growing in the face of great difficulty."
—*Booklist*

"This is sure to be a bestseller. Shreve's prose mirrors the action of the fire, with popping embers of action, licks of blazing rage, and the slow burn of lyrical character development. Absolutely stunning." —*Library Journal*
(starred review, "Editors' Spring Picks")

"I had the sense as I read Shreve's newest and eighteenth novel, *The Stars Are Fire*, that I was in the company of millions of phantom future readers who will adore this novel and devour it and recommend it to all their friends and book clubs. . . . Shreve's storytelling choices feel organically wedded to her writing, a winning and essentially magical alchemy. . . . It's all totally irresistible. Along with storytelling mojo and stylistic verve, this novel has an excellent, suspenseful premise: Grace's life is upended and ultimately transformed by a real-life historical catastrophe, the wildfires that spread through coastal Maine in October of 1947, following months of severe drought. . . . In fact, *The Stars Are Fire* is so virtuosic, so infallibly readable, it could very well sell more copies than all Shreve's others combined."
—Kate Christensen, *Portland Press-Herald*

"It is a book of small moments, a collection of seemingly simple themes that build to surprising and moving crescendos. Shreve's spare, economic prose suits her character's practicality and initial hesitance to determine the course of her own life. . . . Shreve's crisp writing becomes more expansive in the moments when her protagonist consciously stretches beyond the boundaries of her previously narrow life."

—*BookPage*

"One of the pleasures of reading *The Stars Are Fire* is Shreve's ability to impart an authentic feel of 1940s daily life. . . . Shreve's writing is lovely." —"The ARTery," WBUR.com

Anita Shreve

The Stars Are Fire

Anita Shreve is the *New York Times* bestselling author of seventeen previous novels that have been translated into thirty-six languages. She lives with her husband in New Hampshire.

www.anitashreve.com

Also by Anita Shreve

The Stars Are Fire

The Stars Are Fire

A Novel

ANITA SHREVE

VINTAGE CONTEMPORARIES

VINTAGE BOOKS

A Division of Penguin Random House LLC

New York

FIRST VINTAGE CONTEMPORARIES EDITION, MARCH 2018

The Library of Congress has cataloged the Knopf edition as follows:
Shreve, Anita.
The stars are fire: a novel / Anita Shreve. –First edition.
PS3569.H7385 S68 2017 c813'.54—dc23 2016032868

Vintage Books Trade Paperback ISBN: 978-0-345-80636-9
eBook ISBN: 978-0-385-35091-4

Book design by M. Kristen Bearse

www.vintagebooks.com

Printed in the United States of America
10 9 8 7 6 5 4 3 2 1

To my husband, with gratitude and love

Doubt thou the stars are fire;
Doubt that the sun doth move;
Doubt truth to be a liar;
But never doubt I love.

William Shakespeare, *Hamlet*

The Stars Are Fire

Wet

A spring of no spring. Grace pins Gene's khakis to a line that stretches diagonally over the yellow linoleum of the kitchen. Only heat from the stove will dry the cotton. She holds off on the towels, hoping for a good day tomorrow or the next. On the last beautiful afternoon, over two weeks ago, there was wash on the line in every front porch and backyard. With white sheets, undershirts, and rags flapping in the wind, it looked as though an entire town of women had surrendered.

Grace glances at her two children as they nap together in the carriage, the one with the big rubber wheels, the dark navy enameled chassis, and the white leather interior and trim. It is her prized possession, a gift from her mother when Claire was born. It takes up half the kitchen and blocks the hallway when not in use. Claire at twenty months is a hot sleeper and has soaked the collar of her playsuit. Tom, only five months old, is an easy baby. Grace sterilizes the glass bottles and rubber nipples in a saucepan on the stove. Her milk was fitful when she had Claire; she didn't even try with Tom.

When she sleeps with Gene in their marriage bed at night, Grace wears a nightgown, thin cotton in the summer, flannel in the winter. Gene is always naked. Though she would prefer to lie on her back, Gene almost always manages to turn her onto her stomach. She is not built for relations this way. How could she be, never having experienced the *god-awful joy* that Rosie, her next-door neighbor, once spoke of? On the other hand, the position must be good for making babies.

Apart from this unpleasantness, which doesn't seem important and which, in any event, is over fast, Grace thinks Gene a good husband. He is a tall man with thin hair the color of damp sand. He has midnight blue eyes and a short ropy scar on his chin that stays white no matter what color his face: an angry red, a blushing pink, a January pale, an August tan. He works six days a week as a surveyor, five of them on the Maine Turnpike project, a job that sometimes takes him away for three or four days at a stretch. She imagines his head full of mathematics and physics, measurements and geometry, and yet, when he returns home, he seems enthralled with his children. He is talkative at supper, and Grace knows she is lucky in this since so many of the wives complain about dull silences at home. While she holds Tom in her arms, Gene chats with Claire in her wooden high chair. Grace smiles. These are her happiest moments, with her family in harmony. In many ways, she thinks, her family is perfect. Two beautiful children, a boy and a girl; a husband who works hard at his job and doesn't resist chores at home. Every night, Gene washes the dishes, seldom complaining about the heavy line of garments that separates the sink from the dish drainer. They live in a shingled bungalow two blocks inland from the ocean. Good investment, Gene always says.

Before she goes to bed that night, Grace turns on a burner on the stove, correcting the flame to an inch high. She bends down, holding her hair so that she won't set it on fire, and lights the last cigarette of the day. The khakis must be dry by morning, and tomorrow she'll wash the pair Gene wore over the weekend. As she stands by the window, she can't see the pear tree, but she can hear the rain on its leaves, relentless, never-ending.

Please bring a dry day.

She turns on all the burners and adjusts the flames an inch high, knowing that nothing will catch fire in this wet. She weaves her way through T-shirts and underwear and climbs the stairs.

I wouldn't mind seeing the stars either.

Grace pauses at the landing, takes a breath, and then walks into the bedroom. She slips into her white flannel nightgown. The temperature, she reads on the thermometer just outside the bedroom window, is forty-two.

"More rain tomorrow," Gene says.

"How long?"

"Maybe the rest of the week."

Grace groans. "The house will get waterlogged and fall down."

"Never."

"Everything is damp. The pages of the books curl."

"I promise you they'll dry. Come to bed, Dove."

She has never been Gracie. Only Grace. And then Dove, with Gene. Grace doesn't feel like a dove, and she's sure she doesn't look anything like a dove, but she knows there's a sweetness in the nickname. She wonders if it means something that she doesn't have a fond or funny name for her husband.

In the morning, she wakes before Gene so that she can section the grapefruit and prepare his coffee, the grapefruit a rarity that will surprise him. Breakfast will be eggs and toast today, no bacon. Three eggs then. The meal has to last him until his bucket lunch. Ned Gardiner at the grocery store told her yesterday that bakers will now be making smaller bread loaves and one-crust pies as part of the Save Food for Europe campaign. Imagine. An entire continent, starving.

Gene never talks about his personal war as an engineer on B-17s, the one during which he got his ropy scar. The other husbands don't either.

She can hear Gene giving himself a sponge bath in the tiny washroom they have squeezed between the two bedrooms upstairs. They bathe once a week in the tin tub Gene keeps on the screened-in porch and drags into the kitchen. He uses her bathwater because it's too much of an effort to drag the tub out again and empty it onto the ground. Grace has thick brown hair that she cut short right after Tom was born. Gene wasn't fond of the cut, but her mother thought the new look highlighted her cheekbones and large blue eyes. It was the only time Grace can remember that her mother called her beautiful, an exclamation that escaped her like a bee sting. Gene, when he first met Grace, described her as pretty, which she understood as a description less than beautiful.

Grace, at the moment, doesn't mind what others think, because living with short hair, if not fashionable, is easier than dealing with pin curls or a set. She tucks it behind her ears. She looks good in a hat. Whenever she goes out she wears clip earrings.

Slightly above average in height, she is tall in heels. She lost the pregnancy weight fast after Tom: Two children under the age of two kept her running most days. She pictures her husband now, bare chested, wetting and soaping a washcloth, getting his face first, then his neck, and finally his underarms. Often he will scrub his wrists. She can hear him tap his razor against the sink. Is he whistling?

Grace wears no makeup except lipstick, a well-blotted mauve. It makes her lips look fuller, Gene says. When she talks to him, he stares at her mouth as if he might be hard of hearing.

She scratches a match against the box it came in and lights a cigarette, inhaling deeply. First of the morning.

"What section today?" she asks, savoring the wifely pleasure of watching Gene tear into his grapefruit.

"We're resurveying the Kittery portion to register the settling."

Gene has explained to her how he makes three-dimensional elevations and maps for engineers and contractors. She likes the names of the instruments and tools he peruses in catalogs—theodolites and transits, alidades and collimators—but she doesn't know precisely how they work. Once, when he was courting her, he took her to Merserve Hill and brought out his tripod and tried to teach her how to use the transit, but before she could look into the eyepiece, he positioned her by putting his hands around her waist, and she didn't hear what he said. She supposes Gene planned it that way. Grace would like to try the outing again and this time pay attention. If the rain ever stops. They could bring the children and make a picnic of it. Highly unlikely that her husband will put his hands around her waist now. Except for a peck when he leaves the house each day and another when he comes home, they seldom touch outside the bed.

"Doesn't the rain ruin the equipment?" she asks.

"We have special umbrellas. Tarps. What will you do today?"

"I might go over to Mother's."

He nods but doesn't look at her. He would rather she went to *his* mother's house for a visit. Relations between his wife and his mother are not all they should be. Does he wish for Grace to bake a two-crust apple pie and take it to her? Should she mention the bakers' new restrictions? Would he care or would that go into the category of "women's work," a subject that allows him to dismiss it?

"I've fixed up a canvas hood," she says.

"Have you now?" He raises his head and seems impressed. He might recognize a certain amount of engineering in the construction of a canvas hood for a carriage. But she would disappoint him if she told him how she did it. She doesn't use mathematics. Instead she fits and folds and cuts and fits and folds and cuts again, and then she sews. Well, she does measure.

She has rigged up a seat so that Claire can sit up in the carriage while Tom lies papoose-like beside her. Tom, the soft fuzz of his dark hair, the pudgy body with its disappearing folds, the warmth of his skin as he burbles; Claire, her white-blond hair in ringlets, short sentences emerging like radio bulletins through static and surprising Grace. Claire, from birth, has always stolen the limelight, first because of her astonishing beauty and now, as is emerging, because of her feistiness. Grace likes nothing more than to lie on her bed with Tom tucked beside her and Claire rolling to her side to put her face close to her mother's skin. Sometimes they all drift off for a short nap; at other times, they sing.

But as soon as they bump out the door, Claire begins to cry, in seeming sympathy with the rain. Grace knows that Claire's distress stems from the hood her mother so cleverly designed, the one through which the child can barely see. Or maybe not. Grace wants to cry, too.

Her boots have water in them before she reaches the dirt sidewalk. She notes the pink buds of the cherry tree in Rosie's front lawn. Will they bloom in the rain? She hopes so. It trickles down the edges of her clear plastic head scarf and under her collar. Grace turns onto the first set of stepping-stones she comes to, which leads her to Rosie's front door. Her friend will be in her tangerine bathrobe, her hair in curlers, but she will invite them in with enthusiasm. Grace cannot face another day trapped inside her own house. She has read all of her "kitchen-table" books, novels not good enough to put inside the glassed-in shelves at the entrance to the dining room. The "kitchen-table" books are full of plot and romance and intrigue.

"I brought half a grapefruit," Grace crows when Rosie opens the door.

Rosie waves them all in, even the baby carriage, which Grace leaves in the vestibule. Looking at her friend's face, hair, robe, and curlers, all of which more or less match, she imagines Rosie as a column of tangerine flame. Rosie is attractive, even in curlers, but slovenly. Gene once used the word *squalor* to describe the household. Grace objected then, though she partially agrees.

Rosie scoops Claire up into her arms and at once begins to remove the little girl's red rain hat and matching slicker. Claire then sinks into Rosie's chest, and after a moment, Rosie gives the child a fierce hug. But then Claire is on the floor looking for Freddie, the cocker spaniel. Grace, with Tom in her arms, rummages through her handbag and finds the half-grapefruit, carefully wrapped in waxed paper. She gives it to Rosie.

"Where did you get this?" Rosie asks as if she were holding a jeweled egg.

"At Gardiner's. He got a shipment of six. He let me buy one."

This isn't true. He gave it to Grace, and she didn't object.

"He must have a thing for you," Rosie teases.

Grace stares Rosie down, and then she begins to smile.

"Can you imagine?" hoots Rosie.

"No!" says Grace, laughing. Rosie squeals at the image.

Ned Gardiner must eat half his produce in the back room, they have decided, because he weighs close to three hundred pounds. His soft stomach hangs over his low belt, and Grace often speculates about how he and his wife, Sophia, once a dark beauty but now nearly two hundred pounds herself, manage in bed. Then Grace feels a pang of conscience for having laughed at a man who gave her a grapefruit.

"I'll split it with you," Rosie says.

"I've had my half," Grace lies. "You go ahead."

Rosie's house seems to be full of *things,* though Grace notes the lack of a high chair, playpen, or Bathinette. Rosie, too, has a toddler and an infant, a familiar configuration in the neighborhood. Claire has Rosie's toddler, Ian, in a headlock.

"Tim says he's had to go out time and time again to tow cars out of the mud," Rosie remarks as she slowly sucks each grapefruit section. She closes her eyes with pleasure. Tim owns half of an automobile repair shop on Route 1.

"Gene says the ground is so wet, the farmers can't set their seeds."

Grace blows smoke away from Tom's face and takes another pull. "It will end," she says without conviction.

"Coffee, yes?" Rosie asks when she has thoroughly squeezed the life out of the fruit. Grace notes that there's a seed stuck in a fold of Rosie's robe. Eddie, Rosie's youngest, has begun to cry. Grace wasn't aware that the infant was in the room.

She watches as her friend snatches blankets from the couch and picks up a pink baby, Rosie's coloring exactly. Grace might so easily have sat on Eddie, she thinks with a blip of horror. Containerize, her own mother once told Grace, as if imparting the secret of sanity. Her mother meant children as well as dry goods.

"Tonight's shopping night," Grace says to her friend, who has opened her robe to reveal a blond nipple and a blue-veined breast. "Need anything?"

Every Thursday night, payday for Gene, he picks Grace and the children up as soon as he pulls into the driveway, and they go straight to Shaw's. Steak for that night, calves' liver, bacon, codfish cakes, puffed rice, tomato soup, bologna, eggs, butter, chipped beef, canned salmon, canned peas, hot dogs, buns, baked beans, brown bread, and Rice Krispies. Gene removes his pay packet from his pocket and counts out the bills and quarters and nickels and dimes and pennies with care. Everything else—milk, bread, hamburger—can be bought at Gardiner's when needed. Grace tries to have some amount of protein every night, though by Wednesday the meal is Spanish rice with bits of bacon.

"How are you drying the diapers?" Rosie asks.

"I've had to hire a service," Grace confesses, "but I'll let it go as soon as the rain stops."

There's a moment of silence. Tim's pay packet is not as full as Gene's. "Jesus, Grace, how can you stand the stink of the diaper pail?"

————

Rosie once told her, without any embarrassment, that she and Tim made love at least once a day. Grace, who immediately felt poorer than Rosie, wondered if that was why her friend always had on a bathrobe. To be ready. One evening, when Grace and Gene were sitting on the porch, she heard a wail from next door that was distinctly sexual. She knew Gene heard it, too, though neither of them said a word. Within a minute, Gene left the porch.

Grace's house is a testament to containerization. A playpen with toys in it sits in a corner of the alcove attached to the living room. The Bathinette can be wheeled to the sink. The bassinet stays in the dining room in a corner. The toddler bed with railings is in the children's room upstairs, as is Tom's crib. The old wooden high chair that Grace's mother used sits just to the right of Gene's chair in the dining room. The small amount of counter space in the kitchen is free of any flour or utensils. She washes clothes at the basement sink and uses a washboard.

Perhaps because of this, she hates to leave Rosie's house, with its cereal spilled on the kitchen table, the heap of clothes by the cellar door that the dog sniffs at in search of underwear. The couch is a toss of blankets and pillows and magazines and sometimes a surprise: On previous visits, Grace found a hairbrush and a screwdriver. On the coffee table, cups have made rings, and glasses come off as if stuck. But when she's in Rosie's house, she experiences an intensely pleasurable "let-down" sensation in her womb and in her shoulders, not dissimilar to the letting-down of her milk when she briefly nursed Claire. She'd have done a better job of it, she thinks, if she'd lived with Rosie.

In her own house, over the fireplace mantel, Gene has hung an elevation he did of their own property. It's framed in simple black, and below that hangs a rifle that doesn't work. She isn't sure why Gene has put it there, except that it seems to be a common decoration in New England. Around the fireplace stand an old brass bed warmer and a set of fireplace tools. In the winter, she doesn't feel truly warm until the fire is lit at night and on Sundays. Together she and Gene picked out the wallpaper in the living room, poring through sample books until the patterns began to blur. She made the slipcovers herself to match the green of the toile walls, and she fashioned the cream drapes at the windows. She learned to sew in high school, but she taught herself the more advanced skills. Sometimes Gene had to help because she had trouble thinking three-dimensionally.

Rosie is different three-dimensionally than Grace. Grace is softer, though each woman has a slim waist despite two children. As dark as Grace's features are, Rosie's are pale orange. She has no visible eyebrows or eyelashes, and her hair, stick straight and thin, needs the boost of pin curls. Rosie dresses herself and the children, when she rouses them all to go out, in navy or dark green. Anything else, and they would appear to float away.

Grace would spend all day with Rosie if she could, but when she checks her thin gold-colored Timex, she sees that she's already late for her visit to her mother's.

———

When Grace walks into her mother's home, she has a sensation of great warmth and safety. This doesn't occur in her own house despite the fact that at night and on Sundays, there's a man to protect her. Her mother, Marjorie, doesn't have a man to protect her and has learned how not to have one. Even in the vestibule and before she has gotten the children out of the carriage, the familiar scent—from the walls, the rugs, the coats hanging on hooks—transports Grace to a universe before she met Gene, before life became uncertain and even a little frightening.

"Saving the starving of Europe," Grace says as she hoists aloft the apple pie she made in the morning. She skimped on the height and decoration of the crust edges to allow for enough pastry to make two crosspieces over the fruit. The crust browned up nicely, she thinks. She likes the fact that her mother doesn't say, "Oh, you shouldn't have" or "Aren't you a dear?" Merely "Thank you" does for her mother.

Some have taken Marjorie's taciturn manner for a lack of graciousness, but it isn't, and her good friends know this. There are two, Evelyn and Gladys, women who stayed close to her mother long after the refreshments at the church hall had been eaten and her father lowered into the earth.

Grace's father died before the war, his foot catching in a line, the rope hauling him off his lobster boat in forty-degree water in January. Death would have been instantaneous, Dr. Franklin told her mother, which was little solace. The ocean is so cold that most lobstermen don't even learn how to swim. It took until the war was over and Grace married before her mother's crippling mourning came to an end. At forty-six, she has said that she will never wed again, and Grace believes her. So apparently do the men of Hunts Beach, for Grace has never heard of one trying to court her. It is as if her husband's death dragged her mother's beauty into the ground with him.

They eat at the old kitchen table, the pie as good as Grace hoped. Better still, the coffee that her mother percolates with a broken egg to catch the grounds. With Claire in her lap, Grace feeds the girl bits of apple and crust, which seems to ratchet up her appetite to an extent she hasn't seen before. She gives Claire her dish of pie and a child's spoon. Her daughter falls into a frenzy of lust.

"Sweet tooth, that one," her mother says as she croons to Tom. She has her housecoat buttoned up over her gray winter dress. When Tom begins pushing his face into the fabric, she says, "Why don't you put on a pan of water? You know where the bottles and nipples are. I've got fresh milk in the fridge."

Claire, finally sated, sits benumbed in the midst of her blocks on the floor. Grace's mother gets by with monthly donations from the League of Lobstermen, who give part of their paychecks to women who have been left widowed because of the sea. That and the payments from her husband's death benefits tide her over, the policy a result of a life insurance salesman who knew how to talk to a fisherman.

Rosebud cups on hooks. Colonial stenciling near the ceiling. A braided rug under the wooden table. The extra sink where her father washed up to get the fish stink off him before he went to his family. The rubber doorstop. The kitchen cupboard with the drawers that stick. The place where the blue and white linoleum has always been cracked. The six-over-six kitchen window at the sink that her mother has always resisted adorning. The cupboard where the cereal is kept. The mica in the oven door. Grace wonders if Tom and Claire will one day visit her and have a similar sensation of home. Each house has its own signature, unknown to all except the grown children who go back to visit.

Grace would like to talk about what happens in her marriage bed, but no sexual word has ever passed between mother and daughter, a handicap when Grace was twelve and got her period and had no idea what was going on. Eventually she guessed because of the source of the bleeding. She found, in the bathroom cabinet, hidden behind the towels on the first shelf, a package of Kotex and what looked to be a circular piece of sewing elastic with clips hanging from it. She had no choice but to fasten the pad as best she could. The next morning before school, her mother put her hand on Grace's shoulder as Grace sat at the kitchen table eating Rice Krispies. The hand lingered, freezing Grace, but signaling to the daughter that the mother knew. Grace was surprised and yet not. The day before, she'd spent an hour and a half in the bathroom.

While in the bathroom during that hour and a half, Grace explored the cupboard in hopes of finding a less awkward way to secure the pad. She came across, on the top shelf, an aged pink rubber bag with a long hose connected to it, an item that she couldn't imagine a use for but knew it had to do with sex since it had been hidden on the highest shelf. It wasn't until she was about to be married, and her mother insisted on Grace having a checkup with Dr. Franklin before the wedding (perhaps in hopes that the doctor would impart the facts of life), and Dr. Franklin told her that douching wasn't necessary, wasn't even particularly good for the flora of the vagina, that Grace caught on. She blushed, but not for the information. Instead, she colored at the image suddenly planted in her mind of her mother with the apparatus.

On her way home from her mother's, Grace asks herself why it is she can't tell Gene how she feels about the way they make love in bed. After all, there are only two of them in the marriage. Is it that she fears that either Gene or she would explode if she were to do that? Isn't it enough to know her own distress about sex? If Gene were to die, would she go into a deep rocking mourning as her mother did?

That night, after Grace has put the children to bed, she slips her slicker from a hook and walks down her front path to the sidewalk. She has maybe a minute before Gene will notice her absence. It isn't much, but it's everything. She is who she is, nothing more. Free to note the fog rolling in, the leaves letting go of raindrops. That the older couple across the street have already gone to bed. That her hair is frizzing lightly in the mist. That she doesn't care. That her children are inside asleep and don't need her. That by morning she won't be able to see out the windows. That she will probably never learn to drive. That she can move only the distance her feet can take her. That she could begin to go on long walks with the babies in spite of the weather. That someone will notice these errand-free excursions and begin to wonder. That Gene will say, when she returns to her family in less than a minute, that he is going up. That she must listen to the inflection in his voice and watch his face to know if she is to go up with him, or whether she can sit at the kitchen table and have another cigarette.

When Grace undresses for bed that night, she doesn't put on her nightgown, but slides naked into the bed, uncovering her breasts so that Gene, when he climbs the stairs, will see. She doesn't know if she is doing this because the posture is a challenge to him, or if in remembering the early days together she wants to have that again. Gene, when he reaches the room, looks surprised and turns his back to her to undress. Grace wants to cover herself, but doesn't. This one night, is that so much to ask?

Gene comes to bed hard and flings off all the covers. Too late, Grace realizes that there will be nothing gentle tonight. She has set a challenge after all. He enters her at once, when she's not ready, and the thrust is painful. He pounds, as if knowingly, at the cut necessary to give birth to Claire and Tom, the place where she is most tender, and she has to bite her cheek to keep from crying out. She tries once to shift him, but he pins her arms back behind her head with one of his, and that posture and her helplessness set him off. He roars, lets her arms go, pulls out, and faces the other way, leaving Grace to be the one to locate the covers and pull them up and over.

When she returns to the bed, she is sore and has to hold the sheet to the place where she suspects she is bleeding. It seems unlikely now that she will ever have a fond nickname for her husband.

Three weeks after the unspeakable night that has not been repeated, Grace takes what has become her nightly walk to the sidewalk. She notes, in addition to the growing number of puddles that dot the dirt road and the lilac trees bent double with their waterlogged and dead flowers, a swath of blue at the western horizon beneath dark cloud. Her body fills with joy. Tomorrow the wash will hang from an outside line, and she will dry her hair in the sun.

Dry

A gap between two rows of houses gives Grace an exuberant pie-shaped view of sparkling water, the sun high in the east over the ocean. She runs out the door in her flower-printed robe and looks at the blue sky and the cherry tree and raises her arms in a mixture of thanks and relief. She catches a glimpse of tangerine, and Rosie is beside her, laughing at Grace and their good fortune. "Thank God," says Rosie.

"Finally," says Grace.

She opens all the windows to let the fresh air in and dances through the rooms. She empties the linen cabinet, washing the contents and hoping for sun-dried sheets by dinnertime. The towels will dry scratchy in the breezes, the way they should. A soft towel is a coddle, doesn't get the dead skin off.

Before ten in the morning, the town of Hunts Beach has happily surrendered, white sheets flapping along with colored towels and blue shirts and pink dresses and gingham aprons and green bedspreads. It's a marvel, Grace thinks, as she walks the neighborhood streets, the soil underfoot emitting steam in the cool, dry air. Every so often, a slight wind causes a spotty and brief rain shower from tall oaks. Mildew begins to disappear as if by magic. Nearly every window in every house is open, even though the temperature can't be above fifty degrees. She tips her face to the sun as she walks. Life-giving. Grace thinks the fluttering sheets and clothes are not, after all, a sign of surrender, but instead a symbol of survival.

Gene comes home early, before Grace has even started dinner. All the wicker baskets she owns are full of loosely folded laundry ready for the iron tomorrow. She sees his car, towing a trailer, from the side window. He parks at the edge of the grass, close to the screened porch. Grace opens the door to see what's under the tarp, and with a flourish, Gene reveals a secondhand wringer–washing machine, a present to Grace. She knows precisely what the gift represents, a belated apology for a night that doesn't bear thinking about. But she can't help but be intrigued by the object, its big agitator tub and its wondrous wooden rollers that squeeze the water out of the wash more efficiently than any pair of practiced hands can do.

Together, they roll the heavy machine down the shallow ramp of the trailer and stare at it on the grass. All wringer washers are on casters, Gene explains, because they're meant to be rolled to the sink so the rubber hose can be attached to the spigot. It's tough going moving a washer across the lawn, but Grace wants to get the job done before too many neighbors see. A wringer washer is a prize. Only Merle, Gene's mother, and Dr. Franklin's wife have them as far as Grace knows. She and Gene heft the machine up and over the lip of the screened porch and then again into the kitchen. Claire, in the playpen in the living room, squeals when she hears her father's voice.

"We'll do a small wash now," he says, "just to test it out."

Gene picks up Claire, brings her into the kitchen, and sets her on the floor. She, too, is mesmerized by the device, all white and bigger than a person. Gene demonstrates how to use a series of rubber washers if necessary to tighten the seal between the hose and the spigot. As Grace watches the tub fill with water, Gene runs to the car and returns with a bottle of Vano. "You'll need this for the machine," he says.

He lifts Claire to watch the soapsuds grow until they reach the lip of the barrel. Grace rushes upstairs and collects a pile of pillow slips and tosses them into the tub just the way Gene instructs her. When he plugs the machine in, the agitator begins to turn back and forth.

"Amazing," Grace says.

Claire claps her hands.

They watch for ten minutes. Gene turns off the spigot and guides the hose over the sill of the kitchen window. He flips a lever near the bottom of the washer. The soapy water empties onto the ground, leaving the pillow slips covered in suds at the bottom. Grace fills the tub half full and agitates the slips to rinse them. Then, with Gene placing his hands over hers, he demonstrates the right amount of tension needed to pull the slips through the wringer.

With a stiff pillow slip in her hand, Grace feels Gene tilting her face up to his. He leaves a gentle kiss on her lips. He calls her Dove.

Can a wringer washer save a marriage? She thinks the answer a probable yes.

Over the next several weeks, Grace happily launders every piece of clothing and linen in the house, pulling each item through the wringer. She has a few mishaps, such as when the hose with the soapy water falls back into the house and sprays the kitchen, barely missing the radio. Or when, transfixed by the agitator, she drops a piece of toast from a saucer into the washer. She puts her hand in before she stops the agitator and gets a wallop for her trouble. She pulls out the plug and tries to catch the toast with a sieve. The bits disintegrate as she touches them. The next morning when she irons the garments from that wash, she finds tiny studs of toast stuck to her favorite blouse.

She washes so many clothes that all of the outdoor lines fill. She has to put one across the screened porch and one that again bisects the kitchen. The pile of ironing grows massive.

Gene, weaving his way through the kitchen and into the living room, tells Grace that water costs money.

On a summer Saturday, which still seems to Grace like the beginning of the weekend even though Gene goes to work on that day, she dresses the children in light clothing and takes them to the beach. The sand is cool but dry. It seems that everyone from Hunts Beach and beyond has had the same idea because the seawall is lined with cars of every color and make. Grace unfolds the quilt she brought and floats it to the sand. She sets up a tent of gauze for Tom when he falls asleep. Reluctantly, she unbuttons her housedress to reveal her two-piece white bathing suit, the one with the halter top and short skirt. She knows it will flatter her skin when she tans. Though she keeps her eyes fixed on the sea, she's aware of heads turning her way. She strips Claire to her red polka-dotted suit and together they walk to the water. Though the Atlantic is still frigid, Grace waits until her ankles are numb. She plays with Claire in the shallows, each splashing the other. The sound of the surf calms Grace—it wipes out individual voices. Claire likes the gentle action of the ocean drawing her out and pushing her back in again. Grace sits at the edge of the sea and watches Claire until she lowers herself and lets her body be dragged and drawn with Claire's. The daughter giggles to see her mother in the water with her, and Grace laughs, too. The movement of the sea is rhythmic and sensual—she remembers this vividly from her own childhood—and before long, she like Claire has sand inside her bathing suit. They kick their feet and create suds. Grace suggests making a castle, but no sooner has Grace upended a pile of packed sand than Claire smashes her hand through it. She seems to think this is the game at hand.

After another hour, Tom, who has always been an unusually good baby, whimpers. Grace lifts away the gauze she used for a tent and discovers that her son's face and neck are bright pink. When she presses a finger to his cheek, it leaves a clear white spot that slowly fades.

"Oh, Tom," she says, lifting him up.

Would Rosie have given her child a sunburn? Never. Rosie would have come with an umbrella and a little cap for Eddie and would have held the infant the entire time.

A sunburn doesn't fade in a day. By dinnertime, Tom has crinkles around his eyes. Gene says, when he walks in the door and catches sight of his son, "What the hell happened to Tom?"

This is just before he says, "My mother's in the hospital."

"For what?" Grace asks.

"Cancer in the breast."

The news hits Grace at the back of her head. She offers to get a babysitter. "We can go to see her. I've got new roses we can take."

"I've already been," Gene says, putting his equipment on top of the kitchen table, as if the plates and cutlery weren't already there. "I've been there all afternoon."

Grace sits heavily, coffee crystals falling from a spoon. "When did you find out?"

"Last week, when I took the kids over. She's having the surgery Monday."

"And you didn't say anything to me?"

"She didn't want you to fuss over her."

"I don't fuss, you know that."

Gene gazes at his raw son. "They're going to take the adrenal gland and her ovaries, too."

"My God," says Grace. "Why the adrenal gland?" She is fairly sure she couldn't point to the adrenal gland in her own body.

"Get rid of all the estrogen. Same with the ovaries."

"Both?" Grace asks.

"Ovaries?"

"Breasts," she says.

"Of course," Gene answers, looking at his wife as if she were a moron.

When Grace is honest with herself, she finds that no part of her wants Merle to die. If that were to happen, Grace would lose her husband to grief, and her children would have no Nana.

"Maybe after the surgery," Gene says mollifyingly. His mother's illness is not, after all, Grace's fault. "We'll visit together. I'm going back now, just to calm her fears."

"Is she frightened?"

"Wouldn't you be?"

Gene kisses Claire and Tom and opens the door.

"Give her my love," Grace calls, surprising Gene and herself with the word, one she has never used in any situation involving her mother-in-law.

"I will," Gene says, but Grace knows that he won't. Why upset his mother with a name Merle can't abide?

Because Tom's skin begins to peel, Grace deliberately misses an appointment with Dr. Franklin.

After the surgery, Gene's mother wants to die. Specifically, she believes she is no longer a woman.

Gene spends more and more time with his mother, which turns out to be fortuitous, because Mrs. Holland dies ten days after surgery from a blood clot that travels to the heart. Gene believes his mother went willingly. Grace, who never had a chance to visit, believes that when the clot hit, Gene's mother didn't know or wish a thing.

"How's Gene?" Rosie asks a few days after the funeral when she and Grace are sitting in Rosie's backyard watching the children. Rosie has completed several loads of wash in Grace's machine.

"He's managing."

"Truth."

"He's awful. I feel guilty. He makes me feel guilty."

"How so?"

"If I had gone to see his mother once in a while, she wouldn't have gotten breast cancer."

"That's the stupidest thing I ever heard."

"Yes, well." She thinks a moment. "But you know what? It feels true."

It feels true that she might have wished her mother-in-law gone. Not dead, just gone. It feels true that she caused the hurtful night in bed, even though she sort of knows she didn't. She does know, however, that it's been too long since she and Gene have had sex. It feels sort of true that she doesn't want to start up again.

One morning, when Grace is feeding the children, she hears, through the screened window, the surf smash against the rocks two streets over at the beach. It isn't that she has never heard the surf from her house before; it's that it seems especially noisy this clear summer's day, a paradox that perplexes her.

With Claire walking beside her and Tom in the carriage under a small umbrella Grace rigged to the hood of the carriage, she visits the beach. She can't get any closer than the sidewalk opposite the seawall, breeched every time a tall wave comes at it. She has never seen the surf so high. She notes that the residents of the houses that sit directly across from the seawall have come out to stare. Claire jumps up and down and shivers with delight and fear. Just as it seems that a wave will send its spray so high that it will cross the street and catch her, it pounds the wall and slithers away in the undertow.

A woman Grace has never seen before stands beside her and says, "If it takes the house, I got nothing."

"It won't do that. There's no wind."

"It isn't even high tide yet," the woman, in a green house-dress, points out.

If Grace paid any attention to the tide chart that Gene pinned to the inside of the cellar door, she would know this. "There must have been a storm out to sea."

"Beats me. Scary as hell though." The woman seems to have a small head, but it's an illusion because it's covered in pin curls. She must have bad eyesight, though: Few women would wear glasses outside the home. Hers are oval in slender gold frames. "You live on the street, too? I haven't seen you around," the woman asks.

"I live two streets back."

"Oh well then, you're all right." The woman stares at Grace's children. "George and me, we couldn't have them."

"I'm sorry," Grace says, taken aback by the revelation. "If you wanted them, I mean."

"I wanted them all right. As for George, I can't say. He's long gone." Arms crossed, the woman asks through thin, tight lips, "You like your husband?"

"I do."

"You hang on to him. Life's too damn hard without one."

Grace watches her retreat into her house. Will she board up her windows? Fill sandbags? Should Grace have offered to help? How the woman must hate her and her house safely two streets back with a husband and two children in it.

The surf rises as high as the trees behind her. The spray wets the road. What are these messages from elsewhere? It's impossible at this moment not to think the sea menacing. To give it a mind, and an angry one at that.

In the evening, when Grace is making dinner, Rosie calls to her over the side fence to tell her of the accident. When the waves settled, two men and a young boy, maybe seven or eight years old, visited the beach to fish. One of the men went into the water to untangle his line and was swept out to sea in a riptide, a not uncommon occurrence after a storm. The other man ran for help while the boy screamed and did jumping jacks on the sand.

"The fisherman drowned, and the lifesaving service is waiting for his body to wash ashore," Rosie says. "Nobody in town knows the men."

"And what about the boy?" Grace asks.

"It was his father. Awful, isn't it?"

A few minutes later, after Rosie leaves, Grace stands with a potato and a peeler in her hands, her wrists resting against the lip of the sink, and cries. She didn't for Merle, and yet she does for a fatherless boy and a man she has never known. The sea claimed its prize after all.

"What's wrong?" Gene asks as he walks into the house.

"Onions."

She can't tell Gene about the accident without fear of tearing up. Gene will register once again that she didn't weep for his mother.

Gene's grief is as Grace imagined it. He hardly speaks at the dinner table. Even Claire has stopped chatting to him. Usually, he will say one sentence to Grace, as if fulfilling his husbandly duty. More often than not, it's an odd fact she can't do anything with.

"You can go a mile a minute on the Turnpike."

"That's fast."

Gene doesn't respond. He's done for the evening.

Rosie says, "Give him time. When Tim's father died, it took him two years to get back to normal."

"My mother, too," Grace says, rounding four down to two. "But these are important years for Claire and Tom."

"Gene doesn't interact with them at all?" Rosie asks.

"Nothing."

Rosie dips her fingers into the sand. She's fully clothed and has on a wide-brimmed hat and sunglasses while she sits under an umbrella. Even so, she can only stay an hour on the beach. Today the waves run like children up the sand.

"How is he in bed?" Rosie asks.

Grace blushes, hoping her tan hides her embarrassment, her despair, her relief. "The same," she says.

"Tim was a madman. It was all he wanted to do."

"Proving he was still alive," Grace says.

"One part of him was alive all right." Rosie flops back onto the sand, stretching her arms over her head. "I couldn't walk for months," she cries, making it clear she loved every minute.

Grace finds this nearly incomprehensible. Is Rosie to be envied or pitied? Envied, if it makes her as happy as it seems to. It's an arena in which Grace can add nothing, Gene not having been near her in more than two months.

Grace decides it's her duty to help to relieve her husband's grief. She gives herself a sponge bath in the washroom and dresses in her cotton nightgown. She lies on her stomach in the bed and draws the nightgown high up on her thighs. She has left the top sheet to dangle from the foot of the bed. This is as clear a signal as she can possibly give her husband without discussing the matter.

She can hear Gene's tread on the stairway. He walks into the room and stops short. He seems to be looking at her, but she can't hear the sounds of him undressing. No belt unbuckling, no stepping out of his shoes, no sliding of cloth along his legs. She bites her lip and puts her face directly into the pillow. She's aware of him sitting on his side of the bed, the mattress depressing, then the sounds of the belt, the shoes, the pants. He lies beside her and brings the sheet up, making sure it covers her shoulders, almost but not quite touching her with his fingers. Then the slight tug on the sheet as he rolls away from her.

Embarrassment paralyzes Grace, and it's not until she

hears Gene snore that she dares to move her body so that she lies on her side, facing away from him. For an hour, she is awake. Does grief depress a man's sexual drive? It didn't depress Tim's. Does her husband no longer find her attractive? Did he dislike Grace's display? What would happen, she wonders, if she turned in the bed and shook him awake and asked him why he ignored her? Would he pretend not to know what she was talking about?

A new sensation claims her then, a drawing down of hope, of contentment diminishing and sinking into her stomach. She endures the feeling, not quite understanding it, for as long as she can bear it. Then, as if fighting for her life, she wrests the sheet away from her and stands. She descends the stairs and finds her cigarettes in the kitchen. With shaking fingers, she lights one and takes a long drag. The panic eases, and she sits at the kitchen table. The kitchen is hers. Well, it's always been hers, but in the dark there are no chores to do, leaving it an oasis. She lets the air through the screen wash over her face. Her shoulders relax, and she leans against the chair. There's a rustling in the rich summer foliage. From somewhere, a snippet of music, a voice. Under the nearly full moon, the house behind hers shines white. She flips her ashes into a glass on the table, and the disturbance of the ash sends a distinctive smell her way. Gin? She holds up the glass. There's a half inch of liquid at the bottom. Does Gene have a drink when she goes up to bed? A quick one to steady his nerves? To drown his sorrows? She remembers coming down in the morning and finding glasses in the sink. Water glasses, she thought. He must have rinsed those out well. But this one smells of ashes and gin. For how long has he been drinking in secret? She ponders the wisdom of leaving the glass with the ash in it on the table, so that he will know she saw it. She might even leave the stub of her cigarette there, too. Which raises the question of whether she was meant to see the glass, to know that he was drinking.

A succession of dry sunny days is something to discuss, to remark upon. Brides in veils walk out of the Methodist church believing the weather a benevolent sign from Heaven. Grace, with her children in the carriage, watches them and tries to decide which couples will be happy together and which will not. The bride in the satin cap that allows her veil to billow out behind her, and who clearly cares more about the picture that is being taken of her than she does about the groom, even removing his hand from her arm, is doomed, Grace thinks. The bride who flinches at the big openmouthed kiss her new husband bestows upon her, causing her to trip over her own dress, will have a tough go of it. But the young woman in the pale blue bridal gown, who walks out of the church talking in whispers to her husband, who bends down to hear her and then smiles, as if at a private joke, has it made. The brides delight Grace. New life, new possibilities. She holds Claire up so that she can see them.

"Isn't she beautiful!" Grace exclaims.

The muggy days of late August upon them, Grace drops a plate in the sink with the realization that she has missed her period for three months. She sits heavily at the kitchen table, her hands gone cold. She feels her abdomen, which tells her nothing. She balls the cloth of her skirt into her fists. She closes her eyes and counts.

Seconds later, she remembers the only night that could have produced the child. She puts her forehead to the table and counts again.

She sits up straight. The baby inside her is a product of a terrible night. Gene will know. He can add as well as she.

When the child inside her is born, Tom will be fourteen months old. She will have three children under the age of three. Not quite Irish triplets, but close.

She studies the wrinkles in her skirt where her fists balled the cloth. She's aware of sweat trickling inside her sleeveless blouse. She takes a dish towel and sticks it straight down between her breasts to wipe away the moisture there and then lays the towel at the back of her neck. Gene will say they can't afford three children. Or perhaps, feeling guilty, he'll say nothing at all.

She will have to tell Gene. No, she won't. She'll let him look at her and wonder. He will have to say it aloud. By then he'll have done the calculations and will know the night on which they conceived the child. Grace wonders if the way the sperm is put into the woman affects the personality of the child. No, of course not. She knows a wives' tale when she hears one.

The heat reduces them to looser versions of themselves. Grace lacks the energy to cook a proper meal, but can't get away with sandwiches. Some afternoons she picks up the hose in the backyard, bends her head, and lets the cool water

run down her neck and back and hair, shivering with physical pleasure. At night she can't bear the cotton nightgown,
the fan at the window moving sweltering air from outside to
inside. She worries about Tom, who develops a bad diaper
rash. Grace knows she has to visit Dr. Franklin to confirm
the pregnancy. Her mother guesses soon after Grace knows.
Grace says, "I don't want it."

Her mother's eyes widen. "Promise me," she says.

"I promise," Grace replies, knowing there's no alterna-
tive. Perhaps if she lived in Portland or Boston, she would
know where to go for such a thing. But she's never heard of
anyone in Hunts Beach who could help her get rid of a fetus.
Probably Dr. Franklin knows how, but she can't ask him. He
wouldn't do it anyway.

During the first week of September, Grace begins to wish for
rain. All the brilliant sunshine feels unnatural. She knows
others think it, too, but don't mention it for fear of triggering
the endless rains of spring. As if a thought could trigger
weather.

Grace makes herself bigger dresses. Her mother buys her a
maternity blouse and helps her daughter let out the elastic
in her skirts. The first evening she dons these clothes, Gene
says, when he walks into the kitchen, "You're pregnant."

"You noticed."

"How far are you along?"

"Guess."

There's a long silence. Grace knows she's on dangerous
ground.

"Are you happy about it?" asks Gene.

"Are you?"

Grace doesn't expect an answer, and she doesn't need one.

"I hear the water level in the lakes and ponds is low," he says.

"Is that right?"

"I'll be out mowing the lawn."

Through the window, Grace watches her husband push the mower, trailing clouds of dust behind him.

Grace makes an appointment with Dr. Franklin, a man who wastes no time in small talk, who enters houses and walks straight up the stairs to the patient's room before the family even knows he's there. He studies Grace's chart.

"I thought so," he says. "This is your third in less than two years."

"More or less."

With a gesture, he makes her spread her legs. "You need any information about protection?" he asks as he inserts his fingers into her vagina.

"No," she says, "but my husband might."

She has never used this smart tone with the doctor. He knows her as intimately as anyone, she supposes. He brought her into the world.

"You're how old?" he asks as he manipulates her insides.

Grace winces with the discomfort. "Twenty-three."

"You might think of slowing down," he says, withdrawing his hands.

Grace doesn't know how to answer this. Does he mean

slow down the lovemaking? She can hardly slow down something that never happens.

"You can sit up now."

Grace does as asked, drawing the gown across her breasts, which he has already seen and palpated. The office smells the same each time she visits—a mix of chemicals she can't name. When she was a child, the smells frightened her, and she had to be dragged across the threshold. Now she finds them an odd comfort.

"You're not happy about this, are you?" he asks as he wipes his hands. He is getting to be an older man, she sees now, his hair nearly white, his glasses not quite hiding the bags under his eyes.

"It's too soon."

"In some countries they wouldn't say so, but they wear out their women. We don't want to wear you out though, do we?"

She already feels worn out. She thinks of all the extra years of diapers and bottles.

"But you'll be in the enviable position, five years from now, of having had your babies, and of having a close-knit, ready-made family."

She forms a snappy reply, but there's no point in taking out her anger on this kind man who wants only to help.

"The pregnancy and delivery will cost eighty dollars," he says. "I know it's more than Tom cost, but I had to raise my prices by five dollars this year."

"That's fine," she says.

Abruptly he says to get dressed, and then he leaves the

room. If he had something to tell her about the pregnancy, he would have. She and the baby must be all right.

The waiting room is full of patients.

Beautiful day melds into beautiful day. The beach becomes so crowded that not a single blanket will fit after ten o'clock in the morning. Claire begs for the wading pool as soon as she wakes up. Grace dangles Tom in the tepid water. The icehouse runs low, and there are days at a time when Grace has no refrigeration in the kitchen. She and Rosie begin to shop every day at Gardiner's so that they can eat what is fresh and not be worried about cold storage. The corn is good. The tomatoes are fleshy. Cantaloupes are as small as softballs, and watermelons enormous. At night Gene and she eat the watermelons outdoors and spit the seeds into the grass.

One evening, after the kids are asleep, Gene says, "Let's go to bed."

Grace doesn't know whether this means that he is tired or that he wants to make love.

She has her answer in the bed, when he faces her, side by side. His penis is hard, and he makes her feel it, but when she lifts her leg and shifts so that he can enter her, his penis softens. Grace, worried because she knows she has to make this work, begins to stroke him, but she must be doing it wrong, because he stops her hand and says, "I'm sorry."

She says, "Don't be."

After they have broken apart, Grace wonders, for the first time, if Gene is somehow just as perplexed as she is.

Might he, in his own way, be trying as hard to make sense of the marriage he is in? Grace doesn't feel a flood of love, however, but rather a sensation of pity. She doesn't want to pity her husband.

A fine haze is on the horizon when Gene drives Grace and the children to his mother's house, now officially Gene's. It's located four miles to the south of Hunts Beach and sits on a promontory with a view of rocky shore and ocean. Grace has been to her mother-in-law's home only half a dozen times, twice memorably before the wedding when Mrs. Holland was barely able to conceal her distrust of what she called Grace's "wiles," the ones that got her pregnant and ensnared her son before he had completed his studies. Grace thought then, and does so now, that Merle couldn't possibly have believed, during an intelligent moment, that her son shared none of the blame.

The Ford climbs a winding drive to the house, a well-kept Victorian, painted green with white trim that emphasizes the intricate woodwork around the doors and windows and along the wide front porch. Mr. Holland, before he died, owned stocks and bonds, about which Grace knows nothing except that they provided Merle Holland with a comfortable income. Gene takes Tom in his arms, and Grace holds Claire's hand as they step up onto the porch. Grace turns to take in the sweep of the coastline. Gene fiddles with a set of keys, and they are in.

Her husband's face tightens as he enters the dark house with its long hallway to the back, its enclosed sitting room to the right, and the turret room to the left. Grace wonders if her husband is sad or horrified. He opens the French doors to the sitting room. Grace wants to open every window. She rolls a fringed shade to let light in, and Gene scowls as if she shouldn't have done that.

"The view is great," she says.

"The sun will let in the heat," Gene announces, as if parroting an oft-repeated statement of Merle's.

"Do you think the furniture will mind?"

"Don't touch anything," Gene says to Claire, but the warning, Grace knows, is for her.

Ignoring him, she raises the shade.

In the scrutiny of the bright sun, the house shows its age. The wallpaper, a maroon pattern, reveals white plaster where it's peeling. All the woodwork has been stained a dark mahogany. Claire clings to Grace's leg, but Grace has no need to cling to anyone.

Did the lack of light twist the plant that grew here? Moving quickly, she passes through a dining room with a table no child has ever been allowed to eat at and into the kitchen with its back windows overlooking the garden. The room, painted pale yellow and white, is a haven. Claire, feeling it, runs along the linoleum, and Grace finds her wooden utensils to play with.

"This I like," Grace says.

Gene, not looking at her, nods, as if his mother were right. The kitchen is the place for the help. Grace doubts Merle ever visited her kitchen because she had Clodagh to cook and clean for her. When Gene visited with the children, it was Clodagh who had cookies for Claire and a perfectly warmed bottle for Tom. Clodagh, to whom Gene has given her last pay packet. What will happen to the woman?

Outside, the gardens are withering from lack of rain. Grace remembers them as glorious, the result of Merle's expertise and Joe-the-gardener's efforts.

Gene coaxes them out of the kitchen and up the stairs to the second floor, given over entirely to Mrs. Holland's bedroom, dressing room, bathroom, and a piano in the turret. Grace marvels at so much space for one woman, a space much larger, she is certain, than her own home. She touches fabric and silver, writing paper and pens. She fingers necklaces hanging from an ornate mirror, a challenge that Gene doesn't rise to.

He wants me to like it here, she thinks.

He doesn't announce their future until they are on the third floor, inspecting the guest rooms, all of which share a bathroom with wooden fixtures and a chain pull for the toilet. Gene invites her to glance out a window in the bedroom that used to be his. The view is majestic. "You can see ships traveling from Boston to Portland from here," he says.

Grace catches Claire by a foot before she crawls beneath a bed.

"So what do you think?" Gene asks.

"Of the house? It's enormous."

"About moving here."

She has known, ever since the second floor, that Gene would ask this, and though she wants to scream an immediate no, she understands she has to tread carefully.

"It's grand," she says, "but it's isolated. I don't know who the children would play with. They can't get off the property unless they cross the coast road and only then to rocks and sea. How will they walk to school when the time comes?"

"There's a bus," Gene says. "That's how I got to school."

"I do love the kitchen, but the house is too much for us. I'd be working day and night."

"You already work day and night."

"No. I don't."

"Well, this has to be easier in some ways," he points out. "More room to store things."

This seems to Grace a weak argument. What things? "Is it your idea that we would sleep downstairs and the kids would sleep up here?"

"Well, we'd have the baby with us for the first several months."

"And Tom and Claire upstairs where we couldn't hear them?"

Gene sniffs. Grace thinks of Rosie. Who would be her neighbor here? "Aren't the taxes high?"

"There's no mortgage."

"We wouldn't get much for the bungalow," she says of a house that is heavily mortgaged.

"We wouldn't need it if we lived here."

"All our savings would go to taxes and upkeep," she argues.

"I'll get a raise soon."

She sneezes. Then she sneezes again. She apologizes and sneezes a third time.

"It's dusty up here," Gene says. "Nothing a good clean won't help."

Grace had no idea she could fake a sneeze so well.

———

"I can't do it," she says. She hates the house—the Victorian dark, the fringed lampshades, the heavy mahogany furniture. The weight of the dwelling makes her hungry for air.

"I think this is my decision to make, don't you?"

"No, I don't."

"Grace, for God's sake be quiet!"

Claire looks from one parent to the other. Somewhere, far away, someone is smashing a sand castle.

At her own mother's house, after the iced tea and the peek at the layette Marjorie is knitting, her mother asks, "How are you and Gene?"

"Times are a little tough right now," Grace says.

"Financially?"

"No."

"Is it the stress of the new baby coming?"

"I could say yes," Grace confesses, "but that wouldn't be accurate."

Her mother wets Tom's cheek with the icy side of her glass, and he pulls away, giggling. He comes back for more. "What's good in your life?" her mother asks.

Grace, surprised, needs to think. "I have two beautiful children."

"And?"

"I have a house I like, a friend next door, and a washing machine."

"And?"

"We're all healthy."

"And?"

Grace short-stops her mother because she knows where this is going. "And I have a husband who provides for us, who is good with the children, and who is handsome."

She does not add that she thinks Gene is deeply troubled.

Dry turns into drought. The word is on everyone's tongue and is spoken at least once a day. Underfoot, the grass crunches. Men digging at the side of the highway to put in a rest stop report that the top six inches of soil is dust. On the roads of Hunts Beach, vehicles kick up smothering plumes behind them and women begin again to keep the wet wash in the house for fear that tiny particles of dirt will stick to the laundry. Grace isn't certain when the days of sunshine turn from beneficial to unnatural, but she thinks it happens near the end of September, after everyone has returned to school and many of the summer people are gone. The niggling sense of something wrong slowly turns to mild alarm. The mums and roses have withered at the edges of her yard. Grace expects the nights to be cooler, but they aren't. For the first time in over a year, she prays for rain.

Spark

By the beginning of October, inland farmers have to haul water for livestock because the wells have gone dry. Brooks are still, lake levels drop. Dust and woodsmoke lay at the horizon.

The best summer in years, someone says at the store.

The state issues a directive warning its citizens to put out cigarettes and matches in water jugs. During an idle moment, Grace drops a lit cigarette onto the ground just to see what will happen. The grass catches fire and spreads faster than she ever imagined. With her jar of water, she douses the fire before it reaches a pile of dry brush Gene raked to one side. Tendrils of flames, however, have slipped behind her and race toward the house. She stomps and stomps, then runs into the kitchen, stops the washer, and flips the lever to allow the soapy water to fall onto the grass. Catching it in her jar, she soaks the fire until it is well and truly out. Winded, she sits on the porch steps and bows her head, ashamed of her stupid experiment.

She is awed by the wiles of the fire.

———

Hunters report on opening day that leaf drop and pine needles disintegrate upon touch. There's a great deal of talk about whether or not it's safe to shoot a gun.

The colored leaves crumple in the hand before hues can be appreciated. When Grace was a child, she would find the brightest reds, and her mother would iron them in waxed paper so that they could be preserved. Grace remembers satisfying packets of color on the kitchen table. She's sad that she can't do this for Claire, who would love to touch the waxed leaves.

Gene reports that a crew working on the Turnpike set a fire to clear land. Firemen put it out only to discover the next day that it had gone underground and had popped up at the roots of several trees. Again the fires were put out. The next day they broke out in more spots.

"The fire runs underground?" Grace asks.

"Yep."

She imagines secret fires tunneling beneath the house. "But how? There's no oxygen."

"There's oxygen in peat and dead vegetation," Gene explains. The fires move slowly beneath the surface, he adds, burning enough to bring more oxygen into the soil. They can burn, undetected, for months, for years. A fire that goes underground in late fall can pop up in spring.

The idea fascinates Grace. If she were to go out in bare feet and walk in the fields, would she come upon the sensation of heat underfoot?

She finds it difficult not to assign menacing characteristics to the underground fires, just as she once attached them to the sea.

Fall planting isn't possible because dry soil can't be laid over the furrows. Ponds are lower than they've been in thirty years. In one arid pond, a farmer finds what appears to be the remains of an old road. Fire, and not drought, is the word on everyone's tongue.

When Grace is in her fifth month, she climbs into the attic to find her woolens because she still has winter maternity clothes. But as she opens the box and fingers the heaviness of the fabrics, she knows it's too soon. The temperatures haven't been below eighty degrees in two weeks; all the women are still wearing cotton. In ancient times, the natives would have made much of the unnatural season, which seems to have no name. It can't rightly be called Indian summer, because there hasn't yet been a frost. The elders of the tribe would have come together to puzzle out what the summer-into-summer could possibly mean. Had they offended their ancestors? Would it remain summer for months? For years? Would they fear to die? Fear that the planet would die? What was the remedy for such a thing?

Dust enters the house and coats every object. When Grace scrubs her face at night, she can feel a fine grit under the washcloth.

———

Grace has a birthday party for Claire in the backyard and stands ready with a pitcher of lemonade over the two candles on the cake. The girl stands on her chair and blows out the candles with a flourish and is pleased with herself. Rosie, cigarette in hand, takes a long drag and then flips it onto the ground. Grace races around the table and pours lemonade over the butt, splashing Rosie's shoes.

"What are you doing?" Rosie squawks, jumping back.

"I dropped a butt on the lawn the other day, and the fire spread like . . ."

"Wildfire?" Rosie offers, smiling. She pulls another cigarette and the lighter from her purse, but then thinks better of the idea and replaces them.

Grace wakes every morning to see if the world has sorted itself out. The fine grit that she felt on her face seems to have entered her eyes and nose and head, for there are particles in her brain where there weren't before. If Gene is taciturn, Grace is sharp, as if she had broken glass on her skin. She tries hard not to snap at the children, but can't help herself with Gene.

"I thought you were going to clean the screens," she announces the minute Gene walks in the door.

"You've got to find me some ice," she insists the following day.

"How would I know?" she answers when Gene asks, "When's dinner?"

She wants to be a better person, but she can't when there's grit in her teeth.

———

One morning, Grace takes the children to the beach, where other townspeople stand. There's no chatter, no fond hellos, only the sight of fog close to shore. The east light shines through the mist, revealing a lobster boat at work. This is the closest that moisture has come to Hunts Beach in weeks. It seems a promise. Grace and the children wait for the fog to move closer still, as if, were they to wade into the ocean, it would envelop them and put water droplets on their skin and lips. The desire for moisture becomes nearly overwhelming, and she notes that several people, men and women, walk into the ocean. Will they try to make it all the way to the mist, or will the fog peel back as they do so, only a tease?

One by one, the townspeople return to their homes. Rosie and Grace angle toward one another.

"What a colossal disappointment." Rosie sighs.

Grace begins to long for an embrace, a kiss. She begins to associate bright sunny days with marital trouble. She thinks that maybe her marriage has gone underground.

"Have you considered speaking with Reverend Phillips?" Grace's mother asks.

"What?" asks a startled Grace.

"Your minister. You know he went to Harvard Divinity School."

"What's that got to do with anything?"

"He counsels couples," says her mother. "Women. And men too, probably. I know for a fact that Dot Truitt and her husband went to see him for counseling."

"And how did that work out?" Grace asks.

"They're still married."

Which tells Grace nothing. "I couldn't," she says.

"He's heard it all, I'm sure. What's so different about you and Gene?"

Grace, annoyed, says, "We don't talk, and we don't have sex."

Her mother looks shocked and then pained. She purses her mouth in a way that Grace remembers from her childhood and points to Grace's stomach. "So how did that get in there?"

"That was the last time," Grace says, "and it was horrible."

"I don't want to hear any more," her mother says, standing and walking out of the room. When she returns, her mind seems to be made up. "Go," she says. "I'll watch the children. You get yourself over to the church and see if you can find Reverend Phillips."

Grace leaves Claire and Tom with her mother and walks not to the church, but to Rosie's. When her friend opens the door, Grace says, "We don't have sex."

If Rosie is taken aback by the pronouncement, she doesn't show it. "Not at all?" she asks, gesturing for Grace to come inside.

"Not since . . ." Grace points at her belly. "And even then, it was terrible."

Rosie clears a dessert plate, a rubber duck, and a washcloth from the sofa. "The children are napping."

Grace can see from the wrappers on the side table that Rosie was reading magazines and eating Tootsie Rolls during her time off.

Rosie hands Grace a glass of water. "I always knew you weren't completely happy in your marriage. Sometimes it used to waft off you in waves. What's wrong with Gene anyway?"

"I don't know. He doesn't ever want to see my face. He doesn't care if I'm enjoying it or not." She pauses. "Sex, I mean."

"It's always been like this?"

"Pretty much."

Grace can see Rosie try to mask both surprise and dismay. "Have you ever enjoyed it?" her friend asks quietly.

"Maybe I did in the beginning," Grace answers, but then she realizes that Rosie is speaking of the god-awful joy she once gleefully mentioned. "Well, no. Not in the way you're thinking."

Rosie is silent.

Grace can feel heat rising in her face. "I didn't ever want you to know. You and Tim . . ."

"Me and Tim," Rosie says, sighing. "Every marriage has its problems."

"But you like sex," Grace says.

"I do."

"I don't. At least the way it is now. I don't even know if I'd like it ever. Gene's a good man. Well, he used to be a good man. I'm embarrassed I had to tell you this. I started to talk to my mother about it, but that was a big mistake." When she looks down, an inch of brandy has replaced the water.

"Can't hurt," Rosie says, raising her glass. "You've been shaking ever since you walked in the door."

"You're a good friend," Grace says.

"I want to be."

"You are." The two women clink glasses, and Grace starts
to laugh. "Oh, Rosie, you saved me from telling the minister!
That's where my mother thought I was going."

"You were going to use the word *sex* with your minister?"
Rosie asks, incredulous.

Grace reads in the newspaper reports of fires in Waldoboro,
Topsham, and Lisbon Falls. The news is always one or two
days old, and Grace ponders the fate of the people in the stories. What, for example, happened to the house of the man
who soaked it with a hose as the fire approached? Did he
save it? Or to the gentleman who fled with his tax returns?
Did he lose them in the fierce winds created by the fire? Or
to the woman who begged to be allowed to take her refrigerator? By the next day, there are new stories to report and
no follow-ups. How did the woman intend to transport her
treasured appliance?

Many of the stories mention that there is no early warning system for fire in Maine. Often the first sign is the smell
of smoke, followed by a vehicle racing into town with a man
in it ordering citizens to evacuate. Houses go up like bombs.
Animals, trapped in burning barns, die. The ones freed at
the last minute sometimes make it to safety.

Her sweaty arm sticks to the newspaper as she tries to
turn the page.

The women of Hunts Beach are rarely seen walking alone
without a purse or a child or a carriage. Grace, having left
her children with her mother, walks out of her house with

no destination. In a loose maternity skirt and sleeveless blouse, she lets her arms swing as she moves. Because she always heads south toward the village center, this time she goes north. Most people have left the waterfront cottages for home, school, and work—the natives tend to live two or three streets back, as she does—but occasionally, she sees a window open, a rake leaning against a tree, a carved pumpkin on the front steps. As she strolls, the seashore becomes rockier with surf, a pleasant meditative sound. She is thrilled to be moving faster than she can with the kids, stretching her legs, uncoiling the cat inside. She lets her mind empty, or tries to.

What would she take if someone, this very minute, were to tell her she must evacuate her house? Her children, of course, and bottles for Tom, clean clothes for Claire. Perhaps a change of clothes for herself tucked behind the children in the carriage. A photograph of her wedding? Of the children, when they were younger? Yes, one or two. A picture of her father. The layette for the baby? Her purse. An address book? Cigarettes? But then what would happen? She can't outrun a fire. Perhaps she might be able to hoist the children and a suitcase onto the back of a truck. But she can't get rid of the image of herself on foot, pushing the carriage as fast as she can, trying to shush Claire, who would smell and sense, if not actually see, the danger. No one needs to explain a wildfire to a child.

Normally, Grace loves this time of year. It's not just the turning of the leaves or the crisp weather that one expects; it's more a feeling of relaxation while the rest of the world becomes busier. With fewer people in town, streets are less crowded. Quiet descends. This year, however, that sense of peace has curdled to one of nervous watching. It's bound to rain sometime soon, they say. It has to rain someday, they moan.

"Hey, Missy."

The name jolts Grace, who turns to look. A man calls to her from inside a black Ford across the street. At first she thinks it might be Gene teasing her, but then she notices that the driver has a straw hat. Gene never wears a straw hat.

"Lady, can you give me some directions?"

"Where do you want to go?" she shouts back, putting a hand over her eyes so that she can get a better look at the man's face. Middle-aged. A little soft.

"Well, I want to go to Cape Porpoise, and I got a map here."

Grace hesitates.

But why?

As she approaches the automobile, she discovers that the man's shoulders are bare. In the heat, many men have shed their shirts. He must not be very tall, she decides, because his neck barely clears the bottom of the window. How does he see out to drive?

"How can I help you?" she asks.

"Well, I got this map here."

She bends to take a better look. The man is naked and is touching himself. He grins up at her. The missing tooth, the fold of flesh at the belly, the limp penis.

She slowly backs away, ignoring the man's catcalls. She

steps onto the grass, then onto the sidewalk. She reverses direction. She walks with her head bent, her shoulders hunched, praying he won't follow.

To see a soft naked man inside a heavy metal machine. To have been tricked into having to watch, if only for a second, the man fondling himself. She knows her face is red and that sweat is trickling down the inside of her blouse. Why do men do this? she asks herself. Not the touching—she understands that well enough—but the stealth, the wanting to hurt women, to trick them. Rosie would have laughed and said something vulgar about the size of the man's penis. If only she had Rosie's nerve, her ability to think on her feet.

When Grace reaches the beach, she heads for the water. She takes off her shoes and walks in. She did not go home because she didn't want the man, if he was following her, to know where she lives. If he stops at the beach, she won't leave the water. If he gets out of the car and starts to move in her direction, she'll scream and run like hell. But wait, he can't get out of his car. He's naked.

She sits on the sand, knees up, only her feet in the shallow waves. She would love to go for a swim. The coolness, the cleansing, her head diving under the water, coming up for air. How good that would feel.

Why not?

Except for the knee length of her cotton skirt, what she has on is not all that different from a maternity bathing suit. What if the baby weighs her down? No, it won't. With all her extra blubber, she ought to float effortlessly.

The idle thought becomes a desire. The desire takes on a sense of urgency.

She stands and walks into the water up to her knees. She lifts her skirt a bit and runs and stumbles, but then she turns and executes a backstroke the way she was taught so long ago at summer camp. Her skirt floats up beside her, and her legs are free to make any movement they want. She dives, reaching for an underwater breaststroke.

When she comes up for air, she is not at the same place at which she entered. The current has carried her along with it. She squints, and in the distance she sees a black Ford cross an intersection. Lots of people drive black Fords. Her husband for one, the minister for another.

She will never tell anyone—not Gene, not Rosie, not her mother—about the incident with the man in the car.

She floats with her arms out beside her. She lets the waves push her closer to shore. She catches a scent she doesn't normally associate with the ocean. She stands and sniffs again.

A faint whiff of smoke.

Someone burning leaves? Yes, that must be it. But the air seems slightly hazy to the west. The black Ford rounds a corner and begins to come along the beach road. Grace thinks of ducking below the surface, but then sees that there are two men in the car. On the top of the automobile is a bullhorn.

Fire

By nightfall, a reddish glow appears at the western horizon. With Tom in her arms, Grace gazes at the fearful and exquisite disaster. Even Tom seems riveted, and when she looks into his dark eyes, she can see the unexpected light producing a silhouette: tall pines, maples, an electric tower, a barn. How far away is the fire? How fast is it moving?

She imagines the Indians would have seen the glow as a message of doom from the ancestors and would have taken to canoes along the river. Though Grace and her neighbors live near a beach, few of them have boats of any kind. A motorboat can't be launched from a beach. Unless the ocean is dead calm, a canoe is useless. Even rowboats are tied up at the town dock a few miles away. Two families that Grace knows of evacuated themselves by car earlier when the black Ford with the bullhorn cruised the streets telling people to take their most important possessions and get out of town. Over the sound of screened doors slapping, voices murmur and then shout.

Reports of fires in Kennebunk preclude driving south. To drive west is to go toward the fire. To go east is to drive into the ocean. And to drive north is not without risk. There are rumors of small fires along the main road to Biddeford.

Could she and Gene and the children make it to Cape Porpoise just up the coast? Could a boat be found there?

Many of her neighbors are staying put to protect their houses. Few can imagine a fire advancing to the ocean, deliberately moving toward an absolute lack of fuel. By Gene's account, they have at least a day before they need to start worrying. This morning at breakfast, he called her an alarmist.

Three words.

She stares again at the glow of red at the horizon. Who lives out there? Have their homes already gone up in flames? There are no newspapers now, and any minute, according to Rosie, they'll lose power. She urged Grace to assemble candles in every room, which Grace thinks is more likely to produce a house fire than the still distant conflagration.

"I'm frightened," Rosie says when she enters Grace's kitchen at seven in the evening.

"Don't be."

Rosie hunches forward on the kitchen chair to rock Eddie in Tom's old cradle while Claire and Ian color on paper on the floor.

"If the house goes, we've got nothing," Rosie wails.

Grace remembers the woman who stood in front of her home on the waterfront, worried about tidal flooding. She said the same thing. Does that woman now feel safer than the rest of her neighbors, living so close to the water's edge?

"No insurance?" Grace asks.

Rosie shakes her head.

"Oh, Rosie."

"We meant to get to it, we did, but the money was always needed for something else. I suppose it's too late now?"

"I think it might be."

"What'll we do?"

"The fire is still miles away," Grace says.

"What will you take with you?"

Grace has set aside a pile of belongings on the floor of the living room. Clothes, baby food, canned milk, a few photographs, two of Gene's most prized surveying antiques, all the important papers in the drawer of the living room desk, blankets, several bottles of water. How she will manage to get the provisions out of the house with two children in tow is an unsolved problem. Gene took the car in the morning, stating that he was going to help other men create a firebreak to stop the wildfire from nearing Hunts Beach. She wishes he would come home. "Blankets, papers, clothes, water," Grace answers.

"I can't focus. Do I take the sentimental or the practical?"

"A little of the first. More of the latter."

"Will there be any warning at all?"

Does a fire roll down a hill with such speed that it catches people before they can run away? Grace thinks of ancient Pompeii. The population was overwhelmed by moving lava. Is a fire faster than lava?

"I heard Edith on the back porch sobbing this morning," Rosie reports. "I felt sorry for her and almost went over there. And Tim says that the Bakers had the loudest fight he's ever heard."

"Tempers are short. All that waiting for rain. And now the fear."

"We knew in our bones that something bad was going to happen."

"Did we?" asks Grace. "To us?"

"The drought. The unnatural heat."

The early warning they didn't heed. Should they have been more prepared? For catastrophe? Who lives like that?

Grace brings the supplies out to the back porch to be closer to the car when Gene comes for them. Something that looks like a bat skims the screen and startles Grace. But its flight is too slow and too close to the ground to be a bat. It seems to float to the sunburned grass and stay there, weightless. With caution, she opens the door to get a better look, and as she does, an insect flutters against her cheek. She slaps the bug away and watches the pieces drift to the ground. Not a bat, not a bug. Fragments of burned paper, carried on the wind.

Rosie is back at Grace's door. Grace steps outside, and the pair move to the halfway point between the two houses so that each can listen for a child crying. "Where's Gene?" Rosie asks.

"He didn't come back. Tim?"

"Not back, either."

"It's after nine," Grace says.

"You think they're still working on the firebreak?"

"I guess."

"You'd think they'd come home to be with their families," Rosie says.

In the near distance, Grace can hear motors revving. "If

just one of them comes back, we could all cram into a car and get out."

"I can't believe this is happening to us!"

"It's not just us," Grace points out. "If what we've heard is true, half of coastal Maine is on fire. There are inland fires, too."

"Okay," says Rosie, "let's be sensible."

Grace smiles.

"You can fit whatever you have in the carriage, right?" Rosie asks.

"Not all."

"We have to be able to move."

"I heard that people were stealing shopping carts from Shaw's," says Grace.

"Why didn't I think of that?"

"Seriously? Stealing?"

"Do you think that matters when the stakes are the lives of your children?"

Grace guesses not.

Rosie snaps her fingers. "We have a canoe!"

"I don't know," says Grace. "Pretty dangerous to push a canoe into the ocean at night with your children in it."

"No. I'll put the kids and the stuff in it and drag it."

"To where?"

"To the beach."

"And then what?"

"The fire's not going to go all the way to the beach," insists Rosie.

"I don't know."

"It can't."

"Sparks might reach us and our things."

"Simple," Rosie says. "We'll wet everything down."

"And the kids?"

"Oh, Grace, I don't know. Does the fire look closer?"

The silhouette has changed. Two houses, an open field. Yes, the fire is closer, but for now she will keep that knowledge to herself. "Do you know where the firebreak is?" Grace asks instead.

"Near Route One maybe?"

Grace turns back to the beach, certain that she has felt something new on her skin. Moisture, a cool breeze. She inhales deeply. The scent is unmistakable. She grabs Rosie's hand. "Can you smell that?" Grace asks.

Rosie tips her face upward. "An east wind?"

Grace nods.

They stand a minute on the grass, hands clasped, taking in long breaths of refreshing wet air. It seems that other townspeople are just now noting it. Motors stop. Arguments halt midsentence.

"We've been saved?" Rosie asks.

"For now, anyway."

"God, I love an east wind."

Grace floats like a paper fragment into her house and up the stairs to where her children sleep. In a slow dance of exhaustion and relief, she slips into her summer nightgown and lies back on her pillow. She ought to stay awake and watch over her house and her children in case the wind switches direction. She ought to go downstairs and wait in the kitchen for Gene. Will he be covered in soot, desperate for a glass of

water? But won't the east wind have reached the men by
now, signaling a few hours to go home to get some sleep?

She rolls over to put her cheek to the pillow. She will take
a catnap and be refreshed and ready for whatever comes
next.

Hot breath on Grace's face. Claire is screaming, and Grace
is on her feet. As she lifts her daughter, a wall of fire fills
the window. Perhaps a quarter of a mile back, if even that.
Where's Gene? Didn't he come home? She picks Tom up
from his crib and feels a wet diaper. No time to change him.

She scurries down the stairs carrying both children. She
deposits them in the carriage in the hallway and pushes it
onto the screened porch. Claire begins to cough in the smoky
air. "Sweetie," Grace croons, "have you saved us all?"

She stuffs blankets, diapers, baby food, and water into
the carriage behind the children. She loops the kids' clothes
around the upper bits of metal and ties them in knots. She'll
have to leave the mementos.

Because she can't push the now too-heavy carriage over
the lip of the porch, she reverses it in order to drag it down the
step. Claire is crying, and so is Tom, but Grace has no time
to soothe them.

As she maneuvers the vehicle to the edge of the grass, a
bomb goes off, the explosion one Grace can feel right through
her feet and legs. The children are silent, as if awed by the
sound.

"A fuel tank in a house on Seventh Street," she hears one
man shout to another.

Sparks and embers swirl around Grace. There's chaos

in the streets. She hears cars moving, women screaming. Balls of flame seem to leap from treetop to treetop, giving the fire a frightening momentum. A tree catches fire at the top, and the fire races down the trunk and into a house below. Another bomb. The fire turns tree after tree into tall torches.

Fields resemble hot coals. For as far as she can see, there's an unbroken line of fire. Cars are traveling, but where can they go?

An ember lands on the hood of the carriage. Grace swipes it off and begins to run. Heat and common sense push her to the seawall. A deer leaps across the street with her, chased by the freight train bearing down on all of them.

She takes the children from the carriage and sets them on a blanket on the sand. On another blanket, she lays out what few provisions she has brought. Abandoning the carriage, she begins to drag both blankets away from the fire and closer to the water. When the sand feels wet underfoot, she stops.

Smoke adds to the confusion. She spots, and then doesn't, Rosie dragging a canoe.

"Rosie!" Grace calls.

"Grace, where are you?"

"Right at the water. There you are."

Grace helps her friend drag the canoe beside the two blankets. "Where's Gene and Tim?" Rosie wails.

"I have no idea," Grace says, shaken.

"Where are all the people going?" Rosie asks.

"To the schoolhouse, I heard."

"That's crazy. The schoolhouse will burn, if it hasn't already."

Grace kneels on the blanket to change Tom's diaper. His sleeper is dry enough to stay on. Grace can feel heat on her face.

"Oh, God," Rosie cries.

"What?"

"The Hinkel house just went. It's only one street back from us."

Grace has no words. When she glances up, the fire burning on the ground resembles hot jewels among the rocks and pebbles.

"Rosie, take what you can from the canoe and put it near the water's edge. Then push the canoe out to sea."

"But . . ."

"It's wood. If an ember falls inside, it will bring the fire right to us. Wet your hair and the kids' hair."

Rosie follows Grace's instructions. She's glad that Rosie won't see her own house go up. Already, roof shingles are burning.

"Do my kids, too," Grace yells to buy more time.

The splendid maple next to Grace's own house turns orange in an instant, as if someone had switched on a light. The tree collapses. Grace can't see her screened porch, but she knows the fire will consume that next and lead straight into the house. She left the photographs, the papers, the layette, the antique tools.

Rosie's house explodes, the fire having found the fuel tank in the basement. Rosie snaps her head up.

"Rosie, don't," Grace commands, and there must be

something in her voice that makes her friend obey, because Rosie turns to the water and puts her face in her hands.

Grace imagines the fire eating its way through her own home. The kitchen with the wringer washer, the hallway where the carriage is kept, the living room in which Grace made the slipcovers and drapes (an image of the fire climbing the drapes like a squirrel momentarily freezes her), upstairs to the children's beds, her own marriage bed. All their belongings, gone. Everything she and Gene have worked to have, gone.

"Rosie, listen. Go down to the water's edge so that only your feet are in the water. Lay down facing the sand—make an air pocket—and I'll bring you Ian and Eddie. Put a child under each arm and hold them close. Make air pockets for them, too. I'm going to soak your blanket and drape it over you. I'm going to cover your heads. Don't look up and don't reach out a hand or let your hair out from under the blanket."

Rosie is silent.

"Okay?" Grace shouts.

"Okay," Rosie says.

Grace races into the sea to wet the blanket. Men in jackets and caps carry children toward the water, as if in a great and horrible sacrificial act. The women, with provisions, follow. She lays the blanket over Rosie and her children just as she said she would. Then she sets her own children in the sand and wets another blanket. Tugging the dripping wool, she fetches Tom and lies down facing up, pulling the blanket to her face and anchoring it with her feet. She beckons for Claire to come to her. When she has the children securely beside her, she lets go for a second and flips onto her stomach, making three air pockets. She rolls the children over so that they are all facedown in the sand. Holding her hair back with one hand, she drapes the blanket up and over their heads. She checks around Claire and Tom to make sure nothing is sticking outside the covering.

She hears screams—not of pain, but of horror, and she guesses that the waterfront houses are about to go. People who have not managed to get out of town are trapped like rats running for the sea. She prays an animal will not step on her or, worse, try to burrow inside.

The heat on their heads and backs is just this side of bearable. The blanket won't stay wet for long.

"Rosie!" Grace shouts.

Grace can hear nothing.

"Rosie!"

"Still here!"

"Squiggle back into the water till it's up to your thighs, just short of the kids' feet."

"Why?"

"Do it, please."

Grace follows her own instructions and is in water nearly to her waist. She wishes she had thought to make a cave for her stomach. She creates new air pockets for herself and the children.

"Whatever you do, don't look up. Rosie, did you hear me?"

"Yes."

"Did you look up?"

"Yes."

Grace takes shallow breaths, afraid she might inhale sand. She wonders if she and her children will die like this, the fire advancing to the dune grass at the seawall and then igniting Grace's blanket. Would it be too late by the time she felt the pain, or would she have a few seconds to get Tom and Claire into the water up to their shoulders? She might have to dunk herself and the kids if the fire gets that close. Does sand burn?

She can do nothing but wait until the fire exhausts itself. The seawater must be in the mid-sixties, and she has begun to shiver under the blanket. She has on only her cotton nightgown. The children are hardly more dressed than she. She can't tell if the shivering is simply because of the cold, or if it stems from fear. Heat leaves the body quickly when one is lying on the ground, though the top of her feels as if it might sear at any minute. She would rather suffer the cold until the fire is well and truly out. How long will that take?

Around her, she hears timbers crashing, grass crackling. How many people are on the beach now? She doesn't dare look. She wishes she could calm herself, but it's impossible with the shivering. She has only one task now, to save her children.

And then Rosie's children and Rosie.

The shaking becomes so severe, the children seem to catch it. Nature's way of keeping them warm inside.

When she can no longer resist peeking, the moon is red. Burned trees fall to the ground amid showers of sparks. The entire town, for as far as Grace can see, is ablaze. Nothing moves but the fire—hungry, angry, relentless.

This must be what hell is like, she thinks as she lowers the blanket.

Grace worries for her mother. She must be safe, she decides. Her two friends would have rescued her. Gladys has a car. Perhaps they evacuated her earlier, and her mother, having no way to communicate, could not alert Grace. Or maybe her mother is at the other end of the beach, over a mile away, hovering near the water, as she is.

Claire begins to cry. Afraid that the child might inhale sand, Grace removes her arm from her daughter and as best she can fills the hole.

"Look at me," she says to Claire. "Just lie your head down facing me."

Grace brushes the sand from her daughter's face. "Go to sleep now," she says. She reaches back to cover her child with her arm.

When Claire is settled, Grace turns to her son. His face is covered with sand. She fills his hole and turns his head to face hers. She can't understand his strange quiet. His eyes are open, and he is breathing, but he ought to be crying like his older sister. Instead, his expression is solemn, as if he were in shock. She wishes the children would fall asleep. But how can they, when death threatens a mere twenty yards away? They know this is not a game. Not at night. Not in the wet sand.

Grace wants to think of Gene, but her thoughts are muddy because she can't picture where he is or what he is doing.

Does he have a shovel in his hands? Is he cowering in a river as she is in the ocean? Or is he sitting in someone's kitchen having a cup of coffee and a donut in order to keep his energy up?

It would have been impossible, Grace understands now, for him to get a message to her, never mind come home to save her. How is it that they all read the fire so wrong, that no one understood that the town and possibly the people in it would be dust by morning, nothing but hot embers, a whistling wind?

The shaking in Grace's body is so intense that she feels as if her limbs will break apart. Her hands barely work when she reaches beyond her children to make sure nothing is sticking outside the blanket. Not a tendril of hair, not a foot.

She will not allow herself to picture the advance of the fire to the water. They will not burn. They will not drown.

"Rosie!" she yells.

No voice answers her. She doesn't dare open her blanket. The heat has not abated.

She waits another minute.

"Rosie?"

Hour after hour, Grace holds her children. She tries to keep them warm with her body. Her limbs stiffen and ache.

A sensation of natural light. A cessation of sound. Only the wash of the water, the odd comment from afar.

She tries to bring Tom and Claire closer to her, but her muscles are so cramped and numb, she can't move.

"Over here!" a man yells.

Two men Grace has never seen before kneel on the sand and peer into Grace's eyes.

"Are you hurt, ma'am?" one asks.

"Take the children," she manages. "Please. Warm them up."

"Will do," one says, and the two men lift the blanket off Grace.

"Jesus," the other man says.

She knows the skirt of her nightgown is raised, but she can't care about that now. One man takes Claire, the other Tom. Awakened from their nightmare, only Claire begins to wail, a reassuring sound.

"Don't you worry, ma'am. We'll be right back for you."

Grace follows her children with her eyes.

The only signs that what she sees was once a town are the perfectly intact brick chimneys, tall druids with awful stories to tell. In one chimney, two fireplaces are visible, one over the other, the brick of the second-story hearth still protruding.

She spots a large vehicle the size of a bread truck parked across the street. The children are handed over to someone inside. Grace can still hear Claire crying.

One of the two men comes back for her.

"The other man's wife is in there with your children. Can you move?"

The pain in her back and shoulders is searing, nearly unbearable. She shakes her head.

"Have you been here all night?"

"Yes."

She can see only his boots and then his knees.

"I'm going to try to roll you over," he says.

She can feel his hands under her shoulder and hip. She does all she can to help him, rolling with a thud, as if she were a frozen block of ice. She sees him lower her nightgown, but she has no sensation in her legs.

"You're pregnant," he says, alarm evident in his voice. "We've got to get you to a hospital."

"Why? Hospital?"

"You're suffering from hypothermia. Think you could give me your hands?"

Grace grabs both his outstretched hands and tries to stand as he pulls. He manages to get her upright, but as soon as he lets go, she falls onto the sand, her frozen legs not working as they should. He urges her upright again and tells her to put her hands on his head for support. He whips off his blue cloth jacket and rubs her legs with the flannel lining. He is rough with her to get the circulation going again.

He stands, puts the jacket on Grace, and tells her to hook her arm into his.

"Let's give it another go," he says.

She is taken into the truck with many hands helping her. They coax her to lie on her side on blankets. She can hear Claire, from somewhere above her, crooning, "Mamamamama."

"Hi, sweetie. You're a good girl. We're all right now."

The truck lurches forward.

Grace thinks, *I did it. I saved my children.*

Cinders

But, no, she didn't.

The bleeding begins in the truck. Exhausted, Grace drifts in and out of consciousness until she is woken by a pain low in her abdomen. She opens the blanket to see blood on her nightgown and the thin blanket.

"No!" she cries.

She has had these pains before. She knows what they are. She holds her legs tight together and pushes the blanket between them.

"Hold on," the woman says.

"No, no, no, no, no," Grace cries.

She shuts her eyes and prays. She knows by heart only one prayer. She thinks the words as best she can until she is squeezed from within. At each contraction, Grace grabs for the woman's hand. She holds her breath.

Baby baby baby stay inside me stay inside.

Between contractions, she nods off. She can't help herself, even though she knows she must stay awake to keep the child.

The driver races ahead. When the truck stops, the back door is opened by a man in a white coat.

"How many months?" he asks.

"Five."

"Contractions?"

"Yes."

"Intervals?"

"I don't know."

Something in Grace's face must alarm the doctor, because he yells for a cot. While they wait, the doctor takes her pulse. He frowns.

"What?" Grace asks.

"Racing," he pronounces.

Two men help her out of the truck and onto a gurney. They wheel her to the double doors of a brick building. The driver of the truck bends over her to say, "Your children will be well taken care of. We'll be back to see you."

Inside the hospital, Grace is dizzy with swimming over-head lights. She hears deep coughing, yelps of pain, bouts of screaming. Patients lie on cots in the hallway, while others, grimacing, stand against the white tiles. She hopes someone has covered her bloody nightgown. A contraction takes her by surprise with its intensity, and she pushes against the rails of the bed.

"Don't push," the nurse behind her says.

But Grace can't control her body. Once inside a room, she is led off the cot to the bathroom, where her nightgown is removed. She is washed, given a new nightgown, and ordered to empty her bowels. Her body shudders with pain.

She is helped back onto the gurney and a nurse takes her information.

"Grace Holland."

"Eugene Holland."

"Hunts Beach."

"I don't know. It doesn't exist anymore."

"My mother. Marjorie Tate. Her house might not exist either."

"Two. A girl, two, and a boy, nine months."

The nurse looks up at her.

"You'll give birth to this baby today," a doctor, not the same one as before, announces.

"It's not time!" Grace insists.

A mask is clamped over her nose and mouth. Twilight sleep. Scopolamine. She has been here before.

Grace comes to with grinding pain she remembers from less than a year ago. She wants to sit up, to push.

"You can now," the doctor says.

She braces her legs and arms, and with a nurse lifting her torso from behind, pushes blindly, going with the pain, pushing, pushing, pushing.

For the second time, a mask is clamped over her nose and mouth.

She dreams the ocean has overtaken her.

She dreams she is fumbling beneath the skirts of her nightgown, searching for her children.

She wakes to an image of fresh blood on a blanket.

Nooooooo, she cries silently.

———

A doctor stands at the door. Grace wills him not to enter the room. To enter the room is to deliver information she doesn't want, information she already knows.

"I'm sorry," says the doctor as he stands at her bedside. "The child was born dead."

Her eyes fill, even though it's not yet sadness that overcomes her. She's stunned.

"It was a boy," the doctor says. "He never drew breath."

She closes her eyes and nods.

"The woman caring for your son and daughter stopped by to give you her address and to tell you that both are fine."

The doctor doesn't offer Grace a chance to see the thing that she expelled, which only confirms her understanding of the event.

"You need to rest away from the mothers, for at least a week. You nearly died that night on the beach."

She wants to say, No, I didn't. Instead, she asks about her husband.

"I haven't seen a patient by that name. I'll check our records."

Alone, Grace turns her back to the door, rolls herself into a fetal position, and cries for her dead baby, a son. He would have been such a little thing, and she would have loved him to death. To death. She tries to speak to him, to tell him how sorry she is, but she can't find a way to envision a being to talk to.

And what will Gene say when he hears? Will he blame Grace, castigate her? She would prefer that to what she guesses will be his reaction. Silence. Perhaps a word. Maybe two words.

She imagines that Gene made his way back to Hunts Beach, to the cinders that cover the village acreage. Were any houses saved? Is there no one to tell Gene where his wife is? Will he have somehow found his children?

An icy thought slices through her. It's not that he might be dead; no, it's that he might have walked away from his family. He might have seen the fire as an excellent portal to another life. A life in which he would never have to talk to his wife, in which he would never again have to go home.

Grace's shoulders, back, and arms hurt. Her pelvis is heavy and sore. Her legs have needles in them. Having rolled into a fetal position, she thinks she might have to stay that way for days. Curving into herself is bearable. Sitting up is not.

When did she give birth? This morning? Last night? When was she lying on the beach, her legs in the ocean? Has she lost a day? Maybe, as she burrowed into the sand, the fetus wanted to go back to the sea, to squiggle through her legs and swim away, knowing it could never be born.

She will not have another baby. She will not make love again. Her womb will never heal from the injury she has done it.

When Grace thinks about her children, she feels calm: A kind woman said she would take care of them. Grace must send someone to the address that awaits her at the front desk to make sure the children are all right. Perhaps the woman will bring Claire and Tom to the window so that Grace can look down at them and wave.

How easy it is in this white cubicle, the lights dimmed. Has the fire burned itself out yet?

She sleeps a deep sleep with no dreams.

Grace is wakened by a nurse who wants to check the bleeding, take her temperature, listen to her heart. The nurse is abrupt in her commands, a little rough with Grace's body. Does she blame Grace for her current situation, or is this a mannerism left over from the war? The nurse makes Dr. Franklin, by comparison, seem like a lamb.

A lamb. A lamb on the cover of a children's book. Gone.

The entire contents of Grace's house, gone. Even the papers and the children's clothes. Transformed into ashes.

Will an insurance company honor a policy if the insured has no way to prove he or she was insured? She can't remember the name of the company or the man who sold the policy to them. Gene will know. But, then again, where's Gene?

Another, younger, nurse appears with a tray of food. A ham sandwich and a bowl of rice pudding suggests lunch.

"How long have I been here?" Grace asks the younger nurse.

"I don't know, Mrs. Holland. But I can check. I just came on shift."

"That's fine. What's your name?"

"Julie."

Julie has short blond hair under a smart cap, a white apron over a light blue dress.

"You're a volunteer?"

"Yes."

"How old are you?" Grace asks. She slips a spoonful of the rice pudding into her mouth. She might just manage to get this down. She can't even look at the sandwich.

"Seventeen."

"You've graduated from high school?"

"I'm about to be a senior."

Julie hovers respectfully at a distance, her hands clasped in front of her.

"This is a good thing that you're doing," Grace says.

"I had to help, didn't I? It's chaos out there because of the fires."

"Do you have access to hospital records?" Grace asks.

"I can ask someone who does."

"I don't know where my husband is or my mother or my closest friend. I was rescued off the beach with my two children."

"I know."

"You do?"

"Everyone knows."

Grace is surprised. "I need information about Eugene Holland, Marjorie Tate, Rosie MacFarland, or her husband, Tim. Don't you need to write this down?"

"No, ma'am."

"I'd be grateful for any news. Also, there's an address at the front desk for me. It's where my children are. Could you bring me that address?"

"Yes. I'm sorry about your baby."

Grace nods. An awkward silence follows. "You can go now, if you like. I don't want you to forget those names."

"I'm to stay here to make sure you finish your lunch."

Grace examines the tray. "If I eat half the sandwich, will that be all right?"

The girl smiles.

The sandwich half eaten and taken away, the rough nurse reappears to bind Grace's breasts, a procedure Grace didn't think would be necessary since the infant died too soon. But she is reminded of how full her breasts are when the nurse wraps her with a nearly sadistic efficiency.

"I can't breathe," Grace says.

"You can breathe," snaps the nurse, as if Grace had been whining.

In her tight white shroud, Grace is drawn down into a pool of grief. Her body mourns as well as her mind. For the lost baby, for her missing husband, for her unmarriage. How can she possibly bring up Claire and Tom without a father? Would Gene have burned to death with unbearable pain, or would he have succumbed to smoke? Is it possible that he somehow survived?

For hours, Grace is left to contemplate a man on a cross on the wall opposite, a particularly lurid depiction of suffering. Why would a member of a medical staff put a woman in a room with such a grim reminder of death? The placement of the object is dictatorial, suggesting that the patient ought to pray to ease her sorrow, or to realize worse things have happened to countless others, or to contemplate the story that came after the cross, the one about an afterlife, a door that closed to Grace when reason overtook her childlike fantasies.

Is she meant to repent? For lasciviousness in the spring? For the challenge to her husband?

She wonders if she ought to ask to have the gruesome object removed.

On Grace's third day of rest, the rough nurse barges into her room with the news that the bed is needed in the emergency room for a husband and wife with serious burns.

Two people with burns in a single bed?

Grace stands at once, but her womb threatens to fall out of her body. She bends to keep it with her, but it's a sensual illusion.

"You need to squeeze your honeypot tight from inside," says the nurse, appearing to demonstrate what might be a tightening of the vagina, but looks more like a woman desperate for a pee.

Grace can only nod.

"But quick now, get your clothes on. You're going home."

"I have no home, and I haven't any clothes."

"No clothes, really?" the nurse asks, not at all concerned by the disclosure of no home to live in. Who has a house anymore? "All right. Change your pad. Get yourself cleaned up. You've had no fever, no infection. I'll be right back with clothes."

The man with the pickup truck is waiting for her when she emerges into sunlight. The young volunteer has called him on her behalf. He steps around and takes her arm. "My wife and I send our deepest sympathies," he says in the way of a man who has never learned any other words to express the inexpressible. "I'm a little afraid to put you in the truck again . . ." He trails off, acknowledging that it was there that the baby died.

"I'm sorry," Grace says, "I'm not sure I know your name."

"Matthew," he says. "My wife is Joan."

"And I'm Grace."

"Yes."

"Where do you live?" she asks.

"Cape Porpoise."

"When the fire got close," she says, "we thought of escaping to Cape Porpoise."

"Good thing you didn't. The fire did a lot of damage. We were saved only because my son devised a way to suction water from the sea to the house. It worked. The fire passed us over."

Grace studies Matthew. He doesn't look old enough to have a grown son. "Smart young man," she says.

Matthew smiles. "He's eleven."

Grace laughs. "Brilliant boy."

"Well, you know what they're like. A genius one minute, a moron the next."

"I don't yet, but I expect I will someday."

"My wife says your children are super. She's been missing the little ones. She said to tell you straightaway that you're welcome to stay as long as you like."

Matthew and Grace drive through the residue of hell, everything blackened, the trees dark jagged shapes, a gas station exploded, the road itself charred. Shells of automobiles sit at angles to the road, and Grace hopes that the passengers were able to flee ahead of the fire. They pass a lump of metal, an object that might once have been a black Ford, a vehicle to which Grace refuses to assign meaning.

They turn down a winding road that runs through what was once forest. They pass a burned barn, a chimney to mark the spot where the farmhouse stood. Grace notes places where the fire crowned, leaping from treetop to tree-top, singeing the upper branches, but leaving the trunks and the ground untouched. A lone house with wash on the line shocks Grace, not only for its presence amid so much dev-astation, but for the uselessness of a wet wash that will only trap the cinder dust from the mild breeze. By suppertime, the wash will be gray.

But to have a house, to have running water, to have sheets . . .

Grace has on a nurse's uniform with a woolen cape to keep her warm, white nurse's shoes that pinch. She hasn't a dime to her name.

She's aware of coves that lead to the ocean. Matthew turns at one and travels along a dirt road. He stops the car at the only house standing, a shingled cape, the land behind it then dropping off to dark blue tidal water that moves in to fill the cove twice a day.

Before she is out of the truck, Claire runs to greet her. Since Grace can't pick her up, she kneels and hugs her daugh-ter with so much force that Claire struggles to get away. But then the girl is back for more, tumbling onto her mother.

Grace can hear Matthew chuckling. A screened door slams. When she glances up, she sees Joan, Matthew's wife, holding Tom. Matthew helps Grace stand, and with Claire clinging to her leg, she takes her son from the woman. She wants to smell her boy, to make sure he hasn't lost his baby scent. He burbles, a grin across his face. When he starts to kick his feet in happiness, Grace gives him to the woman who has cared for him.

"I can never thank you enough," Grace says.

"They've been a joy to have."

With her prematurely gray hair and wide nose, her dress tight at the waist and at the bust, Joan is not beautiful; but her smile is so warm that she seems beautiful to Grace and, she imagines, to Matthew, who beams at her.

"I'm just fixing dinner," Joan says.

She doesn't mention the lost baby. Good, Grace thinks. Here I can pretend to have moved on until I actually do move on. Will I be able to move on?

Inside the front door is a boy who says, "Hello, I'm Roger. I know you're Mrs. Holland."

"Hello, Roger. I'm sorry you had to share your house with my children."

"Oh, they're okay. Tom isn't up to much, but I'm teaching Claire math."

Grace laughs. "That can't be very rewarding."

"It's all right. She's a little slow."

Roger has on a red plaid shirt and dungarees. She can see soot marks on his knees. He has left his shoes by the door, where there are three other pairs. Grace sits in a chair and takes hers off.

"I spend all day cleaning," Joan says, "but I can't keep the ash out of the house. We do our best, but it's going to take a snowfall to settle the black on the ground."

Grace glances at the living room, where the finest lace of dark dust permeates.

"Eventually, I'll get it all," Joan says, putting on an apron. "I swing wet towels around all day."

In the entrance to the kitchen, Joan has set up a playpen and a crib. Tom raises his hands in the air, a signal for his mother to pick him up. Matthew moves a chair next to the crib so that Grace can touch her son through and over the bars.

"Mom, look!" says Claire. Grace watches in amazement as her daughter folds and then sets a napkin beside each plate on the kitchen table. Her children look months older than they did four days ago.

On the walls, pretty wallpaper. Bright oilcloth on the table. Well-ironed yellow-checked curtains at the windows. All around them is black. Black trees, black underbrush, black ruins of houses. The air they breathe is full of black. On the banks of the cove lie random burned branches and boards, the flotsam and jetsam of a hundred destroyed houses.

They sit to supper, Claire on a wooden booster seat.

"The Methodist church at Hunts Beach didn't burn," Matthew informs Grace. "It's being used as a shelter now. It's a center for information. I'm not suggesting you stay there, but I am saying you might want to have a look at their bulletin board. You might be able to find your friends."

He doesn't say *husband*. He doesn't say *family*.

"I put your name and address up on it a couple of days ago," he adds.

"We don't have a telephone or a post office though," Joan points out. "It could take a while for a message to get to us."

No one has tried to find me, Grace thinks. "I'd like to go there tomorrow," she says. "Can you take me?"

"I sure can," says Matthew.

"I don't have any money," Grace adds. "I can't pay you."

"Good Lord," scolds Joan. "Don't you even think of paying. We're just glad we have a roof over our heads we can share with others."

"And food in the cupboards. Hope you don't mind green beans and peaches. I thought my wife a fool for putting up so many beans. But now I think she's pretty smart."

"And lobster," Roger pipes up. "My dad can pull more pots than any man."

"Now, now," Matthew mumbles.

"You're a lobsterman," says Grace.

"That I am."

"But you didn't go out today."

"Matter of fact, I did. When I got home, I got a call from the hospital. They said you were going home, so I waited with my truck."

Grace, overwhelmed by kindness, can't speak.

Grace and her children have the guest room with two cribs. Grace guesses that either Joan or Matthew has borrowed at least one. Joan has apparently been collecting clothes for Claire and Tom and has for Grace an entire suit of clothing that looks to have been made before the war: a blue tweed skirt and matching jacket, a nylon blouse, a slip and a new package of underwear. How did Joan get her hands on underwear? Grace decides to sleep in the nurse's uniform. In the morning, she'll put on the new clothes, overdressed for breakfast.

"Don't you look smart!" Joan exclaims when Grace and her children enter the kitchen. "It fits you perfectly."

"Thank you," says Grace.

"My wedding suit," Joan explains as she scrambles eggs with a fork.

Grace glances at the fabric, touches the skirt with her hands. "You can't give me this," she says, embarrassed. "It's a treasure to you."

"Truth is, I was busting out of it when I got married. Never had it on since. But now I've found a use for it. Can't be sentimental about clothes when others need them."

"I'll pay you back someday."

"Don't be thinking about that. Get some eggs into you. You've got a tough day ahead."

If she had had a baby, Grace thinks, she would now be lying in the maternity ward for the better part of two weeks while she healed. The baby would be brought to her three times a day for bottle feedings. When she gave birth to Tom, she was offered the option of going home but leaving Tom in the hospital for thirty days, a dollar a day. "Give you a rest and get the little one fattened up," the nurse had said.

But to give birth and go home empty-handed had upset Grace. What was the point?

———

"I'm a fairly good seamstress," Grace announces. "I just need a mill store with remnants. I can work up a dress in no time if you have a machine."

"I'll see if Matt, when he gets home, can go into Biddeford with you on your way to or from the church."

"I have to find a way to make money," Grace says.

Joan glances at the clock. "Matt will come home early to get you to the church. You must be worried about your husband."

"I am," says Grace as she places finger food in front of Tom. Claire insists on using a grown-up fork, which, in her eager hands, acts as a catapult, sending bits of eggs onto the wall and floor. Grace cleans them off as best she can. "You know, I feel fine, but my life ahead seems overwhelming."

"We're here to help, and I think when you get to the church, you'll find lots of people willing to help, too. All the organizations have mobilized: the Red Cross, the Salvation Army, the Grange, any church that didn't burn."

Grace stares through the kitchen window at the unremitting black. So this is what it means to survive a disaster.

The bulletin board is surrounded by a handful of people. Grace, in her blue suit, makes her way to the wall and, when she can, shifts so that she can read the notices.

Henri, I am at Arnaud's. Come at once.

Lost: dark terrier. Answers to Scruff. Leave note here if found.

Mother, we are at Bishop's parents' house in Kennebunk.
Anne.

Please leave any word of David Smith or David Smith Jr.,
father and son, last seen in the vicinity of Hunts Beach.

Any sheep found with red marking on right hind leg
belongs to Piscassic Farm, Route 1, Sanford, Maine.

Grace studies each message. To be doubly sure, she scans the
board again. Nothing. Below the board is a table with scraps
of paper and a pencil. She writes her own message.

Looking for Eugene Holland, Marjorie Tate, and Rosie
MacFarland. Write to Grace Holland, in care of Mat-
thew and Joan York of Cape Porpoise.

She finds a small bare patch in a lower corner. There she pins
her query.

Grace finds Matthew, who reports no luck, and together
they leave the cacophony of the sanctuary for the door. Grace
hears heavy footsteps behind her. She turns to see a haggard
Reverend Phillips.

"Grace," he says, out of breath. "This came for you, directly
to the church. I didn't want to put it up on the board."

Grace waits an eternity for Reverend Phillips to hand the
envelope over. If he expects her to open it in front of him,
he'll be disappointed. Grace folds the envelope and sticks it

into a purse borrowed from Joan. "This is Matthew York. He and his wife are helping me and my children."

"Bless you, son," says the minister. "This is a catastrophe. More and more arrive every minute."

Matthew drives for nearly an hour and parks in front of the Pepperell Mill. "I don't know a lot about fabric and such, so I'll wait in the truck and read the paper."

"Thanks," Grace says.

When she opens the mill door, she sees that the rooms are being used as temporary shelters. She scans faces but doesn't recognize anyone. She studies the bulletin board with no result. Through the large window of the mill, Grace can see Matthew reading a newspaper in the truck. She slips closer to the window for better light. She opens the letter.

Dear Grace,

Rosie was never much good at letter writing, so I am writing you instead. But she's sitting at my elbow telling me what to write, if you can imagine her there. First, I have to thank you for saving her life and the lives of our children. From what Rosie has told me, if it hadn't been for your instructions, she almost certainly would have been caught up in the fire. I cannot even think about that.

Rosie doesn't know where you are, and she asks that you write to the address on this envelope. You might notice that it's a Nova Scotia address. We aren't there yet, we are still driving down east, but we are headed to the

*town where my parents live. There we'll settle for a bit,
see if I can find work. There is nothing for us in Hunts
Beach. The house is gone with no insurance. The auto
mechanic shop burned. As soon as you get this, please
write where you are staying. Rosie misses you so much.
She feels as though she abandoned you, but she had no
choice when the fire department came and made her get
into the truck. They promised her they would go right
back for you.*

*I wish I could tell you something about Gene. As
you know, five of us went to the edge of town to make
a firebreak so that we could stop the blaze from entering
Hunts Beach. Before we knew what was happening, the
fire came roaring down the hill straight at us. Two of us
fled, I and one other man fell flat onto the ground, pushing our faces into the dirt. We were sure we were going
to die. But as luck would have it, the fire crowned and
leapt over us. When we stood, Gene was no longer with
us. One of the men swore he saw Gene walking toward
the fire, which was not a completely insane thing to do. If
you can bury yourself in the dirt, it can sometimes be but
a short moment until the fire passes, and then you're safe
because everything behind the fire has already burned. I
cannot and do not want to say that Gene perished in the
fire. He was the smartest of all of us. I pray that he escaped
unharmed.*

*Rosie says she will die of boredom in Nova Scotia, so
you must be our first visitor when everything is settled.*

Your good friends,
Rosie and Tim

———

Grace slides down the wall to a bench, holds the letter to her chest, and is doubly pained by the true destruction of Hunts Beach: Everyone will move away. What is there to go back to? A barren land with no house upon it. She can't even begin to think about rebuilding. Not without Gene. Even with Gene. Where would they find wood that wasn't charred? How would they come up with the money? How could they, as a family, live alone on a cinderscape?

After some exploring, Grace finds a side shop that sells remnants. Most pieces are too big or oddly shaped to work for day dresses. But she discovers, beneath a small mountain of fabric, a piece of navy blue cotton, enough to make a dress for her and something for Claire and Tom, too. Joan gave her a dollar bill as she left the house in the morning.

The cost of the navy blue cotton comes to $1.04.

"I have only a dollar," Grace says.

The cashier hesitates. Is it worth ripping away a fragment of a fragment?

"Just take it," she says. "What you have is fine."

"Thank you," says Grace, holding her wrapped parcel.

"Matthew, I wondered if you would do something for me," Grace asks when she climbs back into the truck.

"If I can."

"I'd like to go to Hunts Beach to see if anyone I know is still there."

"The fire department has been pretty thorough about searching all standing houses, but it never hurts to try."

"My father was a lobsterman," Grace offers.

"Was he now."

"He died when I was fourteen. Went overboard in January."

No need to explain to Matthew what happened then.

"I'm sorry," Matthew says.

"It would have been quick," Grace says, relying on that not-very-comforting old saw. She has too many times pictured the minute her father was in the water before his respiratory system shut down from the shock and the cold.

"Yes, it would have been."

"It took my mother years to get over it. She lives on what the League of Lobstermen can provide. Some years the money is adequate, sometimes not. I went to secretarial school to help out. But then I met Gene."

"I'm sure she was happy about that."

"Yes, she was."

They drive through blocks of yellow and orange foliage and then through passages of black, as if flitting in and out of a train tunnel. In the green, Grace searches for pumpkins or colorful mums, anything that is a sign of normalcy.

When Matthew turns a corner, she can see from several blocks away that her entire neighborhood is gone. Her mind's eye can trace every wall of her house, every chair, every kitchen tool, her mother's favorite tea mug. What is she already forgetting?

"This is unbearable," she says.

"Can't wait for the first snow," Matthew says. "I'm not sure I ever said that before."

"I need to get out."

———

The setting sun gives the water a shade of blue Grace has always loved. She used to think the sea the one blessing of winter: even though the world around her was bleak, the water seldom lost its color. Today, the contrast between the dead black and the rich blue is almost impossible to believe in.

She removes her shoes and puts her feet into the sand. Two or three inches down, her toes connect with wet. She moves toward the water.

She sticks a foot into the sea and then snatches it back. She is not tempted to go in—she knows the water chill of November, but she has come on a mission, even as she knows how strange it is. She thanks the ocean, that vast indifferent entity, for saving her and Claire and Tom.

News

Alone in her room, Grace sits on her bed, propped up by pillows, and reads the several newspapers she discovered in Joan's kitchen. She learns that fires ravaged Hunts Beach and that 150 of 156 homes in another seaside community burned to the ground. Along with Hunts Beach, five other towns were completely destroyed. She discovers that 3,500 people who were trapped on a pier at Bar Harbor were saved by the Coast Guard. She had no idea the fire had reached so far down east. She reads of a couple who moved all their furniture to the barn, only to have the house saved while the barn burned. Men in planes tried unsuccessfully to make rain with dry ice, fire victims ranged in age from sixteen to eighty, and some farmers would not leave their livestock. Fire damage was estimated at $50 million, home builders planned to build one thousand homes, and Halloween was banned in Maine.

Newspapers are strewn all about her, the collection telling of the immensity of the fire and its terrible toll. From the articles, she doesn't have a precise map of the fire, but it seems to have hugged the coast of Maine from Bar Harbor to Kittery.

The carnage of the fire amazes her yet again. So many

homeless, injured, or dead. She shudders at the report of the sixteen-year-old girl who died in an evacuee motor crash. Grace imagines the panic, the speed, and the horror in the realization that in leaving the danger zone, the girl was put in harm's way. Grace puzzles over the list of the dead and a Mr. Doe from Sanford or Biddeford. Might the body have been named Mr. Doe by a coroner, pending an investigation, while a reporter took the name literally?

Could the body be that of Gene, who left the four other men and walked into the fire, an act she would consider suicidal were it not for Tim's letter? She remembers her fear that he might simply walk away from his life.

Other stories compel her to read them again, such as the one of the man who wouldn't leave without his horse and as a consequence died of asphyxiation. The reports of the cost of the fires make her feel helpless, all the more so because her loss is but a tiny part of the whole, and it might take years for investigators to reach her. But the report of the committee plan to build one thousand homes cheers her. She writes the name of the organization down.

Her eye drifts to a story of the couple who were forced to separate after fifty-one years of marriage because the wife could no longer care for the husband. She was to remain in Maine, while the husband was about to board a plane for California, where their son lived. It isn't a story about the fire, but the human interest of the tale captures her imagination. In the picture that accompanies the piece, the woman, formidable-looking, stands a head taller than her husband, who wears rimless glasses and is rotund. Grace would like to know if the woman is relieved to part from her husband of half a century or is instead heartbroken but stoic in the face of the camera. Grace will never know.

She refolds the newspapers so that they resemble the neat stack she removed from the kitchen. Tomorrow, she and Matthew will likely go back to the church for another look at the bulletin board. Or ought she go straight to the police and inquire about the Mr. Doe? She has taxed Matthew's generosity more than she should have and can't ask for more. But she has to move forward—to locate her husband, to secure a job, and to find a way to rebuild her home.

Headlights play against the window and then stop. It seems the entire house holds its breath. Grace walks to the head of the stairs, and when the door opens she sees a familiar dark green coat.

"Mother!" Grace yelps, running down the stairs. It's not her mother's way to embrace in public, but Grace can feel the force of her relief. Claire leaps from Joan's lap with a cry of "Grammy!" Behind her mother is Gladys, who has driven Grace's mother to the Yorks. Behind Gladys stands her mother's other friend, Evelyn.

"On the night of the fire, Gladys and Evelyn came with the car, and we headed toward your end of the beach," her mother says in a rush, "but the road was blocked, and the heat from the fire so intense, we couldn't get through. They told us that your part of the beach had been evacuated. Oh, Grace," her mother adds quietly while looking at Grace's flat belly.

It seems that everyone stares at her daughter's flat belly.

"Any word of Gene?" Grace asks, as they move toward the kitchen and sit.

"Not yet, but men are still fighting the fires inland," offers Evelyn, who then glances down.

The explanation, which is no explanation, silences the table. No one mentions Mr. Doe. No one mentions the police. Claire, hearing an inaudible cry in the air, slides out of her grandmother's lap and makes her way under the table to her mother. Grace picks up her girl and holds her in her arms.

"Lovely cake."

"Hmmm. Yummy."

Through all of this, Matthew drinks a cup of coffee, answering the polite question that comes his way. Grace can't read him. Perhaps he's uncomfortable in this group of women. She remembers that he has to get up at four.

When the small talk dies down, Grace senses a question on the table next to the cake plate and its crumbs.

By rights, Grace and her children should go with her mother, who is kin. But her mother has lost her house, too, and is living with Gladys. Would Gladys take in Grace and the children? She can't ask that question now, not with Joan and Matthew in the room. But after a second round of coffees has been poured and sipped, Grace's mother addresses Joan.

"I can never thank you enough for rescuing my daughter and her children. We heard of the rescue at the church before we saw the note with your address. And then to have given them food and shelter is above and beyond . . ."

"Our pleasure," says a blushing Joan.

"But we'll take them now. My friend, Gladys, has an extra room at the top of her house where we can set up a bed and a crib and a playpen."

"I'll be sorry to see them go."

"I'll second that," Matthew says. "But of course we all want to see the family settled."

"We'll take them tonight," Grace's mother says, and there, it is done.

Having said their goodbyes and thanked Matthew and Joan, Grace, her mother, the two other women, and the two children are about to pull out of the driveway, when a police car, lights flashing, blocks their exit. The policeman bends down and says to Gladys, who is driving, "I'm looking for Grace Holland. Is she with you?"

"I'm Grace," she says from the backseat.

"Would you step out of the car, please?"

The policeman walks ten feet away from the car, and Grace follows.

"You left this note at the church?" He holds aloft the scrap of paper on which she wrote the address of where she was staying.

"I did, yes."

"Has any of these persons returned?"

"My mother, Marjorie, is in the car, and my friend, Rosie, is on her way to Nova Scotia. I still haven't heard from my husband."

"That would be Eugene Holland?"

"Yes."

He tips his cap higher on his forehead, as a farmer might a felt hat. "We've searched the entire area the fires covered and all the hospitals, and we have no one who answers to that name. We are officially listing him as a missing person."

"Are there many missing persons?" Grace asks.

"In the beginning, we had twenty-seven, now we have two, including your husband. Do you have a photo of him?"

She did, but doesn't now.

"Can you give me a description?"

"About five foot, eleven inches, normal weight, sandy hair, dark blue eyes, he's twenty-nine. A scar on his chin. He was wearing brown pants and a brown jacket. He'd gone to help build a firebreak."

"Yes, we know." The cop removes a card. "When he comes back, you give us a call, so we can take his name off the list. He's probably had a knock on the head, or someone has taken him in." He pauses. "Or maybe the shock of the fire has temporarily addled him."

The policeman doesn't say what Grace knows he is thinking, that Gene is dead. Grace is thinking something else: He's done a runner.

"The idea," says Gladys, "is to ease off the clutch slowly and give it a little gas, then steadily increase the fuel until the car starts to move. You keep it in that gear—first gear—for probably three or four seconds, and when you get this sound, a higher revving of the motor, you ease into second by depressing the clutch and going straight down with the shift. And so on until third, the 'hyphen' over and up, and fourth, down here. It's an H if you can picture it. You'll get the hang of it."

Gladys, in her purple coat and matching hat, offered at breakfast to teach Grace how to drive. Perhaps she'd seen Grace's restlessness, her desire to get a job and support herself in Gene's absence. Four women and two children in one house has at times been trying. Grace is quite sure that Gladys and Evelyn are lesbians, though she never had that thought before living with the two women. It's in the way they brush the backs of their hands together in the kitchen, the tension in the evening, when they have to part in the hallway. Often both Gladys and Evelyn have their hands on the round ball finial at the end of the stairway railing as they delay leaving each other. Grace's mother must know, too, though she's never said a word to Grace. Does she often feel like a third wheel?

"So we're moving," continues Gladys, "but now, suppose I want to make a right turn? I roll down my window, stick my arm out, bend it at the elbow, and have the hand pointing straight up, like this. That tells any driver behind me that I'm going to slow down for the right turn. So now we down-clutch, from fourth to third—watch the shift—to second and possibly to first, though that's seldom necessary. You want to give it a try?"

The night of Thanksgiving, Claire tries to climb onto her mother's lap. Grace lifts her up and senses the fever in the child's limbs even before she touches her forehead.

"Mother, come feel Claire."

Her mother, dish towel over her wrist, puts the back of her hand to the child's forehead. Grace notes her mother's widening eyes. "She's spiking a fever," Marjorie says. "Let's get her to bed."

"On the sofa for now," Grace insists. "I want to be able to watch her."

Gladys appears with a roll of ice chips wrapped in a dish towel. "Put this on her forehead."

"Mother, do you have any aspirin?"

"Yes, I might. Upstairs in my handbag."

"She's shivering."

"Cover her with blankets so she can sweat it out."

Grace thinks the instructions wrong, that her daughter's temperature should be brought down, but her mother has had so much more experience than she with sick children that she does as her mother suggests. Evelyn agrees. Quilts are found to cover Claire.

Grace sits beside her daughter holding ice chips to her forehead. What infection has Claire picked up and where? She tries to recall all the places she has recently been with her. To the police station to deliver a photograph of Gene her mother had in an album. To Shaw's for tins of pumpkin pie filling, and then to bring a pie to Matt and Joan.

Claire begins to shake, and Grace instinctively tries to hold her still. She watches with a mother's horror as her daughter stiffens and goes limp with a froth of white on her lips. "Ohmylordwhatwasthat?"

"She's had a seizure," Gladys says. "This is serious."

With one swift movement, Grace scoops up Claire, praying that the child won't have another seizure en route. "We've got to get her to a doctor."

With the overhead light on and Claire in a fetal position in the front seat, Grace reads the address of Dr. Franklin's clinic and her mother's hastily scrawled instructions as to how to get there. She drives through familiar wasteland and makes the turn onto Route 1. After several minutes, she sees a car coming to an intersection, downshifts, and presses on the brakes. Grace's car slides into a slow skid. Helpless, Grace puts a hand on Claire, pushing her into the seat, and steers as best she can with her left hand, which is no help at all because the steering doesn't seem to be working. Black ice. Grace spins across the highway, the other vehicle missing her by inches and honking, either in recognition of Grace's harrowing near miss, or in anger at the almost accident.

She straightens the car and continues on, never letting the speedometer rise over 15. Because the dark is impenetrable, she has to stop and face the signposts with her headlights. After half an hour, she spots the road she's looking for and follows that for a mile. She reaches the end and parks close to a Quonset hut, with only one other car in the parking lot. She gathers Claire and runs with her to the front door. After several loud bangs, a tall man in a white coat opens it.

"My daughter's had a seizure."

"I'm Dr. Lighthart." He takes Claire in his arms and feels her forehead. Without a word, he walks with her to a room beyond the receptionist's empty desk. Grace has to run to keep up with him. He lays Claire on a gurney, strips away the blankets, raises her pajama shirt, examines her, then listens to her heart. He checks her back, looks at her tongue, and sticks a thermometer in her mouth. "Try to hold this here," he says.

"Where's Dr. Franklin?" she asks.

"He retired after the fire. I've taken over."

A clean sheet is put on the gurney. Claire's body is limp.

"We need to get the temperature down fast," he says,

removing the thermometer from Claire's mouth and glancing at it. "Have you given her anything?"

"One aspirin."

"We'll cover her with cold towels. Then, if necessary, we'll put her in an ice bath. She won't like any of it, so be prepared. You'd best get her clothes off."

For the first time, he glances up at Grace.

"You," he says, puzzled.

"You!" she says, astonished.

Grace holds a bared wrist under the water until the temperature is as low as it will go. She remembers her legs buried in the muck of low tide, the way the doctor and Matthew thought she might be dead. She raised her head then, but couldn't move her arms, and the men had to slip the children out from under her grip.

"When we found you," Dr. Lighthart says, "the high tide of the night before had taken most of the belongings of the families that had come to the water's edge, but here and there, the items were sloshing back in with the new tide. We'd been collecting people who'd been told to evacuate. I remember that I was watching the gas gauge on the dashboard of the truck. It was below empty according to the dial. We talked about how you would have to be our last rescue until we found a gas station that hadn't burned down. Later, after we had you in the truck, I was worried we wouldn't make it to the hospital."

"But you did, and thank you."

Grace wonders if the belongings sloshing in the ocean on the new tide had returned to be reunited with their kin.

———

Claire looks as though she has been wrapped in a shroud. Death. Grace's knees weaken.

"She needs the ice bath now," the doctor insists. "I'll get the ice. As soon as the towels feel warm, unwrap her."

"What do you think she has?" Grace asks, frantic.

"Scarlet fever most likely, though it could be meningitis or polio. She'll need an antibiotic."

Polio.

When the doctor returns to the room, he sets a blue rubber tub layered with ice under the tap, filling it half full. "This is going to wake her up. What's her name?"

"Claire. Claire Holland."

"Age?"

"Two and a bit."

"And what's your name? I don't think I ever knew."

"Grace."

He picks up the child and slowly lowers her into the ice bath. Claire wakes with a shudder. At first she whimpers, and then she screams.

"Hold her there," he says. "I'm going to prepare an injection."

"Of what?"

"Penicillin. In case there's a bacterial infection. We won't know until morning when symptoms begin to present themselves."

"Isn't a seizure a symptom?"

"It's a result of high fever. Not the disease itself. Is your daughter allergic to penicillin?"

"I don't know. She's never had it."

Grace fights to keep the slippery Claire in the tub. The fight goes against every instinct in her body.

After Dr. Lighthart has prepared the injection, he says, "Let's do this over here."

Grace lifts her daughter up and dries her with a towel, thinking, This must be torture for Claire. The child is silent, relieved to be out of the bath.

"Put her on her side facing you. Keep talking to her."

Grace holds Claire's face and croons soothing words, but she doesn't miss the flash of the needle as it goes in. After a split second, Claire shrieks.

"That's good," the doctor says. "Listlessness isn't."

Grace wraps Claire in a dry towel and holds her close. The feeling of momentary relief is intense.

Grace follows the doctor into a small room in which there are two cribs. He lowers the slats on the side of one of them. "I'm going to cover her with only a light sheet. I'll be across the hall in my office. If there's a problem, just yell and I'll hear you. If you think she's too hot, if you spot a rash, if she seizes, if she vomits, if she starts to bark like a dog, anything you don't like, you come and get me."

Grace nods. She understands that he won't tell her that everything will be all right, because both he and she know that might not be the truth.

Claire feels warm. What's the precise point at which warm becomes hot? Grace is reluctant to use the thermometer because Claire is asleep, and Grace knows the child needs rest. She lays her head against the slats of the crib. It's too much, she nearly says aloud. The fire, the loss of the baby, Gene, and now Claire. If something should happen to Claire, Grace knows that she will break apart into pieces that will never be put back together again.

Warm becomes hot, and a line is crossed. Grace stands, unsure. Should she go to Dr. Lighthart or should she try to take Claire's temperature herself? She lays the back of her hand against her child's forehead. She doesn't need a thermometer.

At the threshold to the doctor's office, she pauses. He's fallen asleep on his desk, pushing a manual so close to the edge that Grace is amazed it hasn't fallen.

"Dr. Lighthart?" she calls.

The man rubs his face, and the manual falls to the floor. He checks his watch. Twelve-fifteen, Grace knows from the big clock in the room where Claire is sleeping.

He stands, his white coat wrinkled, and follows Grace. "She's hot," she says.

He feels the skin under Claire's arm. "She certainly is," he agrees. "When was the last time she had aspirin?"

"Maybe seven-thirty?"

He fetches a brown glass bottle in a cabinet. "Wake her and see if you can get her sitting upright."

The doctor crushes the aspirin in a spoon, then fills it with water. "Do you want to do this?" he asks.

"Yes," she says.

Grace lowers the slats and takes the spoon from the doctor while he props Claire up. She gently rubs the back of her

finger against Claire's cheek. The child opens her mouth—
the trick never fails—and Grace gets as much of the medicine into her as she can.

"Give her a second to digest that, and then we'll start the
whole routine again."

"The ice bath?"

"I know of a father who ran out the door of his house and
plunged into the snow with his eight-month-old son. Saved
the kid's life."

"A fellow who's the husband of one of my patients brought
me a plate of turkey," Dr. Lighthart says, "and stuffing
and potato. He apologized for the lack of cranberry sauce,
explaining that the bogs had boiled. Needless to say, I was
grateful. To make up for the sparse dinner, the guy produced
a pumpkin pie. 'Missus had an extra' was how he put it. I
don't know about you, but I could sure use a slice of that pie
right now."

"Thank you."

While he's gone, Grace gazes at Claire and tries to guess
his age. Thirty, thirty-five? The white coat might make him
look older than he really is, but there's a certain gravity in the
face. She wonders why he wanted to exile himself to such a
backwater area when, as a young doctor, he might have been
drawn to a city hospital.

He returns with the pie, two plates, forks, and napkins.
Touching Claire again, Grace watches as he cuts two large
pieces.

The first bite of pie makes her close her eyes with pleasure. It might be the odd circumstances in which she's eating

it, but she thinks the pie the best she's ever had—it's a dark pumpkin, tasting of mace.

"This is delicious," she says.

"I have to do a better job of remembering patients' names. I didn't recall the man's wife's name, but I could see her face as clear as day. The next time I see her, I'll thank her on your behalf."

For the first time all evening and night, Grace smiles. "And not yours?"

"When I saw you last," he says after a time, "you were pregnant."

"I lost the baby."

"Oh, I'm sorry. You *have* had a rough go of it, haven't you?"

"I won't deny it."

"First things first. Let's get this pretty little girl well."

Grace collects the dishes and the silverware and walks with unsteady steps to the kitchen, a long narrow room with a white wooden counter. She covers the pie and puts it into the refrigerator, which is filled with medicines and two bottles of milk. For babies? For coffee?

She locates the dish soap and sponge and washes the few items they used. She dries them with a towel and folds it neatly on top of the counter.

She has trouble with the bathroom lock, though she can't see the need of it. Her hands shake so much that she can barely get her girdle down. When she sits, she examines her fingers, which tremble even when she clamps them together. Her face is wet with tears. She tears a length of toilet paper to wipe them off, a useless gesture since she then begins to cry in earnest. She knows she can't stop—it's the simple act of being alone, of closing a door. And perhaps it truly is the cumulative loss, one after another, but the tears feel different—purely physical, pure release—and when she is done, she feels better, though there has been no change in her circumstances. She puts herself together, washes her face and hands in the sink, dries herself with a towel, and stands back to examine her face in the mirror. Her eyes are swollen, the whites pink. Dr. Lighthart will know that she has been crying. Well, what does it matter? What has she got to hide now?

He has a pad of paper on his lap and a pen in his hand. Making notes.

He's smiling when he looks up at her, but the smile fades. "What happened?"

"Does anything more need to have happened?"

He closes the notebook, clips the pen to his coat pocket. "She's fine for the moment," he says, "but the fever may climb again. We'll see."

"You should get back to your work. We've taken up too much of your time. Besides, you need to sleep."

"I think you need to sleep."

"No," she says. "I need to talk."

"Were you in the war?" she asks.

"I was. A medic. I was in my second year of medical school when war broke out. I finished the year and enlisted."

"What a horrible time you must have had."

"It was pretty bad."

"Do you ever speak about it?" she asks.

"If someone wants to know."

"It's funny, because my husband hardly ever mentioned the war. It's been my experience that most men our age won't."

"You can't blame them. No one wants to revisit horror. Or guilt."

"Why do you say guilt?"

"You're given orders you don't think are right, but you have to do them anyway. Every day, there are choices to make and sometimes you make a selfish one."

"What's a selfish one?"

"Triaging a man you guess won't live past noon though he's in line for surgery. Then you struggle with that decision for weeks."

For a moment, Grace is silent. "If you don't mind my asking, how did you end up here?" she asks.

"After the war, I finished up med school, then just recently set out to hang my shingle. You get a map, and you shop for towns. If you're lucky, someone takes you in and grooms you. I didn't want hospital work. I'd seen enough of wards. I wanted a small-town family practice. After the fire, I'd heard that the local doctor's house had burned down, and that he had a temporary practice here, in this hut. I came here to visit him and to offer my help, and I could see he was in a state. I told him what I was looking for, and he seemed immensely relieved. We brought the lawyers in, and I bought the practice."

She scans the Quonset hut, the metal rivets showing. "I hope you didn't pay a lot for it."

He laughs. "The government owns the building. It's temporary. I hope to build a house with an office attached."

"In Hunts Beach?"

"That's the idea."

"You'll have an awfully small practice," she says.

He glances at Claire, puts the back of his hand to her forehead. "If Hunts Beach were inland, I'd agree with you. Few families would want to rebuild in a place with no infrastructure. No schools, police, fire department. But Hunts Beach will always be valuable land because it's coastal. It will repopulate. Whether it will be with the original inhabitants, I can't say." He pauses. "It's as if you're part of a diaspora now."

Grace is unsure of the word.

"A scattering of a people from their homeland. Displaced."

She nods. The Jews. She has seen the movie reels. Horrifying and unimaginable.

She glances out the window. The snow is still falling. Will her children be taught about the Jews at school?

"But what about you?" he asks.

Grace tells him about her father, the secretarial course, meeting Gene at the small college to which they both commuted, and marrying him before they'd started their second year. She doesn't tell the doctor that when she met Gene she thought him handsome and serious, in contrast to the boys she'd been meeting at parties, and she took that seriousness for depth of character. She doesn't tell him that they married when Grace discovered she was pregnant and that Gene began to shake with either anger or great happiness. *This is good, this is what I've always wanted,* she told herself. And if it wasn't as romantic or as heedless as she had once hoped for, it was fine.

"You mind if I smoke?" the doctor asks.

"Not at all."

He offers her one, and she takes it. He crosses his legs and hangs an arm over the chair. He looks casual and very long. "Tell me more about your husband."

"He's a surveyor on the Turnpike project. His mother died recently. I expected him to mourn, but I didn't expect the silence." She takes a pull on the cigarette. "I used to count up the number of words he said to me in a given day. Sometimes it was only two. When I was a girl, I always thought I'd marry the strong, silent type. But what a bore, really."

"You have friends?" he asks.

"I used to have a very good friend. But after the fire, she and her husband and children went to live in Nova Scotia."

"There you go, the diaspora. Why so far?"

"They have family there. Rosie was wonderful. She made me happy every day." She pauses. "Nearly everyone in Hunts Beach is now homeless. Many are destitute."

"There'll be no charge for tonight."

"Oh, I didn't mean that," she's quick to say. "I'll pay. Of course, I'll pay. You can't very well start a practice without the patients paying."

"I'm going to set up a sliding scale. When I've assessed the general income level of the patients, I'll determine my fees."

"Is that legal?"

"It's time-honored."

"You'll have a bookkeeping mess," she says.

"You know bookkeeping?"

"I do. And I'll pay the standard rate because you just saved my daughter's life."

"You saved your daughter's life by getting her here. Seizures can be very dangerous."

Grace remembers the awful moment in Gladys's house.

"Let's just say she's a lucky girl," he offers.

"Will she really be all right?"

"We'll see in the morning, but I think so."

In the morning, Claire's cheeks are bright red, her tongue white, her throat raw, and she has a rash over her chest and arms. All the symptoms point to scarlet fever, Dr. Lighthart explains. "Any children around her have it?" he asks as the sun rises through the window.

"None that I can think of," Grace answers.

"It can be serious, and it spreads easily. You have another child at home."

"Yes."

"Can you put Claire in a room by herself? She has to be quarantined. You know what that entails?"

Grace thinks about the arrangements, the three of them in the attic. Tom will have to sleep with his grandmother. "Claire and I can sleep together in one room."

"I'd like to keep her here for twenty-four hours, but I'm going to have to put you both in an isolation room. The receptionist and a nurse will be in this morning. I'll leave a note on the front desk as to where you are, as well as the diagnosis."

———

The nurse, Amy, has Claire fill out a card requiring name, address, phone number, blood type, previous illnesses, both for her and for Claire. Grace can do the name and her previous illnesses—measles, chicken pox, tonsils out—but the address and phone number are not her own. She wonders how much money she has in her purse and if she can pay the doctor in full today so that he needn't bill her.

Amy offers Grace a gown, bathrobe, and slippers, none of which fit her well. Her legs are bare from above her knees to her ankles, which would be fine if she were the patient. Not fine as a regular woman. The slippers are small and insubstantial, but she can hardly put her good heels on with the gown and robe.

Claire frets, cries, and coughs most of the morning, which Grace knows is a good sign. Her child isn't listless. According to the doctor, Claire likely has a terrible sore throat and a headache. Grace tries to explain to her daughter that she's sick and will get better soon, but time means nothing to a young child. An hour, two days, four days. It hurts now. That's all she knows.

An hour, two days, four days. It's all Grace knows, too.

Barbara, the receptionist, never makes it in, having skidded into a tree early in the morning. This according to Amy, who gives Claire a cool sponge bath. "I keep telling her, come in later than usual on an icy or snowy morning. Give the plows a chance. But her husband, Burt, tells her that it's best to be the first car on the road—less danger of hitting anyone else if you skid out. Guess he forgot about trees. Burt's an idiot.

He knows all about drilling for wells, but hasn't an iota of common sense. Strange for a man, don't you think? And Barbara, she does what he tells her. I hope she's not hurt, but I've got my hands full now. I have to keep checking the waiting room because there's no one there to tell us someone needs attention."

"Don't bother with us," Grace says. "I can handle everything myself."

"You can probably take her temperature regularly, but you can't do the injections."

"Injections?"

"Yes, she's due at six tonight."

"Of the antibiotic?"

Amy looks at her as if Grace, too, might be dim.

"For ten days," Amy explains.

"But Dr. Lighthart said the symptoms should subside in five days."

"That's true, but you have to do the complete course with antibiotics or else the illness could come back, sometimes in a more virulent form. When the doctor sends you away, he'll give you a prescription for an oral fluid she can take by the spoonful."

When Claire finally falls asleep, Grace climbs onto the adult-size cot and pulls up the sheets. She turns to her side to be able to keep an eye on her daughter. She has to do better by her children; she can't live on the kindness of others indefinitely. She's made good progress in her driving, but what she really needs is a job in a village or a city in which she can walk to work, get a babysitter, and do her shopping on foot. With her mother's help, until she can get a paycheck, she might just be able to swing a one-bedroom apartment in a city. But which city? Biddeford? Portland? Portsmouth? Her thinking stops there as she begins to drift off. Her mind fills with images of scintillating snowfields and someone, a child, in the distance. She strains to hear but can't.

Music

Thirty-eight days after the fire, and Grace has lived a lifetime. Claire is outside, Gladys pulling her on a sled along a path, while Grace's mother, glad that her daughter has emerged from quarantine, seems chirpy on this snow-covered winter day. "I think he's just about ready to walk," Marjorie says of Tom. "All the time I had him, he was holding on between the hassocks and the side tables and the chairs."

"I feel as though I've been away for a very long time."

"When I think of what you've been through—well I may have been mad at you briefly here and there—but you can't imagine the admiration I have for you."

During her week at Claire's side, Grace had hours to try to solve her seemingly insurmountable problem. She, her children, and her mother can't live in Gladys's house indefinitely. Grace has to find another place for them, or at least convince the building commission to put her near the head of the line for a new house. She's a single parent without a home. Won't they view that situation as more dire than that of a family with multiple adults to earn money? But even if she were to persuade an official today, it will take months for the house to be ready.

One night when she can't sleep, she has a thought that at first repulses her and then begins to seem sensible. If Gladys will loan her the Chevrolet, Grace can drive to Merle Holland's house to see if it's empty. If it is, she can bring her children and her mother there; her mother can watch the children while Grace looks for work. They won't have to furnish a home, and in the spring, there will be flowers. There are plenty of bedrooms for all of them, and it has the added advantage of being the first place Gene might go when he returns from wherever he's been. By morning, the plan has solidified.

"Mother, I have an idea. What if I were to take a drive to Merle Holland's house—Gene's house now. And if I found it empty, we—the kids, me, you—could move in there. It would be housing, and it would take the burden off Gladys and Evelyn. We could open all the windows for a few minutes, let in fresh air, see to the linens and pots and pans. It's possible there's an entire house ready for us to inhabit."

"But it would be trespassing," her mother says.

"Not really. Think about it. Gene inherited the house, he's missing, I'm his wife, these are his children, he would want us to have shelter."

"But how could you settle into the house of a woman who never had a good thing to say about you?"

"Times have changed, Mother. I've changed. I could settle into her house just fine. And, if I recall, there's a nursery with a crib and toys. I'll go first to make sure it hasn't been taken over by squatters or by a long-lost cousin of Gene's I've never heard of. I might try to do some dusting, make sure the utilities haven't been turned off. The house has never been listed for sale, because Gene wanted us to move there." She pauses. If he only knew.

"Well, it's a thought. I do feel a bit in the way here."

Grace meets her mother's eyes and knows she understands the relationship between Gladys and Evelyn. How could she not? Grace would like to query her mother further, but now is not the time.

If Grace moved into Merle's, she would have to relinquish access to a car, a hardship after having learned to drive. There has to be a bus, she reasons, that travels along the coast road. It's only then that it occurs to her that Merle's house might have burned to the ground as well.

Her anxiety builds as she drives toward the shore and sees that most of the coastal land is black. When she turns the corner to enter Merle's neighborhood, however, she sees that the houses are intact. She pulls into the driveway as if she were a newcomer to a bridge group. Gene had a key to the house, but she doesn't. There's nothing to search, not Gene's pockets, not a drawer in which he might have left the key. She climbs the stairs, and as she suspected the door is locked. She lifts up mats, sticks her finger into flowerpots, reaches for ledges. She descends the steps and walks to one side of the house, searching for a window that might be partially raised. Now that she's here, the urge to break into the house is strong. She scans basement windows, tries the bulkhead, and attempts to shimmy a window that looks unlocked but is stuck. By the time she's reached the back of the house, she's nearly given up. She tries the porch door, and it opens. She tries the back door, and it gives. How simple. It's then that Grace hears music and freezes.

Someone in the house is playing a record. Or does the music come from a radio left on? She moves cautiously toward the hall, the one that leads to both the sitting room and the turret. The music grows louder each step she takes, and she realizes it's coming from upstairs. It has to be Gene—he's alive! Part of her wants to run up the stairs, shouting his name, and part of her is mortified. If it's Gene, why is he living here without her? Why has he not taken the trouble to find his wife and children?

She can see in her mind's eye a sweep of the keyboard, a rumbling of deep chords, while the melody skips along, and that's how it feels—the melody skipping—and then the two are brought together in a powerful crescendo that causes hairs to rise at the back of her neck and her eyes to close. The sound is pure, sublime. It can't be a record or a radio broadcast. She finds a chair next to a telephone table and ever so quietly, so as not to disturb, she sits. She had no idea her husband was talented in this way.

Grace is reminded of tinkling broken glass, then of someone in great command, then of a deep and primitive growl from the lower notes. The melody, partially melancholic, moves her. It seems to seep through her skin and find its way to her center. Is it from musical notes that true longing is born? The desire to have the same thing again and again? After all, a mother's song to an infant is a melody. Childlike and not always beautiful, but it's a touchstone that one might long for in life. Grace craves the delicate touch of fingers on the keys, which she feels as fingers along the back of her neck. She bends her head.

The music ends.

Footsteps from a room into an upper hallway. Perhaps Gene sees Grace's boots. She can hear him coming down the stairs. She can't stand. Not yet.

There's a moment of hesitation. Both Grace and the stranger begin to speak at once.

"You play beautifully."

"I didn't know the house was inhabited. I beg your pardon."

"I beg your pardon."

"I have nowhere to go."

"This house."

"It seemed uninhabited."

"It is. It isn't. How did you get in?"

"Houses like these are always easy to get into. Impossible to secure."

"I think . . ."

"I think . . ."

"This house belongs to my husband. I'm Grace Holland."

"Aidan Berne."

They shake hands. His grip is warm.

Grace sets the kettle to boil, finding tea, sugar, a little milk, and producing from a cupboard a package of Lorna Doone cookies. She wonders if Aidan Berne, too, lost everything in the fire.

He's at least six feet tall. He wears his light brown hair

long. His eyes are light brown, she concludes, during the brief glances her way. He has on a navy sweater and gray wool pants in the drafty house. She interrupted him in his slippers.

"When did you come here?" she asks.

"The afternoon the fire hit Kennebunk. We were in the middle of rehearsals when men warned us through bull-horns to get out of town. We packed up quickly and fled to waiting cars, and I managed to snag a seat. Then they let us out on Route One with no instructions. They said they had to go back into the village to rescue more. We could hardly complain." He takes a sip of tea and holds out the plate of cookies to Grace. She takes one.

"We started walking away from the fire," he continues. "Those who knew the area slipped down dirt roads leading to cottages, but we could see that the fire was beginning to invade the woods along the coast. We started running. When I looked up the hill, I caught sight of a piano in a round room, just a glimpse, and I peeled off. I played until nearly eight in the morning."

"What were you playing just now?" Grace asks. She has on Joan's blue wedding suit, having decided she should dress up a bit for Merle's house.

"Brahms's Second Piano Concerto."

"You can play that from memory?"

"A lot of people can. Well, not a lot. A few. It's meant for an orchestra and a piano."

"I was moved," Grace admits.

"By what exactly? I've always been curious about this. By how music affects people."

"The melody," she says, setting down her cup. "The passage that keeps getting repeated in different forms. The hairs stood out at the back of my neck." She pauses, embarrassed. "I'm not explaining this well."

"For some, the concerto is purely an intellectual pleasure. You sound as though you absorbed it through the skin."

"Yes, that's it, through the skin."

"Didn't you listen to music in your home?"

"The radio."

"You'll have to get some records."

She nods but wants to protest that she hasn't any money, which leads her to her next thought, the reason why she's here. "I have two children," she says. "My husband, Gene, went off to make a firebreak, and he didn't come home. His body was never found."

"I'm very sorry."

"Yes, thank you, it's awful, but there's another problem. Our house burned down, and I have nowhere to live. At the moment we're living in the attic of a friend of my mother's, but we can't stay there indefinitely. Then I remembered this house. Gene inherited it when his mother died."

"I'll leave of course," he says. "I can be gone by evening."

Grace wants to touch his fingers. How can so much magic come from them? "Are your fingers insured?" she asks.

"My hands."

"They'd have to be, wouldn't they?"

"I can't do anything else except play the piano."

"I don't want to make you leave," Grace admits reluctantly. "I'd like to be able to hear that music again." She blushes and bends her head. "The world is so dreary, so awful now."

"Everything in the house seems to be working fine, as far as I can tell," he offers. "Good hot water, the stove works, can't speak for the oven, the steam heat is better on the second floor than on the first."

"Don't go anywhere tonight," she says. Perhaps, she thinks, he can remain as a tenant. The money would be a relief, a source of income while she looks for a job. "When I come back with the children and my mother in the morning, we'll have made a decision. If you would, could you unlock the front door starting around nine?"

Before Grace can tell her mother about the man at Merle's house, she needs to be sure it's what she wants. It doesn't take her long to decide that the man must stay—somehow, in some capacity. The decision surprises her. She knows nothing about Aidan Berne. He might be an escaped convict, he might be a leech, he might be a spy who will endanger them all. But Grace feels certain he is only an evacuee who was interrupted in the middle of a rehearsal by a fire.

Grace has to wait until two o'clock, when everyone goes up for a nap, Gladys and Evelyn included. Her mother doesn't leave the kitchen, however, knowing that her daughter has news to deliver.

They sit, her mother with a dish towel in her hand. "Well?" she asks.

"The house is open and is in good shape, and we can move in anytime. But it seems we have a tenant."

"A tenant? Paying rent?"

"Well, that's the thing. We haven't established that yet."

"I'm confused."

Grace lights a cigarette. "There's a pianist on the second floor. He was being evacuated during the fire, and he saw the piano in the turret. Curiosity compelled him to enter the house. He's been there since the night of the fire."

"A squatter?"

"A squatter with immense talent. And he's offered to leave."

"Well, then," her mother says, setting the folded dish towel on the table. "That's settled."

"Well, not really," Grace says. "I think we should let him stay."

"Why? Will he pay good rent?"

"I'm sure he will, but that's not the only reason. The music is beautiful. The kids and you and I have had so little in the way of beauty or music in our lives."

"Music won't pay the bills," her mother says. "And what kind of a man just squats in the house without trying to find out who the owners are?"

"Oh, come on, Mother, you know it's been happening all up and down the coast of Maine." She taps her ash into the saucer. Gladys and Evelyn don't smoke.

"If he has no credentials, we can't trust him."

"I'm sure he does have credentials. I just didn't ask. But I talked to him. I liked him. I think he's trustworthy."

Her mother seems about to remind her of instances when her instincts didn't pay off, but she holds her tongue.

"I want to go back with you and the children tomorrow, just to see the place," says Grace.

"It might be good to have a man close by," her mother suggests. "To fix things, I mean."

"There may be one slight hitch. The piano is in the turret on the second floor. It's part of Merle's bedroom. I can only let him stay if he arranges to move the instrument down to the turreted parlor."

"How can he do that?"

"The stairs are wide, but my guess is that they'll take out one of the long windows and use a crane to get it down. They'll have to take out a window in the parlor, too, to get it back in."

"Is all that necessary?"

"I think so. The children and I will take over Merle's bedroom. I want them near me for now. And you have your choice of rooms on the third floor. One of them is a turret room, too."

"I already have my own room," her mother sniffs, doubtless thinking of the house that burned down.

"You don't anymore," Grace gently reminds her.

"But what about the man? Where's he going to sleep?"

"There's a library on the first floor, just off the kitchen. It's a good-size room, and we can move a bed down there. Then he'll have everything he needs, a bed, a bathroom, his piano, and access to the kitchen. Not a bad little apartment."

"You've thought this all out."

"I have," says Grace.

As they climb the stairs, Claire, whose eyes dart from side to side, seems to remember the house. Marjorie holds Tom while Grace opens the front door. Aidan has raised all the shades to let light in, and Grace can't find a mote of obvious dust. They didn't talk about whether or not he should be present, but he seems to have made a decision not to be. The light coming in the windows both enhances and detracts from the rooms. She notes a water stain on an expensive antique table, claw marks from a dog at the side of one of the sofas, a bit of threadbare carpet. It's all fine, even better that way; Grace needn't worry about the children hurting the furnishings.

Grace leads her mother, Tom, and Claire into the dining room and then into the yellow and white kitchen. Perhaps remembering the last time she visited this house, Claire tries to open drawers, looking for the wooden utensils her mother got out for her.

"I like this," her mother says, gazing at the large windows.

Grace shows them the library she means to use as Aidan's bedroom if he agrees. She leads the entourage up the carpeted curved staircase. They enter the room that once was Merle's. Claire runs to the dressing table and wants to touch the jewelry there. "Not now," Grace admonishes. Her mother has wandered into the turret, where the piano is.

"My goodness," her mother says, "how are they ever going to get this thing out?"

"We'll see how badly Aidan wants to stay, won't we," says Grace.

"Aidan?"

"Aidan Berne."

"Where's he from?"

Grace doesn't know. "You can ask him when you meet him. Now to the third floor."

Grace's memories of a nursery are correct. There's a crib and a wall of wooden toys, all neatly lined up. A rocking chair. Childlike paintings on the walls. A small lamp decorated with rabbits. Claire runs toward the toys, and even Tom strains to be put down. "You go explore the rooms," Grace says to her mother. "I'll watch the children."

Grace has them seated around the enameled kitchen table as she pours tea for her mother and her, milk for the children. She finds the bag of Lorna Doones and is glad there are still several left.

"I like this room," her mother repeats.

"So do I," Grace adds.

"Me too!" Claire says.

"Which room did you pick out?" Grace asks her mother.

"I think I liked the turret bedroom," her mother confesses shyly. "The views are very special."

"I'm glad," says Grace. She doesn't mention that it was Gene's bedroom when he was a boy. The doorbell rings in the kitchen as well as in the parlor. Brushing crumbs off her hands, Grace walks to the front door. She thinks, Good timing. She says, "Hello."

"I thought it would be better this way," replies Aidan. "Didn't want to seem like I lived here."

"Smart. Come into the sitting room with me, and then I'll take you out to the kitchen to meet my family."

Aidan has on a good suit, an even better pair of black shoes. His concert clothes, she guesses. He's trimmed his hair.

"I'd like you to stay," she says, "but there's one hitch."

"And what's that?" he asks.

"I want to take over the second floor. My children

and I will sleep there. So the piano will have to be moved downstairs."

Aidan raises an eyebrow, and she can see him pondering that reality. Is he thinking of the size of the windows, the expense to move it, or the possible loss of quality of sound?

"Big undertaking," he says, sitting back.

"Yes. I hate to ask, but can you afford such an operation?"

"I can," he says without hesitation. "Traveling soloists sometimes have good spells."

"You'll agree then?"

"Yes, I'll agree, but you risk harming the piano. And I can't say if the quality of the sound comes from being situated where it is. I guess we'll just have to find out."

"I'd like to leave it where it is," Grace admits, "but I have to have a place for me and my children. I think my mother would find it awkward if we all slept on the third floor with you on the second."

"I'm sure the instrument will survive. Where would I sleep?"

"Have you wandered into the library?" Grace crosses her ankles. Because she couldn't wear the blue suit again, she has on a red sweater and a gray wool skirt. The skirt was Gladys's and doesn't fit her well. "We'll make up a bedroom for you in there."

Aidan nods.

"And there's one more thing." Grace hesitates. "We'll have to sort out some kind of rent." The music ought to be enough, she thinks. More than enough. Grace names a price she thinks is fair. Aidan agrees without further comment. "I should warn you, my mother will want references. She won't say it to you, but I'll have to produce something."

"That's not a problem," he says.

Grace's family stares at the stranger she brings into the kitchen. He walks straight to her mother and says, "I'm pleased to meet you. Aidan Berne."

Bold Claire stands on the table, as if wanting to make sure the stranger notices her.

"And who are you, little girl?" he asks, gently shaking her hand.

"I'm Claire. I'm two. I'm bigger than two."

"Are you now?"

"Claire, please don't stand on the table," Grace warns. Claire complies by sitting on the table.

"And this little one?" Aidan asks, chucking Tom under his chin.

"This is Tom," Grace explains and gestures for Aidan to sit in the extra chair.

"Aidan and I have worked out arrangements," she announces to her mother, who is too polite to ask what they are in front of the stranger.

"Claire, you like this house, don't you?" asks Grace.

Claire, thoughtful, surveys the kitchen, as if assessing it. She gives an exaggerated nod.

"So I think we'll move in tomorrow," Grace says to Aidan. "You needn't move the piano just yet, but I do wonder if you could manage to get a bed into the library."

"I can take a bed apart and bring it down in pieces and then put it back together again," he offers.

"Before we go today, my mother and I will sort out the linens to make sure you have everything you need. And while I have the car, I'll go to the grocery store. When we move, I won't have an automobile. It belongs to the woman whose house we're currently staying in."

"The market isn't even a mile away. I can help you with that when you no longer have the car."

"You're very kind."

"You're very generous," he says.

"I'm not that generous," Grace says. "Would you mind playing something for my mother?"

The adults rearrange the chairs in Merle's bedroom turret so that the seats are to one side of Aidan. Grace wants to see his hands, which she was only able to imagine when she first heard him. With Tom on her lap, her mother to one side, and Claire to the other, she watches Aidan remove his jacket and take his place on the bench. He rolls his sleeves. She has no idea what to ask him to play since she doesn't know the names of classical pieces, but he seems to sense that, or he simply wants to play what pleases him, because he starts in straightaway with his right hand only, and then after a minute, allows the left to crash in. Claire comes alert with a start. Tom claps.

And then Grace can hear the melody, the notes that will repeat themselves during the piece. With her mother beside her, she's careful not to betray, except with a smile, the sensations she experiences. She has a nearly overwhelming desire to bend her head, bare her neck, and let the tensions of the day leave her.

She examines Aidan's fingers—stretching, reaching, confident, fast. She studies his face, a visage of perfect concentration. She doesn't think she has that ability—to focus so acutely on a task that nothing else matters. To be able to do this any time one wants—what a perfect gift. She has often wished she could sing. How heavenly to be able to entertain herself in that way. But the playing is something different. When the piece comes to a close, she thinks it ridiculous that she even mentioned rent.

"He seems a nice young man," her mother says as they leave Merle's driveway. Both children are asleep on the backseat.

"Indeed," says Grace.

"I thought he was very polite. Good manners."

"Yes."

"And very well spoken," adds her mother.

"He is."

"And I liked the way he played children's songs for Claire at the end."

"Nice."

"And the music, really. I'm not sure I've ever . . ."

"Nor I."

"I wonder where he went to school. He must have gone to music school."

"Mmm."

"He's Irish I think. His name."

"Maybe."

"The Rooneys are Irish," her mother points out. "Very nice people."

"They are."

"And I have to admit, he's handsome."

"Mother."

"It's amazing good luck that you found him when you did."

At Gladys's house that evening, as her mother attempts, in an awkward way, to explain why it is they will have to leave, all Grace can think about is Aidan's hands. She imagines them muscular and flexible, the skin soft, the reach long. For how many years has he been playing? Since he was a small child? And how did he come upon such a gift? One doesn't learn talent. And why is he not playing in New York or Boston, with the orchestras they have there?

Gladys, strangely, has tears in her eyes, which immediately produces a teary Marjorie. "You've been so kind to us," her mother says. "I hope you know how grateful we are."

"Gladys is softhearted, if you haven't noticed yet," says Evelyn, sniffing and giving no sign of sadness at the prospect of their four guests leaving imminently.

"And you'll come visit us," Grace adds. "Just as soon as we have the place fixed up. You must come for a meal."

One meal as payback for dozens? Absurd. Somehow Grace will find a way to recompense them for all the provisions. Or would they mind that? She wonders if her mother will stay close friends with the two women, if she's unhappy to be going.

In the morning, they pack, making the beds with fresh linen, leaving the room spotless.

To move from one attic room for the four of them to a house more than a dozen times larger is dizzying. Aidan seems to have had no trouble rounding up a crew of out-of-work men who agree to move the piano. Though the thermometer reads only forty-three degrees outside, the upper window has to be taken out while the piano is attached to a crane that has made deep grooves on the front lawn. Grace's mother can't bear to look and spends most of the day in the kitchen, rearranging the dishes and pots and pans to her liking. She then makes all the beds, including Aidan's. For his part, Aidan is meticulous in his instructions, not wanting to harm the piano in any way, and especially not wanting to leave the piano in the cold for a second longer than necessary. Grace and Aidan move all the furniture out of the way and agree that some of it will have to go down to the basement. Grace, with her arms wrapped tight around her chest, hardly dares to watch the piano come back into the house. Aidan is calm, but quick with an instruction if he thinks something about to go awry. He has on the blue sweater and gray pants he wore the day she met him. Grace has on the same thing she wore yesterday. Claire and Tom haven't been let out of Grace's mother's sight, everyone fearful for their safety.

"My God," Aidan says when the piano finally comes to rest and is correctly positioned. Even the crew seems chuffed at their success. The first-floor window is in place, the lights turned on. Aidan, before he has even paid his men, sits down at the bench, plays some runs, listens, plays them again, listens again, reaches for the bass, repeats that, plays the upper keys and the lower together, produces a small smile, and then launches into "Yankee Doodle Dandy," which causes the men to laugh and then to sing. Grace's mother emerges with the children. Claire, having an audience, begins to dance in her herky-jerky way, making sure everyone notices. Grace's mother produces cider and cookies, which the men accept eagerly. If she didn't know better, Grace might think there was a party at Merle Holland's house.

Her house now.

Sometimes Grace imagines Gene coming to the old Victorian, his surprise and unhappiness at seeing the piano in the front room, Grace and their children and her mother installed in various beds upstairs. Her old way of life seems lonely to her now. She fears it the way one might a recurring nightmare. She knows she must hope for Gene's return, but she's afraid to open the door to him.

Grace's mother, who seems both exhausted and happy, retires with the children shortly after eight o'clock. Grace, with a cup of cocoa, walks into the sitting room across from the turreted parlor and finds Aidan in a chair, reading a book. He stands.

Grace shakes her head. "You needn't stand for me." She sets her cup down on a wobbly side table. "Please use every room. We want you to be comfortable."

"That's very kind," he says, "but you must be tired."

"If I need to be by myself, I can always go upstairs. To my suite. You have no idea how small the house my husband and I lived in was."

"I think I can imagine," he says.

"Are you happy with the piano?"

Does he hesitate just a second? "It's good. I am."

"I'm not sure I believe you," she says.

"Well, there are one or two notes that are slightly . . . off.
I'm not sure the average person would notice, and I'm confident that a piano tuner can fix them."

Grace is silent.

"It's one of the best pianos I've ever played."

"Can't be. It hasn't been used in years."

"I love it."

"It's an odd make. I've never heard of it."

"German. Very rare."

"The moving changed the notes?"

"It's impossible to move a piano and not do something to
it. I'm happy with the tone, though."

Grace feels vaguely guilty. If she hadn't insisted on Merle's
room, the damage would not have happened. But having a
man upstairs with all of them would have been untenable.
She refuses to feel guilty. She can't afford guilt now.

After a time, Aidan picks up his book and continues to
read. Grace removes a slip of paper and a pencil from her
skirt pocket and makes a list of all the items she must take
care of in the morning.

How quiet the house is. How awkward she feels. In another
woman's sitting room with a man she doesn't know. Did the
fire do all of this? She remembers Dr. Lighthart speaking
of the diaspora. Aidan is part of that as well. Where does he
belong?

Gene must have died, she realizes with an inner jolt. He
would not have walked away from this house. He would not
have walked away from his children. A chill settles around
her shoulders as she thinks of him dead, his flesh burned

away, his white bones in a cornfield or on a forest floor, perhaps disturbed by animals. She imagines the agony of such a
death. And to have no resting place, no grave where his wife
and children can go to pay their respects, to remember him.
It's not right.

She shifts in her chair. She wonders how long it will take
to replace all her painful memories with fond ones.

A hundred years, she thinks. At least a hundred years.

Aidan

The sitting room, with all the lights lit, seems a friendly place. Grace has taken to migrating toward the room after the children are in bed because Aidan is often there. She has asked her mother to join her, but the older woman always begs off and goes upstairs.

"Are you Irish?" Grace asks him one evening.

"I am," he says, looking up from his book. He greets Grace when she enters by half standing.

"Do you speak Gaelic?"

"I used to."

"You haven't got a brogue."

"I lost it."

Grace opens her book at the bookmark. "Why?"

"Irish Need Not Apply."

"Still?"

"Still."

"Is Berne an Irish name?"

"It can be. It can also be French." Aidan speaks a French sentence with Berne in it. The *e* in the name sounds halfway twisted around. "Or German." He says a long harsh sentence in a German accent, and Grace can't even tell where the Berne is. "Or even Danish." He spouts Danish and she hears the Berne, with barely a second syllable, like an afterthought.

Grace, in the sitting room, studies him. "You made that all up, didn't you?"

He smiles. "Maybe."

After she has left the sitting room and gone up to her bedroom, Grace checks that the children are asleep and then stands facing the window. She stares at her feet. As she tries a few steps, the rhythm and the dance begin to come back to her. She straightens her back, puts her arms to her sides, and starts to execute the most rudimentary of steps. She wishes she had taps on her shoes. It was the clicking of the metal toes that was so satisfying.

With no one to watch her, Grace stares straight ahead ("never look at your feet") and moves sideways in a linear fashion across the room, then forward and back as best she can remember. After school twice a week, Grace accompanied Patty Rooney to her Irish step-dancing classes. Grace didn't dance, merely watched, but occasionally after the class Patty would teach her a few steps. At a dance recital that Patty took her to, Grace remembers sitting in the audience with Mrs. Rooney, loving the precision that kept the top of the body immobile while the footwork dazzled.

Grace dances until she is breathless. She wipes her forehead and forearms with a handkerchief. She knows a little Irish.

Marjorie outfits Claire and Tom with dark green sweaters she knit for them.

"Where did you find the wool?" Grace asks at breakfast.

"In a drawer full of sweaters. They must have been Gene's. I unraveled one, washed the yarn, and reknit it to make these."

"You have amazing talents," Grace tells her mother.

"In my generation, nearly all women were taught to sew and knit."

"I took home economics, too."

"It's different when you learn at home. Different when it's a necessity."

"I lived through the thirties."

"Yes, but you weren't the one who had to provide."

Grace blows across the top of her cup of coffee. "You've been such a help."

"You're my life now. Just as Claire and Tom are yours."

It sounds like a true statement, but it isn't quite. Grace's life is also Gene and Merle's house and the need to find a job, the necessity to have transportation, the desperation for money, and a desire, buried as it is, for something more.

"I'm thinking of taking the children next door," Marjorie says. "I met the neighbor, Maureen. She seems nice, invited me over. I told her I might have the children with me."

"I'm thinking of applying for a job."

"Are you?"

"If I got a job, would you be able to manage?" She means taking care of the children, cooking the meals, cleaning the house.

"I think so. I'd get Aidan to help with the marketing and any heavy work. How will you get to work?"

"By bus. Walk if I have to."

"Well, it's only temporary, isn't it? Until Gene gets back."

"Right," says Grace.

"Whatever are you going to do for clothes?"

"I'm going to do to Merle's closet what you just did to Gene's drawer."

When Marjorie and the children come home from the visit to Maureen, who turns out to be the cook and not the mistress of the house—"such delicious soda bread; we won't need lunch"—they put Claire and Tom down for a nap. Grace, not willing to open Merle's closet without her mother, makes a flourish of it when her mother is beside her.

"Oh my Lord," Marjorie says, "it's enormous."

Together they enter the massive closet and stare at the racks and racks of clothes.

"She must have had quite a social life." Marjorie gestures. "Look at all these silks and furs. And this is no mouton coat, I can tell you that!" she adds as she holds the arm of a fur.

"I don't know where to start," Grace says.

"You explore while I decide what to have for dinner. Pick out a few things, and I'll see if I can alter them to fit you. You're about the same height, though I'd say Merle had a good fifteen pounds on you."

Grace enters the parlor, where Aidan is sitting at the piano. She drops a pile of dresses onto a chair. "My mother wants to alter these so that I have something to wear when I look for work."

"Where are they from?"

"Merle's closet."

Aidan's sleeves are rolled to his elbows. He hasn't shaved yet.

"You think I shouldn't be doing this," Grace says.

He turns around on the bench. "No, I think you have to."

"The rules have changed, haven't they?"

"They do in a disaster."

"Is this stealing?" she asks.

"No, not now."

"So what do you think of this one?" Grace holds the dress by its shoulders against her body. Her mother liked the jade green silk with gold trim at the sleeves and gold buttons. She thought it suited Grace's coloring.

"Where are you going in that?" Aidan asks, crossing his arms.

"You don't like it."

"It's a little . . . I don't know . . . fancy?"

Grace whips the dress around and studies the front. She tosses it onto another chair. "What about this one?"

Aidan tilts his head. "It's red."

"Yes?"

"And it has polka dots."

"So?"

"Maybe you should choose something a little more conservative?"

"You're a bore."

"Not usually."

She smiles. She rummages through the heap of dresses and reaches for a navy blue with a white collar. She holds it up.

"Is your mother good enough to put a waist in it?" Aidan asks.

"You think it should have a waist?"

"You have a very nice waist."

"Thank you, but this has short sleeves. Too cold for winter."

Again Grace separates out the dresses. She spots a light gray dress with a slim skirt and a little jacket to cover her arms. It's wool, and it will keep her warm.

Aidan nods and points.

"This is it?" she asks.

"That's what you should wear. Are you nervous?"

"A little," she says, laying the gray dress on top of the others. She sits on another chair. "Do you have a cigarette?"

"You *are* nervous."

She pulls a cigarette from his pack and leans his way while he lights it for her. She inhales and rests against the upholstery. "Do you get nervous before a concert?"

"Sometimes I start to sweat. When it's really bad, I get the hiccups."

"You can't go onstage with the hiccups. How do you get rid of them?"

"I find a knife and stick it in a glass of water, put the blunt end of the knife to my forehead and take ten slow gulps."

"And that works?"

"Always."

"Did you just make that up?"

"No."

Grace stubs out her cigarette and slides out the green and gold dress—the dress deemed too fancy—from the bottom of the pile on the chair and begins to dance with it in a free-form movement she makes up as she goes along. Aidan, catching the game, plays waltz music. Grace swoons herself into the dance as if she were wearing the fabric that swirls with her. She waltzes around the parlor, encircling Aidan and the piano. When he switches to the Charleston, Grace holds the dress to her bodice and swings one sleeve back and forth as she executes the footwork of the dance of her mother's generation. Aidan's segue to jazz is Grace's cue to occupy in a languid manner an empty chair, the dress still clinging to her. She pantomimes leaning forward to have her cigarette, in its holder, lit for her. Relaxing into a louche pose, she crosses her legs.

Aidan laughs, rolls his sleeves, and draws her into a slow jazz piece she thinks he must have learned at a Harlem nightclub.

"Merle's closet is enormous. She has dozens of dresses and fur coats," Grace says as she sits with the fancy dress folded over her lap.

"Someone should wear those clothes," Aidan says.

"There have been pleas for clothing since the fire. Maybe I can get someone to pick them up."

"And when your husband comes back? Won't he mind that you've given away his mother's clothing without consulting him?"

"Yes. For a minute. But then he'd see the necessity. If we'd moved in here, which he wanted to do, I suppose I'd have been given the contents of Merle's closet."

"Do you see yourself in furs?"

Grace laughs. "No. Can you imagine? Where on earth would I go?"

"You could come to one of my concerts. You'd be beautiful in a fur."

A blush climbs the sides of her neck. "I hated the house when I first came here," she remarks, glancing away.

"Why?"

"My mother-in-law wasn't fond of me. She thought I'd ruined her son."

"And did you?"

"Seen from her point of view, I suppose I did. He was meant to go places. Marry up."

In her bedroom, Grace finds a hassock and climbs onto it. She strips down to her slip. In the triple mirror over the dressing table, she can see her reflection. She can't see her head, only the body and the slip. Her skin is pale, and the slip hangs from her shoulders, not as fitted as it used to be. Common sense tells Grace that it's her body in the mirrors, but she moves her arm just to make sure. She dips her head down to make double sure. How insubstantial she has become.

"I've got everything I need," her mother announces as she enters the room. "You can get down from there. I have to do the fitting before I can hem anything. Which one did you pick out?"

Sometimes, as Grace walks the rooms of the large house, she thinks she's won a prize. She thinks she's stolen a prize.

In the large kitchen, when she and her mother first entered it, they discovered a wringer washer and a gas clothes dryer.

At first Grace didn't recognize the appliance. It was three feet high, two feet across, and low to the ground. When she opened the enameled hopper, she learned that there was a metal drum inside. The appliance had only one switch—on or off—and she and her mother concluded after several tries that it took only fifteen to twenty-five minutes to dry a load of wash. Towels and flannels didn't need ironing. She and her mother were amazed. When Grace thought of the time needed to dry sheets in the wet spring, she could only shake her head.

Grace is certain that Merle never used the machine. Laundry would have been Clodagh's province.

"They're building tin houses for the homeless," Aidan says that evening as he and Grace are reading in the sitting room.

"How do you know this?"

"I heard it at the post office."

"Is that where you go when the kids are napping?"

"Either there or the market. The houses are temporary until the new ones can be built."

Grace remembers the aluminum clinic. "Won't they be awfully cold?"

"They must have some kind of insulation. They can't be comfortable, but people are desperate to get them."

Grace is silent. "We should be taking in refugees here."

"You already did," he says.

"What do you and Aidan talk about at night?" Marjorie asks Grace the next morning while they are eating oatmeal.

Grace stares at her mother. Why this question now? "We don't talk a lot. We're polite, but mostly we're just reading."

"Reading?"

"Yes," Grace says, avoiding her mother's gaze.

She rises to rinse out her tea mug and sees Aidan giving the children a ride on a sled he must have found in the barn out back. Because the barn is farther up the hill than the house, he's able to work up some speed as he sleds down. The children squeal and beg for more. In order to get Tom back up the hill, Aidan puts Claire on the sled and tells her to hold on tight to her brother. Grace watches as Aidan digs in his boots to fit the foot-size ledges in the snow he's made earlier. It produces the illusion of him climbing a flight of stairs.

Grace snatches her wool coat off a hook and steps outside at the front of the house, and for a few minutes, she is free. She slides down the slippery hill of the driveway, crosses the coast road, stumbles through the brush, and arrives at the beach. In her haste, she forgot her gloves and hat. Her ears sting. She puts her hands into her coat pockets, where she finds a quarter. Where did that come from?

The sea has a chop to it that produces a deep blue-green. Living on the water is like watching a movie in color. She happens upon a large rock and sits on it and covers her ears until her hands are too cold.

She's not sure she's ever been this happy—with her children and her mother safely in a large house; with Aidan to help and to talk to. She remembers sitting at her kitchen table at Hunts Beach, smoking a cigarette, and staring at the sink. How lonely and grim that seems now.

"You forgot your hat and gloves."

Aidan settles the hat on her head and hands her the gloves, and she realizes she wished him here.

"Thanks," she says, glancing up at him. "My ears were stinging."

"It's pretty cold out," he says, drawing his black wool coat tighter. He claps his gloved hands together. He wears a black watch cap.

"The children are in?" she asks.

"Tom got a snootful of snow and started to cry. I had to take them to your mother."

"It looked like fun."

"They're wonderful."

Grace smiles. "I agree."

He stands beside her, staring out to sea. Perhaps he's as mesmerized by the chop as she is. It makes the ocean seem alive.

"I'm always amazed that we're not looking at England, but at Portugal," she says. "And it's warmer in London than it is here."

"The Gulf Stream," they say simultaneously.

"Do you ever wish you could go back to Ireland?" she asks.

"In the war, I went to every Allied country on the European front, which didn't include Ireland or Switzerland because of their neutrality. Yes, I'd like to go back there sometime. I still have brothers there."

"Do you?" Grace asks, surprised.

"Two of them. They were older than I and more settled when we left."

"It must have been painful for your mother to leave them."

"My parents planned to save money for their passage, but the oldest refused to leave and the other followed suit."

"I can't imagine growing up in a large family. I was an only child."

"How old are you?"

"Twenty-four," Grace answers. "You?"

"Twenty-nine last September."

"So you just travel from place to place whenever they need a pianist?"

"I've done it all," he says. "Taught music in school, soloed with orchestras, tried to put some bands together."

"You don't mind not having a place to call home?"

"I didn't used to."

"It's wonderful to have such dedication," Grace says.

"It's a gift. I won't deny that. But I admire you."

"What for?" she asks, squinting up at him.

"Finding a safe place for your family, keeping life sane when you must be worried sick about your husband."

After dinner, Grace meanders into the sitting room with her book and is glad to see Aidan there.

"I'll go out tomorrow and start looking for a job," she announces. "There's a bus I can take."

"Where will you start?"

She tilts her head. "I'll tell you when I get one."

"I'm breathless with anticipation."

She reaches a leg out and kicks his boot. "How is your search going?" she asks.

"I've half a dozen queries out. We'll see what comes of them."

"Where are you looking?" she asks. She notes his knitted vest of brown wool. Hand knit. A mother? A lover? A sister? A wife?

"Boston, New York, Chicago, Baltimore."

"So far away?"

He sits up straight and clears his throat. "I've got to go where there are orchestras."

"What are you reading?" she asks.

"It's a biography of Antonín Dvořák."

She doesn't know who Antonín Dvořák is.

"He was a Czech composer. Brahms was his mentor. What are you reading?"

"The plays of Eugene O'Neill. I found the volume in the bookcase beside you. Right now I'm reading something called *The Iceman Cometh*."

He nods.

"You know it?"

"Yes."

"I try to picture the play as I read it," she says. "O'Neill was Irish American."

"Are you enjoying them?"

"He's very dark and full of pain."

"Our national heritage."

"Are you dark and full of pain?" She means it as a joke.

"Sometimes."

Grace's evening conversations with Aidan often end abruptly. She wants to tell—ask him—so much more, but like in her exchanges with Gene, they talk in bits; unlike her exchanges with Gene, the bits fascinate her.

Grace removes a pile of papers from a drawer in Merle's bedroom and sets them on the bed next to her as she sits up, her back to the headboard, to find out how the house is run and what the bills might be. The date, 1947, is affixed to the first page by a paper clip, and after that the papers have no obvious organization. She locates an invoice for shoe repair under an account for electricity, but there's no indication as to whether either of these has been settled. No dunning notices, no checkbook. Did Merle pay only in cash, sending it through the mail? Grace unearths a breathtaking statement for a bracelet containing ten one-carat diamonds in gold. She hasn't come across a bracelet of that description and imagines that Merle squirreled her best jewelry in a hiding place. Perhaps a safety-deposit box.

Several doctors' bills are clipped together—first, those of Dr. Franklin, then of a cancer specialist, then from the hospital. Was Merle supposed to pay these as she lay dying? There has to have been a will, accounts with a bank. Gene would know about these. It's odd he never mentioned anything but the house.

She comes up with an invoice from Best & Co. in Boston for four dresses with detailed descriptions. "Satin belt with paste clasp." "Navy wool skirt cut on the bias." "Blush pink silk Fortuny skirt with thirty-six pleats." "Mink hat, turban style, lined with royal purple silk." Where did Merle go in these clothes? Would she have worn the Fortuny silk to a cocktail party? The skirt cut on the bias to play bridge? The satin dress with paste clasp to a winter wedding?

At the bottom of the pile are three bills clipped together, each dated a subsequent month, for a case of Edgerton pink gin.

O'Neill's words swim on the page. Across from her, Aidan has on a striped shirt and a black V-neck sweater. She notes onyx cuff links. She catches these details in quick glances.

She reaches into her pocket and pulls out her cigarettes. She leans forward an inch to ask if he would like one, but then notes his pack, Camels, and a box of matches on the table next to him. She wishes she could read the name of the restaurant on the front cover. Is it from New York or St. Louis?

His shoe jiggles once. She takes a long drag. There's so much she never noticed about this room. The Delft clock. An array of silver boxes atop a desk. A darkened portrait of an important man. No, a self-important man. But then, it was for the painter to say, wasn't it? The man in the picture might have been told to stand with his chin elevated, his fingers inside his buttoned coat. In his other hand, he holds a book, a fact that changes her idea of both the man and the painter. A book, not a Bible, suggests learning as opposed to commerce. When she glances down from the portrait, Aidan is staring at her. She smiles slightly.

"Have you had a good day?" he asks.

"Yes. At least I think so. I can hardly remember it."

"You're a busy woman."

"I suppose I am. I was looking at that painting and trying to decide what the man did for a living."

He turns to examine the picture. "A reader, certainly. Perhaps a teacher who thinks a lot of himself. I suppose your husband must be related to the man."

"What era do you think it's from?"

"Judging from the clothes and mustache, mid- to late nineteenth century. He could have been your husband's grandfather."

"You'll have your portrait done," she says.

"Why do you say that?"

"You'll be an important musician, and someone will want to do a painting of you."

"A photograph for a poster, maybe."

"I was thinking that there's so much talent in your hands." She has seen his fingers move so fast they created a blur as she watched.

"There has to be dexterity," he concedes, "but they're only producing what's in the brain."

"All that music in the brain. It must be full up."

He laughs. "There's room for plenty more."

Grace tries her book again, but reads the same sentence three times. "Have you ever been married?" she asks, pulling a piece of lint from her powder blue sweater.

"No, my work doesn't lend itself to marriage. I travel too much, work nights."

Her hand trembles as she turns another page. She lays her fingers hard against the open book. Does she only imagine the connection between them? Not that of landlady and lodger, though they are that. Not that of mutual refugees from a catastrophe, though they are that, too. And not merely friends, or even friends, as she and Rosie are to each other. Grace is married. Why does she keep forgetting that?

She thinks that her body, if it could, might speak. Touch my hand. Let me touch your hand. Put your hand at the back of my neck. Nothing more. Her body can't ask for more.

Her mother called him handsome. The straight brow and the eyes, a soft brown. His hair curls slightly and then doesn't, as if it can't make up its mind. His mouth is straight and hard, not cruel in any way, but . . . serious. Yes, she would say he has a serious mouth.

"I like this house," he says.

"You do?"

"I'm a man of hotel rooms. This is grand, isn't it?"

"I suppose so. It housed a woman who hated me, but I've come to appreciate it without having to think about her."

"Even children couldn't break the ice?"

"Apparently not."

"Your husband must have been torn."

"Yes, he was." But was he? Maybe not.

How might her life have been different if she hadn't married Gene? Would she be a secretary now? An unmarried daughter, living with her mother? Might she have met someone who truly loved her?

"What are you thinking?" he asks. "You look pensive."

Should she tell him? "I was wondering what my life might have been like had I not met Gene when I did, but then I quickly realized I wouldn't have my children as they are, and that was the end of that."

He is silent.

"Do you imagine alternate lives for yourself?" she asks.

"No, not really. I can't see having another life. I wouldn't want one."

"You've worked too hard."

"Something like that."

She watches him return to his reading. Do the words swim on the page for him? She lights a second cigarette. If she keeps this up, she'll become a chain-smoker. A year ago, Grace discovered, during a hectic morning, that she'd left a cigarette burning on the edge of the bathroom sink while another was going in an ashtray in the kitchen, and the realization shook her. She vowed to be more careful. Again, she looks over at Aidan and discovers he is again staring at her.

She smiles, and he looks away.

She crosses her legs, aware of a silky rustle. She puts out her cigarette. She ought to go up.

"What are your plans for tomorrow?" he asks.

"Pretty much the same as today. I thought I'd start looking for work, but they say the storm we're expecting will be a bad one. I don't want to leave my mother with the kids alone."

"I'll be here," he says.

"Thank you, but I think I'll start looking on Monday. Fresh start."

He rolls his sleeves, and she can see from the dial on his watch that it's well after nine. She would stay until one in the morning if he asked her to. He does want her to stay, she can feel it.

But after another minute, Aidan says, "I suppose I'll take my book to bed now."

"Good night then," she says.

He stands and is careful not to brush against her.

She feels bereft even before he has left the room.

Grace lies on her four-poster, the children asleep in the room with her. She stares at the ceiling and feels heat rise and then drain from her face. She wants to put her mouth to Aidan's skin. She wants him to run his fingers through her hair. That's all. Does there have to be more? There must, because she wouldn't feel like this. She understands that the act might be wrong, but the desire for it is not.

In the morning, Grace bundles the children into their winter woolens, and together she and Claire walk down the gravel lane. Grace shows Tom, in her arms, the ocean. She wonders if he remembers it from the night of the fire, if he will always carry with him a vestigial love for or fear of the sea. What will the hideous night do to Claire? Or did the fact that their mother held them tight through the natural horrors give them a protective coating that will serve them well?

The snow crust has grown soft, which makes walking easier. Grace reminds Claire to look both ways before they cross the coast road, even though there hasn't been a vehicle on it for half an hour. On the other side, they struggle over low prickly bushes, cut grass, and mounds of snow-covered sand. Claire loses a boot, which Grace finds and puts over Claire's wet sock. Because the tide is low, the beach gravel and the sea's leavings are plentiful. When she was a girl, Grace used to search for sea glass among the pebbles. She shows Claire what to look for and notes as she does that there are hundreds of emeralds strewn among the debris. When she bends to look, she discovers they are small bits of emerald sea glass, each the size of a stone in a ring. There are no other colors that day, no other shapes. It's not a configuration she's ever seen before. What caused this unique and even offering?

"Claire," she says, "see these little bits? They're sea jewels. Very valuable. Let's look for them and put them in this handkerchief, and when we go back, we'll make jewelry."

Claire's eyes widen. She has seen the strings of jewelry hanging from her mother's dressing table. Grace sets Tom on a tuft of sand right next to them, and as she searches for emeralds herself, she keeps a close eye on Claire. But her daughter seems to have intuited that jewels are not to be eaten. She can't pick the emeralds up with her mittens so drops the knitted items where she stands and grasps as many bits of color as she can find. When she hands the treasures to her mother to put into the handkerchief, there are just as many pebbles as pieces of sea glass. Tom has a shell that occupies him. Grace stands to stretch her legs and glances up at the house on the hill, which she has never seen from this vantage point. She catches Aidan, hands in his pockets, looking at her and the children. She waves. She kneels next to her daughter.

When they have collected all the gems that will fit into the handkerchief, Claire's fingers are red with cold. Grace ties up the bundle and puts it into her pocket. "Let's get your mittens on and go up and make some jewelry. We'll ask Grammy how to do it."

Tom, who has poured a shell full of beach over his face,

has sand stuck to his nostrils and tongue. Grace hefts him
into her arms and glances up again at the turret window.
Aidan isn't there.

In a drawer of odds and ends in Merle's room, Grace finds
an old brooch, most of its seed pearls missing. When she
brings it downstairs, she asks her mother if she has come
across any glue. Her mother knows of some in the sewing
basket upstairs. Grace and Claire bend over the brooch, glu-
ing the emeralds that haven't stuck to Claire's fingers against
the silver backing. While they are working, Aidan enters the
kitchen to pick up a sandwich that Grace's mother has made
for him. Aidan asks Claire what she's doing, and Claire
answers she's making "julie." Grace smiles.

In the afternoon, Aidan asks Marjorie if it would be all right
if he practiced through the afternoon. She says yes, especially if he'll help her get the children's beds up to the third-
floor nursery, where they will sleep better. Grace, who has
been listening from the bottom of the stairs, watches Aidan
carry first the collapsible playpen, then the crib across the
landing. Her mother follows with bedding.

Sitting out of sight of Aidan, Grace listens while he plays.
It's the same piece he was practicing when she entered Merle
Holland's house, and she has physical sensations similar to
the ones she had that day. Occasionally, Aidan breaks off and
repeats a passage or he trills up and down the piano, practicing scales. Then he launches into a later part of the concerto.
Grace lays her head against the back of the chair and travels
with him.

———

After Grace has finished the dishes and put the children to bed, she hesitates as she descends the stairs. In seconds, she'll walk into the sitting room with her book. Does Aidan look forward to these evenings as much as she does? When she turns the corner and sees him sitting in his usual chair, her relief is almost audible.

"How did the brooch come out?" he asks as she sits.

"Pretty good. Well, you know . . . Did you hear anything back from your inquiries?"

"Yes, I did."

Grace looks up.

"I have an audition with the Boston Symphony Orchestra."

A fist strikes her chest. "That's wonderful news. When did you hear?"

"When I went to the post office this afternoon."

"Oh," she says, registering the implications of the audition. "When is it?"

"Tomorrow."

"Tomorrow? So soon?"

"They need someone right away."

She closes her book. "That's why you were practicing all afternoon."

"I hope I didn't keep the kids from their naps."

She notices that he didn't bring his book to the sitting room. "They were fine."

"Grace, I've enjoyed my time here."

Stop, she wants to say. She hates his elegiac tone, his building up to a farewell. He stands and begins to pace. He walks the length of the sitting room and back again.

"How will you get to Boston?" she asks.

"By train."

"It might snow tonight."

"It might."

"It looked like it this afternoon," she adds. "If it snows tonight, the trains might not run."

"Perhaps not."

Only the reading lights illuminate the room. When he walks to the far side, she can barely see him. Time and time again, he returns to her. When he's tired of pacing, he leans against a wall. "I don't want to leave here," he says. "I don't want to leave you."

She says lightly, "Maybe I'll come to one of your concerts."

"In a fur coat," he says.

She'll never go to one of his concerts. She can barely afford the bus fare to look for work, never mind a trip to Boston. And she could hardly take the kids with her. Nor would she ever dare to wear one of Merle's furs. She's done enough damage to her mother-in-law's closet. Besides, isn't it now her role in life to wait for her husband to come home?

"Maybe I'll get back this way," he says.

When? In three months? Six? A year? Two?

Her head is bent, and she knows he's studying her. She's afraid to look up; it will be her undoing. She bites her lower lip.

"If I play the piano softly, will I wake your mother?" he asks.

"They're back up on the third floor tonight. After hauling all the equipment up there for the naps, it seemed too much trouble to bring it all back down."

He takes her hand and leads her into the turreted parlor. She sits on one of the "audience" chairs.

His playing is subdued, so as not to wake anyone. The notes tickle her skin and soothe her mind. He's trying to tell her something, and she understands it, she does, though there aren't any words attached. Music doesn't translate. She feels the chords envelop her, but not in the way a mother might hold a child.

Four sconces light the room. She imagines Aidan on a stage in evening clothes. That will be his world—this man who will make men and women sit up and listen.

The music is both commanding and sensual. No child could ever make sense of this embrace. It's something she's longed for, longs for even now. The music rises to a crescendo and then falls as softly as a pillow. She closes her eyes and lets the piano take her somewhere she's never been.

This is what they will have, these next several minutes, these next few measures. She knows she'll remember it always, that if in the future she hears a snippet of this music, she'll be transported to this room, this evening. She opens her eyes and studies him as he plays. His gaze seems to be focused on a distant point out to sea, and only occasionally does he glance at his hands.

She wants to absorb every note, every combination of notes. She wants it all, especially the intimacy of it. It's not the god-awful joy that Rosie once spoke of, but it must be close. Or perhaps this is an even grander sensation, one she will never be able to explain to her friend.

Grace wishes she and Aidan had never spoken, from

the first day she met him until now. How wonderful if they had communicated only by music every one of the nine days they have had together. She wouldn't have seen that he was good with the children or that he could make her smile with his charm; she wouldn't know who Dvořák was. But every night, he would have done this to her as she sat in her chair, helpless and spellbound.

He plays, and she drifts along the curvature of the earth.

He plays, and her body is flooded with gratitude.

He plays, and she understands that the end is coming.

When he stops, she can't speak. Words will break the trance, will sound trivial and trite. She'd have to wish him good luck, and he'd return the phrase. Perhaps he'd tell her that he would write to her. And everything they had just experienced would be punctured by the commonplace.

When he walks by her, he holds out his hand.

Wordlessly, in the dark of the library, he lights a candle by the bed. The music has already undressed her, so that the removal of the sweater and skirt, the brassiere and slip, the girdle and her stockings, seems unremarkable. When she is naked, he gazes at her in the low light, and she isn't ashamed. He drapes the sheets back, and she slides into the bed, the sheets silky and smooth. She does what she has wanted to do for so long, she bares her neck as she drapes herself across his body, and he kisses her there, allowing her to kiss his skin. He touches her everywhere, sliding his hand down her calf to her foot; running his hand from her breast down her flank. Neither says a word.

Inside her head, the music is still playing, or perhaps this is an entirely new piece, one with more urgency, the beat faster, the fingers flying. He pauses to protect himself, to protect her, and he slides into her with ease. As he raises himself up by his arms, his eyes scan her face. She shifts her hips and arches her back to take him in. She grips his back. Another man might say that he loved her, but Grace doesn't need that. Aidan is slow, holding back, and she experiences the buildup of a different kind of crescendo. She feels it rise up through her toes to the insides of her thighs, a crescendo with many more notes in it than any piece of music, one that continues to climb, and she knows that he can see the moment of her intense pleasure, which feels like liquid flooding through her veins. She's certain she said something, an ecstatic word in a language all her own, a word that causes him to focus on his own crescendo. His eyes fix on hers. He makes his own sound and bends his head.

He pulls her toward him, so that her head rests in the crook of his arm. She floats—placid and perfect. His breathing changes, and she knows the moment he loses consciousness. She thinks it lovely to have him sleeping beside her, as if they were indeed a couple, as if they had all the time in the world. She will leave him before he wakes so that there will be no need to say goodbye.

For the first time in a week, Grace sleeps so deeply that when she opens her eyes, the children are already up. She puts on her robe and runs downstairs.

"He's gone," her mother says.

Grace is silent.

"He took his suitcase."

Again, she doesn't speak.

"He stripped his bed," her mother adds.

Snow

Against the windows, the snow falls in dry sheets. The wind thumps at the front of the house, and from some of the rooms Grace can hear it howl. She prepares a fire, but won't light it until the power goes out, nearly inevitable in a nor'easter. Her mother collects all the candles she can find and sets them in holders or sticks them to dessert plates by lighting the wicks and letting hot wax drip to the dishes. Grace checks the cupboards and refrigerator for food and supplies and decides that Aidan has done a good job of provisioning the house. They can live on what they have for at least five days.

Aidan. She puts her forehead to the cold glass of the window. She wants to howl like the wind.

She won't wash Aidan's sheets until the storm is over. If she did, and the machine stopped mid-wash, the linens would be coated with soap for days. Alone, in a darkened corner, she lifts the bundle to her face. She can smell Aidan on them. Would she be able to smell herself? She is tempted to look for evidence of their time together, but she drops the sheets to the floor.

She pictures the train he was on moving away from the storm as it made its way toward Boston. There, she imagines, he will walk to his audition if he can't find a taxi. She glances at her watch: 11:20. How many hours since he made love to her? Thirteen?

By two o'clock in the afternoon, two feet of snow has fallen. When the sun sets, three feet push against the sides of the house. All day, Grace has been shoveling to keep the steps and a short path clear, though what good it will do them, she can't imagine. It's a path to nowhere—not to a car, not to the street. She supposes she ought to have shoveled to the barn, but for what purpose?

She has a wild and desperate urge to put on her coat and hat and gloves and slide down to the street and walk south in hopes of catching a ride to Boston. Can it be done?

The snow is too deep and she wouldn't be able to tell the road from the beach. She might wander into the sea. She might lose her balance in the blizzard and fall into a snow-bank and die there.

She has children.

The onset of evening begins well enough—the snow has been steady—but by seven o'clock, the wind picks up again, and shortly after that, the electricity stops. A tree, perhaps weakened by the fire, has fallen onto an electric wire.

"We're in it now," her mother says.

Grace tucks Claire into a soft armchair and sees apprehension in her daughter's face. "Mommy, stay next to me." Grace kneels on the floor to rub her daughter's back until she falls asleep. Grace has made a nest for Tom and herself with a pile of rugs on the floor in front of the fire screen. She makes up a bed for her mother on the sofa. The high upholstered back will help to capture the heat.

"There's a fair amount of wood on the back porch," her mother says. "I hope it outlasts the power outage."

"It has to."

Grace then remembers the water pipes. In the kitchen, she turns on the tap at the sink, running as little water as possible, but keeping the flow steady. She doesn't want the pipes to burst in what will shortly become a frozen house. She does a similar thing with all the faucets in the bathrooms, making sure there are no stoppers in the sinks and tubs, and when she ventures down into the basement, candle in hand, she discovers a large sink with a faucet.

"We have the stove for warmth when we need it," Grace says to her mother. "Refrigeration won't be a problem—at least not yet."

"Wish we'd listened to the radio before the power went out. Then we might know how long it will snow for."

What good would that have done? Grace asks herself. It's not as though they have somewhere else to go. She remembers the families in the tin houses. Electricity only, and when that went . . . She hopes the people were evacuated before the storm got rough.

Despite exhaustion, Grace periodically untangles herself from the nest, lights a candle, and brings a pile of wood into the sitting room via a red wagon her mother found in the nursery. Because the journey is cold, she works fast to build up a good fire. When she's done, she holds the top blanket close to the fire screen and then lays it over Tom and herself.

———

The four eat in the kitchen, their hats and jackets on, the warmth from the stove saving the room from being intolerably cold. Marjorie prepares oatmeal, determined to get a hot breakfast into them. She warms the maple syrup, which is as thick as sludge from the cold, and pours it over the cereal. Marjorie urges Grace to eat an entire bowl. "This is no time to be fussy about food."

Grace wants to tell her mother that her lack of appetite has nothing to do with fussiness.

"I have an idea," Marjorie announces to Grace. "The sitting room is massive, and the heat dissipates. We could move into the library instead, which is smaller. There's a fireplace and a bed. You could sleep there with both the children, and we could bring in the sofa and put it against the wall, and I'll sleep there. If we shut the door, we'll be fine."

Grace experiences her mother's proposition as a gift. To sleep in Aidan's bed is to stay connected to him, if only for a few more days.

"I'll find some clean sheets," her mother burbles happily, "and we have plenty of blankets. We'd better bring in toys for the children and books to read by candlelight."

In the library, Grace starts a fire in the grate. She and her mother drag the sofa in. Her mother makes up the two beds, so that they are ready for evening, though it is only ten in the morning. After Grace gathers her small family into the library, she wants to lie on the bed and think of Aidan.

She changes the children's clothing, and then enters the

frigid bathroom just off the library to change her own. It's so cold, she doesn't want to sit on the toilet seat. She has brought from Merle's closet a wool sweater, pants, and a scarf. After she wraps her coat around her and puts on her gloves, she places Merle's mink turban on her head; there's a great deal of wood to bring in and to store just outside the library door. From her mother-in-law's closet, she's taken the warmest and smallest items she could find for her mother. Marjorie swims in the mink jacket but doesn't refuse it.

Before Grace leaves the bathroom, she opens the medicine cabinet to see if Aidan left anything behind. But the metal shelves are empty.

By eleven o'clock in the morning, Grace, Claire, and Tom have made a fort out of all the pillows and cushions; they play in it in woolen coats, as if they were outside and making an igloo. Marjorie has braved the frigid kitchen to bring spoons and small plates, so that Grace and Claire can delineate the "kitchen" from the "living room." Tom, delighted to be playing with his mother's and sister's full attention, crawls and rolls and delivers deep belly laughs. He sits on plates and knocks over cushions, eliciting his sister's fury. When it's time for their naps, Grace crawls into the fort, her legs sticking out, and reads them stories. She, too, falls asleep with her head in the kitchen.

Grace stumbles, snow-blind, outside. She squints in the bright sun. The world is covered in white, which seems, with its crusty surface, to be a heavy blanket of sparks stretching as far as she can see. Even the ocean has frozen near the shoreline, and she can see blue water only a hundred feet out to sea. These blasts from nature that make it so hard to live are sometimes beautiful. The fire, in its essence, was sublime; the quiet world around her covered in snow is as still as glass.

The beauty makes her miss Aidan with an ache that feels unbearable. She replays the night they had together, moment by moment. Will she spend her life missing him?

Two boys with shovels call to her from the bottom of the long driveway. She can't hear them, but she nods vigorously. Whatever they will charge her when they make it to the top, she'll pay. She steps inside the house to search for stray coins.

The silence in the house is haunting. The music, which was magical, has vanished. When she entered the old Victorian, she heard the piano and Aidan playing it. The loss is in her skin, along her backbone.

Grace takes the children out to see the magic blanket. Tom claps his mittened hands and laughs. Claire steps into the snow, which swallows her. To help Claire, Grace sets Tom, for just a moment, onto the shoveled path, itself now deep in snow. She stops Claire's tears by making a snowball and teaching her to throw it. Turning, Grace discovers Tom facedown in the snow. She brushes him off and sits with him on the stoop. Claire makes tiny ineffectual snowballs that barely dent the white blanket.

The following day, the power returns, but it's an hour before anyone notices. It's only when Grace rounds the corner to the sitting room with a reading lamp lit that she sees Aidan in his usual chair. She gasps with happiness; he's returned to her! The illusion lasts only a second, however: She covers her eyes and bends forward to protect what little self she has left.

After a few minutes, she enters the kitchen and flips all the switches.

"Oh, thank God," her mother says.

Grace might say the same, though she is fizzy with longing.

That evening, Grace and her mother wash all the bedding, dry it, and remake the beds. The children seem to like sleeping on the third floor with their toys and their grammy. Marjorie is pleased, and Grace is relieved. She needs a night to herself.

In her room, Merle's room, she turns the light on in the closet to look for warmer clothes suitable for job hunting in the snow. She happens upon a brown wool suit, half hidden and overshadowed by the more beautiful dresses surrounding it. She tries on the jacket and decides that if she wears a sweater under it, it will fit her. The skirt, however, is too wide. Grace takes the skirt to the bed, examines it, and realizes that it has an elastic waist. If she gently gathers the elastic, she can make the skirt work. It will have bulges at the hips, but the jacket will cover them. She removes the brown skirt from its hanger and sits with it on the bed. While studying the hem, she feels hard lumps inside the wool. Weights. Women sometimes put them in the hems of thick material to give a skirt more drape. With a pair of snipping scissors from the dressing table, Grace begins to cut the stitches of the hem. After a foot, Grace tilts the skirt so that the weights will fall out. Instead of a weight, however, a ring falls into her palm.

Grace drops it onto the bedspread as if it had singed her. A large sapphire is surrounded by diamonds in a gold setting. The ring is too big for Grace, but she isn't at all interested in the fit. Instead, she's curious about why Merle felt it necessary to hide it in the hem of a dull brown skirt.

She shakes all the weights out of the hem. There are six rings: a large diamond set in gold; a silver dinner ring with a massive emerald; a ruby surrounded by pearls; another diamond ring, this one set with two sapphires on either side; and a large ruby, multifaceted, in a gold setting. Grace lays them out side by side on the bedspread. Apart from movie reels of Jewish refugees hiding their valuables in their coats, Grace has never heard of such a thing. Did Merle not trust her staff?

Hundreds of dollars' worth of jewelry dot the bedspread. Did Gene know about this? Did Merle tell Gene as she lay on her deathbed? To think that Grace might so easily have taken Merle's clothes to the Salvation Army! Did Merle undo her own hems when she wanted to wear the sapphire and diamond ring? Was the large diamond her engagement ring, put away after her husband died? More curious still, are there other treasures hiding in the wardrobe?

Grace stands and paces Merle's room, glancing from time to time at the gems on the bedspread. She slips a cigarette from the pack in her pocket, lights it, and inhales deeply. With the rings alone, she would have a deposit for a house for her mother. Grace could buy a car. But the treasure on the bed is contraband. It doesn't belong to her. If anything, it belongs to Gene, and until Gene is declared dead, if he did indeed die, it's his to keep or to sell. But does she really believe this? If she has assumed that the house is hers by right of marriage to a missing husband, isn't she entitled to its contents as well?

No. Sleeping in Merle's house was an act of desperation. Selling her jewelry is a tacit admission that Grace's husband is dead. Grace doesn't know the contents of Gene's will, or even if he has one. She has never seen such a document, having always assumed they would get around to writing them someday in the future. But did Gene, knowing what he stood to inherit, write one after his mother died?

Merle wouldn't have put her jewelry in her best clothes— too great a chance of ruining an expensive dress. Grace wanders into the oversize closet and begins to feel the hems of lesser dresses. With several items selected, she brings them to the bed, having put the discovered rings into a clean ashtray. She picks up her snipping scissors.

Grace lays the additional treasures in the center of the bedspread. A string of pearls. A pair of diamond clip earrings. A gold bracelet with ten diamonds. An emerald brooch. A diamond and ruby brooch. A diamond hatpin. A massive diamond necklace that dazzles with its beauty. A heavy gold bracelet. An emerald necklace with twenty-two stones. A gold watch, diamonds encircling the face. At least a dozen screw earrings with precious gems.

The pile in the center of the bedspread scintillates.

The pile in the center of the bedspread screams an unspeakable amount of money.

The pile in the center of the bedspread isn't hers.

———

Grace fingers the gold bracelet with ten diamonds, the only item for which she has a record. In the morning, she'll carry the bracelet into Biddeford with the invoice and explain that her mother-in-law has died and can no longer pay the bill. If the jeweler takes the bracelet back from Grace, that will be that. If some portion of the bill has been paid, the jeweler might take the bracelet back and give Grace a small amount of money for it. And that will be that. She can't pocket any of the rest of the jewels. They aren't hers. For the first time since Grace entered the Victorian to stay, she wishes whole-heartedly that Gene would come back to her.

She won't tell her mother about the diamond bracelet.

The journey into Biddeford lasts an hour longer than it ought to. Some of the roads are plowed, some are not, resulting in a tortuous route of detours. A few of the passengers mind; Grace is patient, enjoying the views outside the window.

When she is let out in the city, she climbs a long hill of brick buildings and realizes these are the mills. She notes the snow still bundled at the sills and sides of the long paned windows, and as she passes close to them, she can hear the din from the sidewalk: wooden shuttles sound like iron machines clanging against each other as if in battle. Through a pane of glass, she catches sight of a powder of tiny cotton threads released into the air. She crosses the street hoping to find the center of town only to discover she is already there. Branching off Main Street are rows of multistory board-inghouses. Trolley cars, tethered to electric lines overhead, scoot along faster than the automobiles, stopped in traffic. It has been a long time since Grace has found herself within a bustle of people. She asks a woman, waiting at a curb, how to find the jeweler she has come to see. The woman names a street and gives Grace directions.

She turns where the woman indicated and, five doors up, encounters a sign that reads, JENSEN, JEWELER TO THE WORLD. How does a man become a jeweler to the world in a barely visible shop on a side street of a poor mill town? The sign must be more of a wish than a fact.

The jeweler has white hair, poorly trimmed, yellow teeth, and wrinkles that might have been cut by the diamonds he sells.

"How can I help you?" he asks.

Grace opens her purse and lays the bracelet on the glass.

"Oh yes, I remember this," the jeweler says. "Mrs. Holland had it specially made for her. She'd seen it in a magazine, I think."

Before the man can ask how Grace came by it, she offers, "Merle Holland was my mother-in-law. Her son, Gene Holland, is my husband. I'm Grace Holland. Merle gave this bracelet to Gene to give to me, and now we're in a bit of a fix because of the fire. We have two children, and our house burned down. I'm looking either to sell the bracelet back, or if it hasn't been paid for, to give it back. I have the invoice."

Grace sets the bill beside the bracelet, dazzling in the lighting of the store.

"Yes, that's us," the jeweler says. He turns the bill around. "But this is an appraisal. Mrs. Holland always paid for her jewelry with a check on the spot. One of my best customers, actually. So sad about her death."

"Yes, it was." Grace clears her throat. "I'm wondering if you'll buy the bracelet back."

"It's not our policy."

He puts a loupe on his eye and examines the bracelet. "It's got some denting here—gold is soft—and a residue of some substance encircling one of the diamonds." Pink gin, Grace thinks. "You understand I can't give you the price Mrs. Holland paid for it. It's secondhand now, and there's not a lot of demand for diamond bracelets these days, with most people around here barely coping. But still, I have quite a clientele."

I'll bet you have, Grace thinks.

"Do you have any identification?" the man asks. "How do I know you're not a maid who stole the bracelet or waited for Merle to die before stealing it?"

"I'm not a maid. I'm the mother of Merle's two grand-children. My birth and marriage certificates burned in the fire."

According to the appraisal, the bracelet cost eleven hundred dollars, a staggering sum of money.

"I can't give you more than seven-fifty for it."

Grace nods, unable to speak, the sum he's named staggering in itself.

"I don't carry that sort of money in the shop," he explains. "I'll have to go to the bank. Are you all right with meeting me back here, say, at one o'clock?"

"Yes."

"Then it's a deal. Take your bracelet—here, let's get a box for it."

Grace leaves the shop in silence.

———

She has almost two hours to wait. Will the jeweler call the police and have her checked out? Will the police tell him that Gene is missing? Or will Jensen reveal to her, when she goes back into the shop, that the value of the bracelet has dropped to seven hundred dollars? What good would it do her to point out that they already had a deal? She would take the seven hundred, of course she would. She must find a restaurant and settle in for a long lunch, even though she has only seventy cents in her purse. Bus fare home, a twenty-five-cent lunch, and twenty cents to spare. She will pick up apples for the children.

Noting the blue plate special, three courses for a quarter, Grace decides to order that and make each course last. She starts with a cup of tea, moves on to tomato-cheddar soup, picks at a bacon and lettuce sandwich, and has Grape-Nut pudding for dessert, followed by a cup of coffee, over which she lingers.

The jeweler has the money in a fat envelope. He counts it out for her in tens and twenties and the occasional fifty. He asks her if she would like to count it, too, but she responds that it won't be necessary. She receives the envelope into her hands.

The worn leather handbag she borrowed from her mother (who in turn had borrowed it from Gladys) glows with the envelope of money inside. She holds the purse to her chest, afraid that someone might snatch it. When she gets home, she'll put the envelope at the back of the closet in a hatbox and remove money only when absolutely necessary.

She'll find a job. With her first paycheck, she'll fill the

pantry, buy clothes for the children, and pay the utility bills that have been accumulating in a basket in the kitchen. With her second, she'll dip into the hatbox and buy a used car. She'll say she bought it on time with her paycheck. She hopes her mother knows little about financing or the price of cars.

The following morning, Grace enters the doctor's clinic to ask about work and finds a full waiting room with no one at the desk. She walks beyond the desk and into the corridor of rooms and discovers Amy in the first room, taking a child's temperature, the mother eyeing her watch. Grace doesn't want to intrude, but she remains a second longer. Amy turns to shake down the thermometer and nearly shouts, "Grace."

Grace steps away from the door to wait for Amy to be free.

"Are you okay? What are you doing here?" Amy asks.

"I've come looking for work."

"Barbara never came back; she fractured her hip and elbow."

Grace asks where Dr. Lighthart is.

"He's in the back."

Grace waits. She sees Dr. Lighthart darting across the corridor, and several times Amy comes back with a patient, ignoring Grace.

"Hello," Dr. Lighthart says, slightly out of breath. "I've often wondered about you. Amy told me you were here and wanted work."

"I do."

"How's your daughter?"

"Fit and healthy, thank you."

"Can you start now?"

"Yes," she says, "I can."

"The front desk is a mess. Do you think you could sort through the piles of paper and put them in order and label them so that I could take a quick look after work?"

"I will."

"Good."

He disappears as suddenly as he came. Grace finds Amy and asks if she knows the order of patients and who came in first. Amy shakes her head and replies, "If you can, practice some triage. If a person looks as though he or she is deathly ill, I'll take those first. And any child with a high temperature."

Grace swallows.

In the waiting room, Grace asks the crowd a simple question. "Do you know who got here first?" There's a moment of silence, and a woman points across the room. "That man there."

"Okay, I'm going to go around the room in the order you all think is first-come, first-serve. Just tell me your name and how you feel."

In the next few minutes, Grace crisscrosses the room, writing down names and symptoms on the back of a telephone bill. With a frightening uncertainty, she develops her own triage, putting some names at the top of the list.

"Are you in labor?" she asks a woman with splayed legs.

"Not yet, miss, but this is my sixth, and I can tell something isn't right."

The woman should be in a hospital. Grace puts her at the head of the line. When Amy appears in the doorway,

Grace gives her the list. Amy calls the name of the pregnant woman, who can barely walk across the floor.

Grace sits at the desk, and tries to look official in the gray suit her mother remade to fit her. She finds a clean piece of paper on which she can write the names of the newcomers to the clinic when they come in. After that, she stacks all of the papers that were already on the desk into a large pile. She whisks off all of the coins and dollar bills and puts them into the top right-hand drawer. When the rest of the desk is clean, she lifts a handful of material and sorts by dates, the most recent first: bills in one pile, checks in another, Dr. Lighthart's notes, letters from patients, medical reading material, official forms. She opens every envelope, reasoning that she can't complete her job without doing so. She tries, when she scans a letter, to ascertain which pile it belongs to without reading all of the details. She's invading privacy, she knows, and she doesn't want to pry. As she works, individuals enter the waiting room and walk to the desk, where she records their names and symptoms. Amy and the doctor will be working nonstop for hours.

When Grace is finished with the sorting, she hustles to the kitchen to find plates to lay on each of the piles so that they won't blow about when someone opens the door. She writes notes identifying the piles, and tapes them to the plates. The scheme looks unprofessional at best, but it's all she has to work with. When finished with the top of the desk, she begins to search through the drawers. There are five, two on either side of her skirt, a horizontal one in front of her. One drawer is so stuffed with material, Grace can't, without a knife, get it open.

———

Amy says, "You missed your lunch."

"I lost track of the time."

"You could eat now; you seem to have the room in hand."

"If you're sure," Grace says, standing.

She takes her paper bag with her peanut butter sandwich to the kitchen at the back of the building. When she enters, she can see that Dr. Lighthart is asleep at a table in a darkened corner, his head on top of his arms. She steps outside the kitchen to unwrap the waxed paper so that she won't wake him. She doesn't dare pour herself a glass of water.

Already the sun is lowering, setting the tall barren trees outside the window alight with an orange color she has loved all her life. She checks her watch. Three-fifteen. She has no idea when she should leave. A six o'clock bus will take her back to the coast road.

Though she has been as silent as possible, Dr. Lighthart slowly lifts his head, stretches, and stands. It's only then that he notices her by the window. Grace moves toward the sink to pour herself a glass of water.

"Amy says you're a lifesaver."

"She exaggerates."

"Amy? Never. Comes from an old Yankee family."

"Do you want me to work here on a permanent basis?"

"Yes," the doctor says.

She doesn't dare ask about a salary. "My hours would be . . . ?"

"Let's try for nine to five, though it might go over a bit."

"My bus leaves at six."

"Leave in ample time to catch it. I paid Barbara thirty-five dollars a week. Will that suit for now? We can always revisit the subject."

"That will be just fine," she says.

His dark eyes fix on hers. "Did your husband return?"

"He hasn't come back."

"I'm sorry to hear that," he says.

On her way home from her fourth day of work, Grace falls asleep on the bus and has to be woken by the driver. When she drags herself up the hill and into the house, her mother and children are in the kitchen with dinner on the table. They look at her as if they might not recognize her. Claire comes around the table and hugs Grace's knees.

"What happened?" her mother asks.

"Nothing. The hours have caught up with me. It's a long day, eight to seven."

"I gave Claire a snack at four today so that she could hold out for dinner, but I'm keeping Tom on his regular schedule."

Grace nods and sits in her chair without removing her coat.

"Which means," says her mother, "that he has to go to bed in half an hour."

"I'm so grateful," Grace manages before she starts to cry.

"Now, now. Let's just get some food into that scrawny body."

Grace puts the files in the oak cabinet in order. Often she's interrupted by patients, some of whom understand their symptoms, while others just admit to feeling lousy. Occasionally, a woman will enter with a fairly accurate diagnosis, which she recites in great detail. These are the women who have had experience nursing family members, Grace guesses. She makes notes, sometimes resorting to an agreed-upon shorthand of five phrases that both Amy and Dr. Lighthart understand. Almost always, Grace can locate the proper file. She attaches her notes to the first page inside the file, and hands it to Amy when she comes to the door.

"We're going to need more files," Grace tells the nurse.

"There's a fund for petty cash in Dr. Lighthart's office. You can get what you need there."

When Grace first opened the door of the cabinet behind the desk that contained supplies, there was so much disarray she wasn't even sure what the cabinet was for. After sorting, she makes a list of necessary items: envelopes for sending out bills, a roll of stamps, paper clips, several new pens, a new ream of paper, and a new ribbon for the typewriter. Finishing that task, she sits before her clean desk. She enjoys her little fiefdom, though she has arranged everything so that Dr. Lighthart and Amy can find what they need without trouble. Grace has become, in five days, adept at diagnosing illnesses. She can spot a patient with pneumonia almost as soon as he or she enters the waiting room: a certain hunching forward, as if protecting the lungs, the awful coughing, and the mouth hanging open, making it easier to breathe. She guesses the children with fevers by their glassy eyes and general listlessness. The pregnant women, even if they aren't showing, are also readily identifiable: they almost always have hands on their abdomens.

At five o'clock, Grace makes her way into Dr. Lighthart's

office before she realizes she has no idea where the petty cash is kept. Nor can she just take the money without asking the doctor, whom she can't find at the moment. She lingers at his desk, noting photographs at the edge. One of the doctor with a beautiful blond woman, both on skis, each wearing ski pants and a thick sweater, catches her eye. It must be a girlfriend, she guesses, since the two look nothing alike. Their smiles are exhilarating, their faces flushed.

"You've come for your paycheck," Dr. Lighthart announces as he enters the room.

Grace senses a blush rising from her throat to her face.

"Actually, no," she says. "I came in to ask for money from the petty cash box to buy supplies. Amy mentioned one, but I didn't want to look without asking you first."

He opens the right-hand drawer of his desk, which reveals a familiar sight: papers having been stuffed into it over a long period of time.

"I keep the cash at the bottom in a tobacco tin. There's not enough in here to tempt a thief. I worry more about the drugs."

He means the contents of a cabinet, hidden within a tall kitchen cabinet, which can be opened only with a key.

"Well, let's see," he says. "I have at least five dollars here. Will that do?"

"I should hope so."

"I took a look at what you've done out front," he says, searching underneath a pile of papers on his desk. "I'm extremely impressed. How long has it been since your last job?"

She folds her hands. "I've never had a job."

"Really?" he asks, much surprised and looking up at her. His hair needs a comb. "You've taken to it like a, well . . ."

"Duck to water," she finishes. "I was ready for a challenge."

"You mean surviving a fire, taking care of your children, and trying to find housing wasn't challenge enough?"

"Mental challenge was what I meant."

"I know I have my checkbook here," he mumbles, frustrated.

Grace can see the checkbook near the edge of the desk in front of her. Ought she point it out? Will she seem too eager to be paid? But what's the sense of not seeing what's right in front of her?

She slips it off the surface of the desk. "Is this it?"

She watches while he begins to write out her check, the first she has ever received. But then he stops. "Do you have a bank account?"

"Not yet."

"Well, let me know when you do," he says, ripping up the check. He reaches into his pants pocket and removes a large wad of cash. He counts out thirty-five dollars. She feels awkward taking the stack of money from his hand.

"I was wondering," she says, making a sweeping motion over his desk, "if you'd like me to tidy up your desk and your office. If there are things here that are personal, please say, and of course, I won't go near them. But I can see from here that there are papers that need to be filed."

He examines the mound. "I can't think of anything in here too personal. Did you read the patients' files?"

"No," she answers, "no more than their names and addresses really."

"I want you to. The information doesn't leave this building, but you should have an idea of the patients' medical history. Also, if they've come from somewhere else and are first-time patients here, please make sure you have the name and phone number of the physician they used to see. Though you'd be surprised how many of them have never been to a doctor. The women have, usually, but not the men."

Grace nods. "I'd better go. I have to get those supplies."

"You won't be able to get them now," he notes, checking his watch. "Nor before you come in on Monday. Do you know how to drive?"

"I do," she says, "but I don't yet have a driver's license."

He smiles. His teeth are white. Only children, in her experience, have such white teeth. "I'll send you out on Monday morning in my car. You can get the supplies and your license in the same trip."

"And open a bank account," she adds.

Dear Rosie,

I'm guessing by now that you know that we survived the fire, that Gene didn't come back, and that I lost the baby I was carrying. It was born dead, which was a great sadness to me, but I'm determined not to write about sorrow in this letter. I've had enough of it. The good news is that my mother and I and Claire and Tom have moved into Merle Holland's big house on the water, ending our homeless period. There was a fellow squatting in the house when we got here, though that's not a fair thing to say. He inhabited the house. Seeking shelter from the fire, he saw a piano in the upstairs turret and headed for it. When I entered the house for the first time, I heard music and discovered that the man was on the second floor playing the

*piano. He left us when he learned that he had an audition
with the Boston Symphony Orchestra. We haven't seen
him since, so I gather he got the job.*

*My other news is that Claire came down with scarlet
fever, and as a result, I drove her (yes, Rosie! I can drive
a car!) to a clinic, where there was a doctor who success-
fully diagnosed her and cured her. After the pianist left,
and it became clear that if I didn't find work our little
family would starve, I went back to the clinic and asked
for a job as the receptionist. The place was busy when I
entered, and they hired me. There's a thing going around
here that's a form of pneumonia, due to smoke and ash
inhalation during the fire. It's pretty serious, so I thought
I might mention it in case Tim shows any signs—a bad
cough, listlessness, loss of appetite. But since I can't imagine Tim not eating, I'm pretty sure he'll never get it.*

*Oh, Rosie, my life has changed so much in three
months, you would hardly recognize it as the life I had
with you. I work, my mother takes care of the kids, we live
in what you and I would have called a mansion. I've met
new people—well, a few—and I feel different. I wish I
could explain in depth what I mean, but that wouldn't be
something a woman could put in writing, if you catch my
drift. I hope I haven't shocked you.*

*One benefit of living in Merle's house (me in Merle's
house—can you imagine? She'd be spitting out the nails
of her coffin!) is that if Gene does make it back, he might
search for us here. Worse, as far as Merle is concerned,
is that I have raided her closet. Rosie, you would have
shrieked if you'd seen it! It's filled with very expensive*

dresses, fifty at least, and five fur coats. I wear her mink hat all the time. I can't imagine where she wore all those clothes to. I certainly never saw them, but of course when she was coming to our house or we there, which hardly ever happened, she always wore something plain. I imagine she thought herself slumming or that one of the kids would spit up on her. I never liked the woman, and she certainly never liked me, but I admit I felt like a thief raiding her closet. I feel less so now because I really do need the clothes. My mother sews and knits all her free hours, but she loves doing it, so I don't try to stop her. One night this week I came home and saw the children in a dress and in overalls made from a navy corduroy skirt I'd seen in Merle's closet. We don't touch the beautiful clothes, though sometimes I wonder why not. She's certainly never going to wear them again. If I was ever asked out somewhere nice, I think I might choose a dress. But a working mother with two children is never going to be asked out, is she, so I don't think I need to worry about it.

I try to picture your life in Nova Scotia. I have a bad sense of geography, but I think it's part of the Maritimes, yes? Can you see the water? Is it beautiful? Are you all living in one house, or have you and Tim managed to find your own? Please tell me about the kids—they grow so fast. You wouldn't recognize Tom, and Claire is already a string bean. My mother makes long hems in her dresses so that she can let them out.

Thank God for my mother. I can't imagine what I'd have done without her.

Do you ever think about our former life, how safe it seemed? With the war ended, we thought all danger was behind us. Nothing ahead but prosperity and children growing older. I have never been so afraid in my life as I was the night of the fire. When they came to rescue us, my arms and legs wouldn't move, and they had to slip Claire and Tom from under my arms. Please tell Tim that I don't begrudge the fire department rescuing you first. Not one bit!!

If I know you, you are focused on only one sentence in this entire letter, and that if you were here, you'd be asking, Which one? All I can tell you is that the music was sublime.

Love and kisses,
Grace

Dear Grace,

You know me so well. Have you really never heard from the musician again? You will, you will, I am sure of it. But it would be best for you if it happened after Gene was declared dead—what a horrible thing to hope for.

But I'm happy for you. When you come to visit, a fantasy I persist in believing, you will tell me everything. Every tiny detail!

Winters in Nova Scotia are harsh, what can I say. You and I used to complain about the wind off the water in Maine! This winter, you could magnify that by ten. Our hats have to be buttoned under the chin, our coats belted. I dare not take the children out unless they're tied to me.

Tim is now part owner of a Ford dealership, thanks to a gift of money from my parents. We had to decide between the down payment on a house or the business. We chose the business, reasoning that Tim could make enough money so that in a year's time we could put down our own deposit. But I have to tell you, he entered the business at the wrong time of year. There have been no sales since Christmas, and, truthfully, there aren't a whole lot of cars in Nova Scotia. Tim is hoping that when spring comes, business will pick up and be strong over the summer. I can't wait for spring, Grace. I think of last year, how we complained about all the rain. But at least it was better than this terrible moaning and whistling weather. I don't know how the fishermen do it, but they are out on the water all the time. I hear of men dying more often than I should. Tim takes us for outings on Sundays, his day off, if the skies aren't spitting sleet. Fortunately Tim's mother has a washer and dryer, which I could hardly believe when I entered her house. (How we are relying on our mothers now!) Since the kids are a little older, I usually have a couple of hours to myself. I'm reading books and not just magazines, mainly because Tim's mother doesn't get magazines and she has a lot of books. Children's books, too. I enjoy reading them to Ian and Eddie. I can't wait for spring, for their sakes, too. They need to run! But then I'll be terrified that one of them will fall into the water. It's a very rocky shoreline.

I envy you your job. (I think even without the clue at the end of your letter, I would not have guessed the doctor. Too hazardous with a boss.) How I would like to

*have a new dress and be able to go into a store each day
and sell . . . what? . . . gloves maybe. But I'd make it into
work only half the time, since the snow piles in drifts here
and the cars can't get through. Grace, I have never been
so cold in all my life!*

*I guess now we will always live in Nova Scotia. Tim's
business will tie him here for years. And now that our parents have got us back, I doubt they'll let us leave without
a fight. And truth to tell, there's something in this way of
life that appeals to me. It's slow and though I sometimes
long to go into Halifax, to a movie or to a nightclub, I feel
in my bones that we were meant to be here. For one thing,
my carrot top doesn't stand out! I'll have to join some kind
of organization in the spring to meet people.*

*Some of my best times were when we were out in the
yard with the kids.*

Love from your Rosie.

Dr. Lighthart

"How was the skiing?" Grace asks, shrugging off her coat at the office. It's Monday, nearly noon.

"Spectacular. How did you do on your driver's test?"

"I can drive your car legally," she answers.

"Good for you. You'd better put your coat back on then. Here are the keys. You've made a list? Stupid question. Of course you have."

"Are you happy here running the clinic?" the doctor asks the next day in the kitchen.

"I don't run it, you do."

"Nonsense," he says. "Amy would agree with me."

Amy and Dr. Lighthart can't take their lunch breaks together. Ideally, none of them should, but Grace was already in the kitchen when Dr. Lighthart entered, washed his hands for a long time, and dried them on a clean dish towel. "I don't want to sound like a parent, but do you wash your hands thoroughly before you eat here and when you leave for the day?"

She smiles. "I, too, have heard of the germ theory."

"I deserved that."

"Who makes your lunches?" she asks.

"I've hired a woman to provide food for the clinic when needed. She prepares my lunch and dinner, and I put my own breakfast together. Today it's . . . drumroll . . . roast beef!"

Grace would die for a roast beef sandwich. With mustard. "You're still living here."

"I haven't had a minute to look for a place. I think I'll be stuck here forever."

She likes the way he crosses his long legs. He has an elegance to his masculine frame that was either learned or inherited. "You must be making money," she says.

"Well, I appear to be, now that you've uncovered a treasure trove in cash and checks in all that mess out front. Most of that will have to go back into the clinic, for supplies and so on. Amy's salary."

"Anything left over for you?"

"I hope so."

"Maybe I could get the newspaper in the morning and look through the classifieds for you, call the landlords and ask them some questions."

He takes a sip of water. "You'd do that for me?"

"What sort of place are you looking for?"

"A one-bedroom, not too far from here so that I could walk to work if I had to. I like a lot of windows. And all the regular things—heat, good hot water, electricity, some privacy, a bathroom to myself, a kitchen."

"Furnished or unfurnished?"

"Furnished."

"I'll see what I can do," she says as she finishes her sandwich.

"The Soviet Union has begun to jam broadcasts of the Voice of America," he says, frowning.

Grace is startled by the abrupt change in subject. "Is it serious?"

"The VOA was the hope of freedom for thousands of people. Now there's only silence."

"Can the government do anything to override the jamming?"

"I think we'd have heard about it if they could. Do you listen to the radio?" he asks.

"I listened to the radio in your car when I went to get supplies."

She doesn't tell him that she was hoping for classical music. Instead, a soap opera was playing, and she became so involved in the plot that she missed the stationery store the first time she passed it. "That picture on your desk," she says, spreading out the waxed paper to save, "is that your girlfriend?"

"No, she's my brother's wife, Elaine. He's taking the picture. I sometimes go skiing with them and their kids. My nephews. Impossible to get a picture of all of us, since the kids are long gone the moment they hop off the J-bar."

"Where do you ski?"

"Gunstock or Abenaki. They're both about two and a half hours away," he says, balling his waxed paper and trying for the basket, which he makes.

"Five hours driving. That's a lot."

"My brother has a place near Gunstock. If I have the time, I stay overnight with them."

On clear days, Grace can see Mt. Washington in New

Hampshire to the west from the top floor of Merle's house. Majestic when the sun sets, lighting the snow ablaze.

"Someday you'll go skiing with me," he declares.

"I highly doubt that."

"I keep the photo on my desk to discourage patients I see in my office from trying to fix me up. When they ask if it's my girlfriend, I say yes, and the conversation usually ends there."

"Why didn't you do that with me?"

"Were you planning on fixing me up?" he teases. "We seem to have begun our conversation months ago by not lying to each other, which was why I told you the truth about the picture. Do you know how rare that is?"

"Telling the truth? Yes."

"It's interesting. We didn't have these pneumonia patients in the beginning. We had burns in the throats and lungs and a lot of coughing up blood, but that was different, those were emergencies. Why the pneumonia cases now?"

"Do you think that the stuff the men inhaled stayed in their lungs and has only recently grown infectious?"

"Possibly," he muses, "but the infections should have happened sooner. The body reacts to an unwanted foreign substance by trying to get rid of it—hence infections. That's why, for instance, you have to get a bullet out of a person as soon as you possibly can."

She wonders about all the men involved in fighting the fire. To be laid low by pneumonia after having exhibited such bravery seems cruel. Though Grace knows, at least as well as anyone, how cruel nature can be. "You could put up signs," she says.

"How do you mean?"

"Something like, WERE YOU FIGHTING ON THE FRONT LINE OF THE FIRE? DO YOU COUGH A LOT? IF SO, SEE YOUR PHYSICIAN AS SOON AS POSSIBLE."

"And put them where?"

"Here for one. Post offices, grocery stores, gas stations, churches, anywhere men go."

"Anywhere women go, too, since they're often the ones who get their husbands to a doctor."

In the waiting room, Grace has the task of telling each patient that Dr. Lighthart will be at least forty minutes with his current case and that he has another waiting for him in an adjacent room. If they would like to leave, she'll book them first thing in the morning.

"I already took one afternoon off. I can't get another."

"My mother's babysitting the kids. I'll have to wait."

"Okay," says a man, coughing badly. "But it won't be tomorrow. I can't get time off until next Friday."

Grace asks the coughing man, who must have come in while she was in the back, to wait a minute. She explores the examining rooms and finds a clean, empty one near the kitchen. "Come with me," she says when she returns.

She walks him down the corridor and into the room. "Why don't you lie down here and rest," she suggests.

"Can't lie down. Just cough more. Can't sleep at night less I'm sitting up, and I can't sleep sitting up."

"Does the cough hurt?" she asks.

"Son of a bitch, it does. Sorry, miss."

His color is bad; Grace would say gray if asked. He strains for breath. Another case of pneumonia.

"What's your name?"

"Busby," he says with a harsh rasp. "Harry Busby."

She'll have to have another conversation with Dr. Lighthart about posting signs.

In the evening, Grace leans against the doorframe in her coat, waiting while Dr. Lighthart writes out a check for her. When she opened a bank account, she put in ten dollars. He hands her the check but seems to want her to stay. For the first time since she started working at the clinic, two weeks ago, the waiting room is empty. "Hell of a day," he says. "Thanks for your help."

"The man you saw after Mrs. McPeek has pneumonia, doesn't he?"

"I think we may have a statewide epidemic, or rather a state-long epidemic. If we could just get the men to come in sooner, before they're so compromised . . ."

"That man will die?" she asks.

"I'd be surprised if he didn't. He could hardly breathe when I saw him. He'll get closer observation at the hospital, and they have better equipment. We need an X-ray machine for the clinic. Listen, let me drive you home."

"I couldn't let you do that."

"Why not?"

She can't think of a good answer.

———

Grace wills herself to enjoy the ride in the Packard with Dr. Lighthart beside her. She knows now why he bought it—the room between the driver's seat and the pedals is ample. She has never seen him in his suit coat, since he always wears the white coat at the clinic. When she gets to the office in the mornings, he's already there; he's there when she leaves for the day.

"This is much more luxurious than the bus," she says.

"I should hope so. You strike me as someone who's philosophically opposed to luxury."

"Yes," she says, "when it's luxury I haven't earned. Though I have to warn you, when you drop me off, it will be in front of a large Victorian house on a wealthy street. That's my mother-in-law's house."

"She must be waiting, too, for her son to come home."

"She died before the fire. I took my family there because we were homeless."

"That's not unearned luxury. That's necessity."

"That's how I've chosen to see it. The mink hat isn't mine either. I got it from her closet. It keeps me warm."

"Again, a necessity."

"Well, I could have knit myself a hat."

He laughs. The car seems to float over the road. He tunes the radio to a station he must like. In the darkness, with only the lights from the dashboard and the seductive notes of the jazz ensemble, she can't believe the pleasure of a simple ride home. In the morning, she'll take the bus into Biddeford and buy her own car, but it won't be anything like the vehicle she's in now. The warmth from the heater coddles them. Will her car even have a heater?

She tries to savor every minute. She wants to close her eyes, but she can't risk drifting off. Somehow that would be insulting.

"I loved driving your car," she says.

"I forgot to show you where the controls are to bring the seat forward. I hope you found them."

"I wouldn't have been able to leave the parking lot if I hadn't," she says. "I put them back to where they were when I first got into the car. It purrs."

"Listen, Grace, I mean it when I say you've improved my life. And Amy's. And certainly those of the patients who were turned away by the chaos of the waiting room. Or the ones who just got sicker and sicker as they waited. I should never have let it get out of hand like that."

Grace leans her head back against the soft upholstery.

A hand squeezes hers, and she comes awake. Dr. Lighthart is in the driver's seat next to her, and her mother-in-law's house is up the hill outside the window. Damn, she thinks, she did fall asleep.

"I'm sorry," she says. He withdraws his hand. "It's just so comfortable in here."

"That's a compliment."

"Thanks for the ride," she adds as she turns to get out of the car.

"Anytime."

She watches the taillights for as far as she can see.

"You're home early," her mother comments. As usual on Fridays, Marjorie's hair is in pin curls under a red bandanna. She washes her hair on Fridays and always has, which Grace thinks stems from the days when her mother and father were courting: a fresh set for going out.

"I got a ride."

"From whom?"

"From the doctor. He had a patient out this way."

Grace doesn't think she could utter a lie to Dr. Lighthart, yet it's so easy to do to her mother, who is undeserving of any lie. Who, without the slightest complaint, has taken over the care of her grandchildren and the enormous house they are living in. Whenever Grace and Marjorie have words, it's because her mother is worried about her, trying to keep the marriage, which threatens to roll down the hill and out to sea, intact. Grace can hardly blame her for that.

She gives her mother a peck on the cheek.

"What's that for?"

"No good reason," Grace says.

After Grace has cooked teddy-bear pancakes for Claire and Tom the next morning (Claire annoyed that her bear is misshapen), Grace's mother comes down late. "I hope you didn't mind my not being up to cook."

"Mind?" says Grace. "On weekends, you should sleep all you want. I'll bring you a tray for breakfast. I'll do it tomorrow in fact. I've been thinking I might go look for a car today."

"You're going to buy a car?"

"I hope to."

"With what, may I ask?"

"I'll put this week's salary toward the purchase as a down payment. I've heard you can pay as little as ten dollars a month."

"But money is so tight."

"I have to have a car," Grace argues, drying the dishes. "It will be much easier for us to shop, and I can skim an hour off my commute. I'll leave here at eight-thirty and be home by five-thirty. I'll see the kids more." Grace knows it's this last point that will win her mother over. "So I thought I might go into Biddeford today. I saw a used-car lot there."

"When were you in Biddeford?" her mother asks, startling Grace.

Thinking quickly, she answers, "When Matt took me there to buy material to make the kids clothes."

"You ought to write to them," Marjorie says as she brings the kettle to the sink.

"I should."

"All used-car salesmen are crooks."

"And you know this how?"

"Everyone does," her mother says. "Oh, by the way, there's a letter for you on the telephone table."

Grace picks the letter up and studies the return address. The Statler Hotel, Boston. She walks into the sitting room, slits the letter open, and reads.

Dear Grace,

I've wanted to write to you ever since I got on the train to travel south. I left without saying goodbye because I couldn't. Simply could not. I hope you'll understand.

I was hired by the Boston orchestra for several solo performances and have already been asked to travel to New York and to Chicago.

It is not my place ever to hope we will meet again.

I enjoyed every minute I was in your presence, and the memory of our last night will be with me forever.

I can't say more than that, just as you cannot.

With deep affection and love,

Aidan Berne

(Italian accent)

In her room, Grace reads the letter half a dozen times. During the second and third readings, she dots the paper with tears. On the fourth reading, she laughs at the words *Italian accent.* During the fifth reading, the word *love* causes her to feel like a balloon leaving the earth. After the sixth reading, she folds the letter and puts it into the hatbox.

Grace stands by the outer wire fence of the used-car lot pretending to be searching for something in her purse.

"This one's a beauty," the salesman says to a young couple, the buyer in a long taupe coat and hat, his wife in a green wool coat and shivering. The salesman, in only a suit (a show of strength?), points to an old Ford. It's been washed and polished, but nothing can hide the considerable rust on the front bumper, or the dent above it. He has had the car pushed so close to the wire fence that the buyers, unless they ask him to pull the car out for them, are unlikely to see the damage. Grace wants to call to them to check out the front, but she probably shouldn't alienate the salesman. She's here to buy a car, too.

"A young woman bought this," the man says, "used it to go back and forth to her mother's in Kennebunkport, and inside of six months, turned it in when her daddy, competing for her attention, bought her a Lincoln. Hardly used at all."

But what about the owners before the young woman, if she even exists? Grace wonders. The car has to be over a decade old. No mention of them. Grace needs someone who knows cars.

She knocks, then remembers the layout. She knocks again, harder. The doctor's car is still in the lot, indicating that he hasn't gone skiing yet. She knocks a third time, giving it everything she's got.

He's dressed but hasn't combed his hair. "Grace, are you all right?"

"I am, I'm fine," she says quickly, "and I'm sorry to intrude on your day off. But I need advice, and I can't think of anyone else who could help me."

"Come in, come in. Let's go back and get some coffee."

"I had half an idea that you'd already be off on your skiing trip," Grace says as they walk the corridor to the kitchen.

"I begged off. I need sleep, and I have to catch up on my reading."

In the kitchen, he puts the water and grounds on the stove to bring to a boil. Grace removes her gloves but not her coat. "I need to buy a car. I went to the used-car lot in the middle of Biddeford and just happened to overhear a conversation between a young couple and a salesman, and I could see that he was cheating them. I wanted to warn them but I was on the other side of the fence. And I suddenly realized that a woman alone in that car lot would be viewed as an instant sale. I know enough to have them take the car from its parking place and to walk around it. To get in and look around. Even to take a test-drive. But I ought to be able to have them lift the hood and look at the works and see if it's in decent shape. That I can't do. I've never seen under the hood of any car."

"I could teach you everything you need to know out in the parking lot. But I'm intrigued. I'd like to get a look at this sleazy salesman. I think I'll just turn off the coffee, and we'll go."

"I'll buy you coffee afterward."

"Deal."

"I should tell you this before we go. I found a bracelet belonging to my mother-in-law and sold it last week. I needed the money to buy the car. I told myself a story in which Merle gave the bracelet to Gene to give to me so that rightfully it was mine."

"That's probably pretty close to the truth."

"No, it isn't. Merle hated me. She would never ever have given me a piece of her jewelry. I could make the argument Gene probably inherited the contents of the house, and he would want me to have a car in order to support his children, but even that isn't true, technically. I have seven hundred dollars in my purse."

"Cash?" he asks, surprised.

"Yes."

"I thought you had a bank account."

"What was the point of putting the money in the bank if I knew I was just going to take it out again?"

"If someone stole your purse, you'd be out a car. By the way, you're going to be my sister, and you should call me John."

"John?" she asks. "That sounds so strange to me."

"I wasn't born Dr. Lighthart."

The gleam in the salesman's eye is brighter, having seen the Packard drive in. "What can I do for you two?" he asks as soon as Grace and John are out of the car. "Ralph Eastman," he says, putting out his hand.

"My sister needs a car. I'm thinking of a used Buick."

"Buick," the salesman muses, as if trying to remember his inventory. "I've got a sensational mustard yellow with a black convertible top, gorgeous car. Nineteen forty. Last convertible made by Buick prewar." He waits. No response. "And I've got a green Super coupe that's a stunner."

"How many seats in the Super coupe?" John asks the salesman.

"Two, but the trunk is good-sized."

Grace shakes her head.

"A sedan?" the doctor asks.

"Yes, one. A navy 'forty-one. The chrome is a little pitted, but that can't be helped around here. The sea salt."

"Why don't you pull her out and we'll take a look?"

"Yes, sir." His bluster leaking like air from a balloon, Ralph all but runs into the showroom to get the keys. When he parks the Buick in front of John and Grace, the man seems even smaller in the driver's seat.

Grace lets John do the walk-around, the inspection under the hood, the kicking of the tires. "What's the story on this one?" he asks the salesman.

"Bought by a twenty-two-year-old guy, who used it only seven months before he enlisted. It was kept at his mother's house in Biddeford Pool for the duration of the war. She didn't have a garage. When the war ended, he drove it for a while, but he didn't like the pitting. Brought it into our lot. Very little mileage. You can see for yourself."

"I did," says John. "I think it's time for a test-drive, what do you think?"

"Yes, sir. You drive, I'll get in, and your sister here can wait inside where it's warm."

"No, my sister will sit in the passenger seat," says John, "and you'll get in back if you don't mind."

"If that's what you want," Ralph says, disgruntled. He probably had part two of his pitch all set to go.

"I'm going to take Route Nine, let it open up," John says. He seems to be listening to the innards of the car as he drives out of the city. "Radio work?" he asks.

"It certainly does," says the salesman, inching forward in his seat so that his face is just behind his customer's ear.

"The heater?"

"You can turn it on with that button there. Honey, why don't you just press that green button and then turn the dial?"

The doctor chooses that moment to press down hard on the gas pedal, slamming Ralph back. Grace wants to smile, but knows that wouldn't help the negotiations. Once out of the city, John steadily increases the speed until they are going fifty-five miles per hour along Route 9. The dial reads sixty. He takes it to sixty-five.

"I must remind you about the speed limit!" Ralph squawks from the back.

"Yes, of course," says John, bringing it down to thirty. The car feels as though it's barely moving. Even so, according to signs, they are still five miles over the limit. Wisely, the salesman keeps his warnings to himself.

When they pull into the lot and exit the car, the doctor asks the price.

"I can't let this beauty go for less than eleven hundred."

Inside, he and Ralph retreat into an inner office, while Grace, tempted by the coffee but remembering that she has promised to buy Dr. Lighthart one after the sale is complete, sits and waits.

It isn't long before he emerges from the office. He sits next to Grace and speaks in a low tone. "I got him down to nine. He'll take the seven today, and you can pay the balance in installments of twenty dollars a month for ten months. He agreed to waive the interest."

"How on earth did you manage that?"

"He's got his eye on my Packard. Worth his while to keep me happy. The Buick begins to shimmy at sixty-five, so I wouldn't take it over sixty."

Grace laughs. "I'll be amazed if I ever go over thirty-five."

"After I made the deal, I got him to agree to fill the oil and the radiator and gas her up. As soon as we do the paperwork, we can go get that cup of coffee."

"I'm buying you lunch," she says.

———

They both order meals that will take them twenty minutes to eat. "I told him we'd be back in half an hour."

Grace nods. Now, alone with the doctor in the luncheonette, an awkwardness settles over her. Her mouth is dry. She isn't at all certain she can call him John. He sits back in the booth and lights a cigarette and asks her if she wants one. She says yes, mainly to quell her nerves. If they were in the office right now, there wouldn't be any nerves. It's the change of venue and possibly the excitement of buying her own car that's causing her anxiety.

"You're smiling," he says.

"I was thinking about Rosie. I told you about her. She almost always makes me smile."

"Why is that?"

"She's a little zany, and she wants to have fun. If she were still living next door, and I drove up with the new Buick, she'd shriek with happiness. She'd want to put all our kids in the backseat and go for a ride and let our hair blow in the wind and smoke cigarettes."

"You must miss her."

"I do."

He puts money on the table.

"No, it's my treat," she says.

"Okay," he says, withdrawing the cash.

Grace fetches seventy-five cents from her purse.

He stands. "Let's go take your new car for a spin. I'll leave mine here. You're driving."

———

Having adjusted the seat so that it suits her, she maneuvers out of the city. The doctor leans back.

"Where shall I go?" she asks.

"Get us out of the city, and then take Route Nine again," he says. "We'll head toward Kennebunkport."

She follows his directions.

"Now bring it up to thirty-five," he instructs.

"I don't want to get a ticket my first time out."

"You won't."

Grace brings it up to speed and lets the Buick go. She's too nervous to turn on the radio or the heater. Her hands feel as though they're cemented onto the steering wheel.

"Take it to forty."

"Speeding tickets are expensive."

"I know. Trust me. How does it feel?"

"Good."

He laughs. "You're supposed to be thrilled."

"I'm too nervous to be thrilled."

"I can see that. Here." He holds out a lit cigarette. Grace reluctantly lets go of the wheel to take it, and then again when she wants a puff. "Now hit fifty-five," he says, "and roll down your window."

She holds the steering wheel with her right hand, which has a cigarette in it, and rolls her window down. The cold air blasts into the car and lifts her hair.

"Relax," he says. "Smoke your cigarette, let your hair blow around, and think of Rosie."

When they reach the town limits of Kennebunkport, Grace reverses direction and heads back to Biddeford.

"Wait a sec," John says, reaching into his coat pocket. "I wrote down two addresses from this morning's paper for apartments that sounded promising. How about you come with me? I could use your opinion."

Grace imagines telling her mother that it takes a very long time to buy a car.

The first place was clearly once a boardinghouse with its bare door and at least six vehicles parked in the driveway. The building is painted sky blue, the shutters pink, and there are rusted farm implements and children's toys in the front yard.

"What do you think?" Grace asks. "Worth a try?"

John raises his eyebrows. "I don't think I could stand coming home to a pink and blue house, and to judge from all the stuff in the yard, I'm guessing the interior isn't up to much either."

"If it were me," Grace says, "I wouldn't go inside."

"That's it then," he says and gives her directions to the second place.

Grace pulls to a stop at the head of a driveway. It's hard to tell if it's a working farm or not. The buildings are well kept.

They are presented with three doors to choose from.

"Pretty barn," Grace murmurs.

John heads for the main house. "This must be the kitchen door. With farm folk, that usually means the front door because the real front door is never opened."

"How do you know so much about farms?"

"When I was in medical school, a doctor let me go

with him on house calls." John knocks, and a middle-aged woman, with her hair in a bun, and her face red (heat from the oven, Grace decides), opens the door.

"Hello, we're here to see about the apartment to rent," John explains.

"Yep," the woman says, stepping aside.

Grace would like to rent the kitchen. The scent of sweet spices floods the room. She breathes deeply.

"It's this way," the farm woman says, opening another door. Grace has a sense that they're now in the ell attached to the kitchen. "This used to be a sheep farm. Last October, when the sheep were out to the far pasture, fire come roaring down the hill like a dragon and burnt nearly all of them. They couldn't get away. You could smell cooked meat for weeks. That's why we're renting out rooms, to make ends meet."

"The fire didn't touch the house," Grace says.

"Nope."

"You were lucky."

"Don't feel that way." She stops and makes a short gesture with her hand. "This is it."

Grace scans the room, large enough for a small sofa, an armchair, a table and two chairs. The woman has made an effort to transform what was essentially a place for tools into a cozy living room. The focal point is the fireplace. When the farm wife notices Grace's glance, she says, "Fireplace draws good. I only put a hot plate out here case you want to make your own coffee. You always have access to the kitchen, and I make three meals a day. They're included in the rent. You can eat with one of us, or bring your meal to the table here. As we go along, you can give me some idea of what you'd like. You plannin' on having children?"

Grace and John look at each other.

"We're not married," John says. "Grace is my sister, and I'm John Lighthart," he says, offering his hand. "Pardon my manners. I should have introduced us right away. Only I will be renting the apartment."

"I mentioned it because I don't rent to families. In the next room there, you'll find the bed and the bathroom. Water pressure is good. It's got electric heat, but you get too cold, just build up the fire with the wood."

The apartment comes with a porch that faces out to pasture. Grace wanders into the bedroom as John emerges. There's a white iron bed, a white bureau, fresh yellow and white striped wallpaper, a desk, and two more windows. A closet has been made by a curtain pulled across an alcove. She checks the bathroom. Old but clean. Well kept. Plenty of linens.

When she exits the bedroom, John blocks her way. "What do you think?" he asks in a low tone.

"I like it. The shared meals, I don't know."

"It's perfect. I can't cook, and I haven't the time to do it."

"You've certainly got a lot of scenery, four big windows. If I were you, I'd take it. Make the lease flexible in case the husband is intolerable." She turns around. "Yes, this suits you, and look, it has bookshelves. You'll get the cooking smells, since it's attached to the kitchen. Eventually, you'll have to tell them that you're a doctor and have long hours. But I'd take it," she says.

"One good turn deserves another," he says. "You followed my advice; I'll follow yours."

Dr. Lighthart moves toward the farm wife. "I think I'll take it," he says, "if we can work out terms."

"It's sixty-five dollars a month, with meals, heat, hot water, electric, and laundry included. Rent due the first of the month. We live our life the way we live our life. You'll hear sounds from the kitchen, I don't doubt, and the cars coming and going, but the walls are as solid as can be. The house was built in 1720, this ell in 1790. Built as a passageway from the barn to the house. Man was supposed to get hisself clean before he come into the kitchen. I don't like a dirty kitchen, and my mother didn't either."

"Well, can we just assume this is the first of the month?" the doctor asks, counting out the bills for the farm woman.

"You moving in today?" she asks.

"I thought I might. I don't have much."

"What's your livin'?"

"I'm a doctor. I work in a clinic in North Kennebunkport." She nods, taking this in. "You'll be wanting supper tonight."

"Yes, if you have enough. What time is dinner?"

"Five. On the dot."

"Ah," says the doctor, "the earliest I can get here during the week would be seven. Six-thirty on a slow day."

"Well then, I'll save your dinner for you. I can always whip up another batch of popovers if they go flat."

"I'll be here for dinner tonight at five. And tomorrow at five," he says, shaking the farm wife's hand.

Grace smiles at the woman as she follows John out to the

driveway. They don't speak right away, thinking it rude to do so in full view of the wife.

In the car, however, Grace says, "You just got yourself a good deal. She doesn't seem like the type to want to pry into your life. I liked the place. It was charming, and in the spring it will be magnificent."

"You paint a nice picture."

When they reach Biddeford, Grace double-parks beside his Packard. He lingers in her car a second longer than he might. "Maybe we could go on another drive next weekend, take the kids sledding. I know a great hill."

"That sounds like fun."

"Great day, Grace," he says as he leaves the Buick.

When Grace pulls up the driveway in the navy blue Buick, her mother pushes the back door open. "Oh my Jesus Christ Almighty!" she exclaims and holds her chest as if she thought her heart might explode.

"Are you angry?" Grace asks, sliding out of the car.

"Angry? Oh no."

In the doorframe, her mother stands in awe, as if her chariot had come for her, as if all the dates of her youth had shown up at the right moment, just when her hair is perfect.

Grace's responsibilities at the clinic expand. She is asked to see to the billing of patients and to keep the accounts at the bank. When the waiting room is overcrowded, she is charged with bringing patients to rooms in which she takes their temperature, weighs them, gives them a robe if necessary, and records physical complaints. In this way, the patients can wait in a private room for Dr. Lighthart.

By midweek, she asks the doctor if there's enough money in the budget to buy side tables and lamps and to subscribe to *Time* and *Life*. She wants to make the waiting room more appealing.

"Sure," Dr. Lighthart says. "Saturday afternoon all right with you? I could leave right after lunch, say one o'clock?"

Surprised that he has invited himself along, she tells him she'll just check with her mother.

"Your car or mine?"

"I'll collect you." Grace can't have Dr. Lighthart come calling for her at Merle's house.

Grace invents an outing for her mother and the children for Sunday: a car trip with a picnic to a scenic vista. After explaining the trip (to her mother's pleasure), she mentions that she'll need a couple of hours on Saturday afternoon to buy furniture for the office.

"Not new furniture!" her mother exclaims.

"I'll find a good secondhand store. It's just side tables. They have to be respectable and more or less match the chairs there."

"What's that then?"

"Wood with a mahogany-like stain."

"And to think I used to have side tables that would have been perfect," muses her mother.

"I wouldn't have taken your tables."

"Maybe you should get a coffee table, too," her mother suggests. "To put flowers on."

"We're getting subscriptions to *Time* and *Life*."

"Well, you'd better get *Good Housekeeping*."

On Friday night, wanting to confirm their expedition the next day, Grace leans against the doorframe of Dr. Lighthart's office. He hands her a check. "So we're all set for tomorrow?" he asks.

"Yes. How do you like your new place?"

"Meals are outstanding. There's a widow living in one of the bedrooms upstairs in the main house, a shoe salesman in another. I gather he's giving her samples." He wiggles his eyebrows, and Grace laughs. "I'm not there much. Heat's surprisingly good. Bed's comfy."

The bed must indeed be comfortable because the doctor appears, for the first time since she met him, rested. Maybe another weekend at his apartment will be even more beneficial. For her part, Grace can't imagine living alone. Sometimes she wants to picture it, but to do so would mean obliterating Claire and Tom. "I've heard of two places we can try," Grace suggests.

"And there's always Salvation Army."

"They must be cleaned out by now," she says.

On Saturday morning, in Merle's room, Grace hems a pale wool skirt she wants to wear on the shopping trip. Sunlight, bouncing off the snow, makes the windows shimmer, but the glare darkens objects in the room. She tries on the skirt and stands before the mirror. Because her hair hangs straight from the winter dry, she decides to put it up in a French twist. Maybe a little lipstick to punctuate her facial pallor.

The skirt is part of a suit from Merle's closet and still loose, though more tailoring would leave the garment misshapen. She puts her hands on her hips, turns, and notes that she's gaining back some of the weight she lost when Aidan was in the house. Her hands move up her rib cage to the undersides of her breasts, but she can feel almost nothing through the thick brassiere and her white blouse. It's the same with her girdle: running her hands down the front of her skirt, she would never know of the contours within.

The scream is so loud, so guttural, so not like a child's, and yet a child's, that Grace yells Claire's name as she runs downstairs and into the kitchen. First she sees the terrible apparition and then, in the corner, her mother holding Tom with Claire's face buried in her skirt. Claire has wet her overalls.

In a voice as calm as she can manage, Grace tells her mother to take the children upstairs. When she turns to her husband, it's all she can do to stand straight and not cover her mouth.

He is hideous.

The left side of his face seems still to be on fire with its skin resembling a gruesome picture in a medical textbook. His ear is gone, his scalp raw, and his left eye appears to have melted. His right eye and his mouth are mostly normal, though the left corner of his lip is indistinct. He wears a silk scarf around his neck, and she realizes that the arm of his tattered coat is empty. She can't imagine what the skin on his torso looks like.

"Are you in pain?" she asks, her first words to her husband.

"Yes."

"What can I do for you?"

He tries to shake his good arm out of his coat, and she understands: he wants his coat off. Without looking at his face, she begins to lower the empty sleeve from his shoulder. He yelps—she must have touched him too hard. She lets the coat fall to the ground, then picks it up and drapes it over the back of a chair.

"Sit," she gestures, staring at the pinned sleeve.

"Can't sit."

"Can you lie down?" she asks.

He nods. "I need water."

She pours a glass of water at the sink and hands it to him. He raises it to his mouth and at least half of it dribbles down the left side of his face and falls onto his shirt, made of an unusually thin material.

"Come with me," she says.

The irony of Grace leading her husband to another room in his boyhood house is not lost on her. And can't be on him.

Her hands shaking, she checks her watch. An hour before she is to collect Dr. Lighthart, which will not happen now. She doesn't know the telephone number at the farm, and she isn't sure she ever gave him the number of Merle's house. How long will he wait before he realizes she's not coming? Would he then dare to drive to her house? She prays that he won't.

She points to the sofa. In what looks to be a torturous set of moves, Gene manages to lie on his right side. She finds a pillow and puts it under his head. As she backs away from him, the entire construct of her life collapses. She will live in this house with this injured man on the couch until one of them dies. She will never again go to a job. She will never make love again. She will not have friends. Slowly, she sinks into the armchair under the tremendous weight of her future.

Gene

"I have to go to Claire and Tom," Grace says to Gene. He barely moves his head. He has an inner look she's familiar with from the clinic—the anticipation of pain.

She finds her family upstairs in her bedroom. Grace walks first to Claire and holds her in a tight embrace. "You were scared, weren't you?" she asks her daughter, whose clothes have been changed.

Claire, sucking her thumb, nods.

"Do you remember Daddy?"

Claire gives a more exaggerated nod.

"Well, Daddy went to help others on the night of the fire, and he got burned. What you just saw was Daddy with some burns on him."

Claire drops the thumb and opens her eyes as wide as they will go. She stares into the middle distance, caught halfway between fear and incomprehension.

"He was a hero, your daddy. And sometimes heroes come back with cuts and bumps on them. That's what happened to him." She sets Claire on her lap so that she can see her daughter more easily. "Would you like to go out and see him? He's lying down."

"Nooooo," Claire keens as she whips her head from side to side.

Tom, crawling on the bedspread, stops to listen to his sister.

"That's all right," says Grace, holding her daughter close and rubbing her back. Grace catches her mother's eye, in which she reads an agitated mix of fear, despair, and stoicism.

"We need to make some decisions," Grace says.

"Is he staying?"

"We'll have to put him in the library. I'm not sure he can make it upstairs."

"The police said he'd been in a coma. Came to a week ago in a New Hampshire hospital, but couldn't remember his name until yesterday."

"How is Claire?" Gene asks from the couch as Grace sits across from him.

"She's fine," says Grace. "She just needs a little time is all."

"My own children didn't recognize me."

"I'm sorry," she says.

"Don't be. It's reality." He swivels his good eye, taking in the room. "I was never allowed in here. My bedroom and the kitchen were my playrooms. I was brought in here only to meet company and then disappear."

"I'm sorry."

"I wish you wouldn't keep saying that. What are you doing here?"

Grace crosses her arms in front of her chest. "Here? In this house? Our own house burned down."

"So I'm told. But my mother's house?"

"Your children were homeless. My mother, too. I didn't have a choice." She pauses. "Were you in a coma?"

"I didn't know who I was until a week after I woke up. For that week, I didn't want to be alive."

She waits.

"The arm, but mostly the pain."

"Why did they take your arm?" she asks, unable to look away from the pinned sleeve.

"Gangrene."

"Oh, Gene. Tell me what I need to know in order to take care of you."

He closes his eye. "You won't want to do it. I'm going to need some things."

"Such as."

"Gauze, Vaseline, iodine, a bedpan." He studies her. "Lots of towels. The sheets will need to be cleaned every day. A rubber sheet."

Grace takes in a sharp breath.

"I told you you wouldn't like it."

"We'll do whatever has to be done."

"And aspirins. I get terrible headaches. Where are you sleeping?"

"On the second floor."

"In my mother's bed?"

Grace nods.

He glances at Grace's skirt. "And if I'm not mistaken, you're wearing her clothes."

"We had nothing when we got here."

Fluid leaks from inside Gene's shirt. She leaves the room, finds a clean towel, returns, and lays it with care over his left side. "I'm sorry if I'm hurting you," she says.

"Please don't pity me."

"I don't." But she does.

"You lost the baby," he says.

"I did."

"Was it bad?"

"It happened the night of the fire."

He rolls his head to the side. For a moment Grace wonders if he will cry. But, no, he's angry. "If only they'd let us go home, I'd have got you out of there!"

"Can you lie here for half an hour?" she asks.

"You're leaving me?"

"Just to get a doctor."

"Old Man Franklin?"

"He's gone. His house burned down, so he retired. We have a new one now. His name is Dr. Lighthart."

For a few seconds Gene is silent. Then he snaps his fingers. "Injun!" he says.

"What?"

"Injun. You can always tell from the name. Two names put together. Whiteman. Yellowhair. Manygoats. Watchman. I knew some of them in the war and later working on the Pike."

The prominent cheekbones. The high color of his skin. The straight black hair. Indian and something else. Maybe a lot of something else. What difference does it make?

"He's a good doctor," Grace says.

———

Grace's hands shake so much she can barely shift the gears. Backing down the hill, she veers into snow-covered bushes at the end. I'll kill myself this way, she thinks.

When she turns onto the rural street on which the farmhouse is located and pulls to the top of the drive, John Lighthart is pacing. She's a half hour late for their appointment.

"Hello," he says with a grin as he swings open the passenger door and gets in.

Grace turns to him and holds up a hand. "John." She pauses, gathers herself. "My husband, Gene, came back this morning. He's badly burned and not yet healed. He can't sit. If you're willing, I need you to come to the house and examine him and tell me what to do."

The doctor searches her eyes. "Are you all right? Your face is white."

"It's just the shock."

"You shouldn't be driving, but I'd better take my car. You go on, and I'll catch up. I have to put a few things in my bag."

"Thank you," says Grace. "Please don't mention that I work for you. I haven't told him yet, and . . . I'm not sure I'll be able to continue at the clinic."

"That would be a shame."

"He's crude. He's not himself."

"You go back to him. I'll be right behind you."

Grace parks the car and reluctantly walks into Merle's house. Her mother, with a yellow apron on, stands in the center of the kitchen. "I don't know what to make for him to eat!" she sputters.

"The doctor is coming."

"I nearly fainted when the police showed up. It's dreadful, isn't it."

The sharp light from the window etches every defect in Gene's face. Grace partially draws the maroon drapes.

"Where did you get that schmancy Buick?" he asks.

"A friend lent it to me."

"Rosie?"

"Another friend. Rosie and Tim have moved to Nova Scotia. Can you walk with me to the library? There's a bed in there."

"Why?" he asks.

"We had a power outage that lasted four days. We all slept in there with the fire going."

She watches as he reverses the agonizing process that enabled him to lie down. She moves toward him to help.

But he limps ahead of her, indicating that he's master of the house now.

Grace greets Dr. Lighthart at the back door without a word. She remembers how Dr. Franklin used to walk in unannounced and take the stairs to the bedroom where the patient lay. Another world. Another country.

"Gene, this is Dr. Lighthart," she says, introducing her husband.

"You can leave us alone, Mrs. Holland," says the doctor.

Grace closes the door.

Mrs. Holland.

She sits on an upholstered chair in the hallway that may

as well have been placed here for this very purpose: to wait to
be summoned. In less than two hours, her life has been transformed. To think that at this very minute she might have
been selecting side tables and lamps for the office with a nice
man, a good man. She was planning on purchasing something quirky or useful for him as a house present.

She hears murmurs, a quick stab of a cry, and then silence
behind the closed door. Dr. Lighthart signals to Grace to
move with him toward the sitting room.

"The burns are bad," he says as they walk. "He'll need
constant care. He has to wear loose silk pajamas and lie on
silk sheets and silk pillowcases, all of which will have to be
laundered every day. I've treated the burns, but I've not put
on gauze. I want them to dry in the air under the pajamas I
brought." He pauses. "I'll see what I can come up with and
send along with Amy. I've left the supplies he'll need for the
next day or two on the dresser. Amy will bring more. The
most important thing at the moment is to keep the wounds
clean and to keep him hydrated. Whenever you're with him,
make him drink. Water, apple juice, and more water. I'd
put a small table right next to the bed and set a plate of finger food on it. He can manage that better than, say, soup.
He'll pick at it when he wants to. Amy will try to get him to
sit up tomorrow. She'll be firm, and I expect your husband
will holler like crazy. Then you'll have to continue with that
treatment yourself if you're physically capable." He sighs.
"Grace, it's unfair, I know. I'd like to see you hire a part-time
nurse. Full-time would be better."

She shakes her head. "He'd want to know how I was paying for it."

"You have more jewelry," he says in a lower voice.

"I don't know. He's very sharp."

"I noticed that."

"I'm sorry about not being able to work for you. I loved the job."

"And I was happy to have you there. Truly."

As they head for the back door, he collects his hat and pulls a piece of paper from his pocket. "This is the phone at the farm. Call me anytime. If I can't get here myself, I'll send someone. Below that is the number of the ambulance service. An emergency would be pain terrible enough that he can't keep from crying out for, say, fifteen minutes; excessive oozing from the wounds; any sign of blood from the wounds; and fever. I can't do anything for his headache today because I don't yet understand what's causing it. It might just be dehydration."

"Thank you for coming. You've been a good friend to me."

"I hope we'll continue to be good friends." He puts his hand on her shoulder before he turns the doorknob. "I want to feel sorry for the man."

The doctor has left a glass with a bent straw on the mahogany dresser so that Gene, in new navy silk pajamas, can drink water without sitting up. She notices that he has given himself a sponge bath in the bathroom nearby. The good part of his face looks shinier, and his nails are clean.

"Was someone here?" he asks.

At first she thinks his brain is addled. "The doctor was here."

"No, I mean before."

"I don't understand." She sets a small blue plate with pieces of deviled ham sandwich and apple on it by the bedside table.

"I saw a razor blade on the floor of the bathroom, half hidden by the claw foot of the tub. I couldn't bend to pick it up. Someone could cut a foot on it."

"I'll get it later," she says.

"But who left it there?"

"I have no idea."

"Well, some man was here. My father's been dead for years."

"Gene, honestly, how would I know?"

She pulls a chair closer to the bed. Her husband doesn't smell as bad as he did before the doctor came. "Do you need a toothbrush?" she asks.

"I need it all."

She holds the straw to his lips.

After Grace has played cowboys and Indians at Claire's request, she returns to Gene's room and sees him struggling to get out of bed.

"Here, let me help," she says. She lifts the blanket and sheet away from him. He pushes himself off the bed with his right hand. There are stains on the sheets.

"What do you want?" she asks.

"What do I want?" he says when standing. "I want to be a normal human being again. I want to go back to work. I'd like to take a shit in a toilet. I'd like to sit at a table and eat a bowl of soup. I'd like to not have to worry about moving in a certain way and causing pain. I'd like my face back. That enough?"

Gene's bitterness, however well earned, could eat through walls.

He says he wants to walk into the parlor because he's sure he left something there. Again he moves ahead, and Grace obediently follows.

"There!" he says. "I knew something was wrong."

"What is it?"

"Why's the piano in here?" he asks.

She glances at the piano, gathering dust. Grace has no choice but to lie and lie and lie. "I thought it was always in here."

"No, no, no, no! It was on the second floor. In the turret. Just off my mother's bedroom."

"Are you sure? Who would put a piano on the second floor?" she asks.

"For crying out loud, I should know. I took lessons on it for years. I know this house a lot better than you do."

"Of course," she says.

The business with the bedpan is awful. He tells her how to prop him up with pillows under his head and back and knees and to put the pan under him and to go away and close the door. Grace does as asked and wants to walk straight out the front door and not stop until she falls down.

The sight of her children as she puts them to bed is a flicker of joy in a dim cave. She gathers them around her on the floor and sings a dozen verses of "Hush, Little Baby," making up the lyrics as she goes along. From the corner of her eye, she sees her mother scurry about folding laundry and picking up toys. Grace sings until the children feel heavier in her lap, and with her mother's help, she carries them to their beds. She would like to lie down on the floor between the children and have her mother float a blanket over her.

Amy arrives at the house with an enormous green suitcase full of supplies. For the first time, Grace sees the extent of Gene's burns along his torso and hip and upper thigh. Her gorge rises. Keeping up a constant chatter, the nurse instructs Grace how to clean the burns, let them air-dry, apply iodine or Vaseline where necessary, take his temperature and his blood pressure, examine the skin, bathe the back of his body, and help him dress himself. She leaves a list of instructions next to the supplies.

"Now the hard part," Amy says. "He has to stay as flexible as he can without cracking the protective layer of skin he's building up. That's why I've put the Vaseline on so heavily. Later, we'll dab it off."

She turns and addresses Gene. "Do you want to be able to sit on a chair?"

"Yes."

"Do you want to be able to get down onto the floor and play with your children?"

"Oh, come on," he says, "what's with the interrogation?"

"I need to know how badly you want these things, Mr. Holland, because if you really, truly want them, you're going to have to work hard."

Grace watches as Amy lays Gene flat on his back in the bed, which already causes him some pain as his left side comes in contact with the sheet. She takes hold of his left leg with one hand on his calf and one on his knee. She bends the knee and pushes it toward his face, in and out, in and out. Gene grits his teeth. Whatever Amy does to one side of Gene's body, she does to the other. She has Gene scoot down on the bed. After he has done so, she climbs onto the bed up by the headboard and asks him to lift his head and shoulders as high as he can. As soon as he rises off the sheet, she gets her arms and her full weight under him and slowly angles him higher and higher until he is nearly at thirty degrees from the flat surface. He cries out and tries to turn and hop off the bed.

"Grace, hold his legs down by the ankles."

Grace leans over the footboard and pins her husband's feet to the bedspread.

When Gene's cries reach a certain pitch, Amy lets him rest. Grace hopes her mother is on the third floor with the children and the door shut.

"Good work, Mr. Holland," she says. "We'll rest a minute and give that another try."

"The hell you will."

"Do you want to be able to sit on a toilet one day and get rid of the bedpan, because really, that is what this is all about. You getting back your independence. So do you want that?"

"I guess so."

"No, I'm serious, Mr. Holland. Do you really want that to happen?"

"Jesus Christ," he says in a louder voice.

"Then bend your head and shoulders as far up as they will go, and we'll give this another try."

Without being told to, Grace grabs her husband's ankles while Amy repeats the process. Grace knows she'll never be able to do this therapy for Gene, both because she can't hold his feet and push from behind at the same time and because she doesn't have Amy's strength. After the third exercise, Gene says to Grace, "Get that bitch out of here."

"You're going to have to toughen up."

"I don't have your strength."

"You're afraid of him," Amy says as she puts on her heavy wool coat.

"I've always been afraid of him," Grace confesses.

"Do you want him on a bedpan the rest of his life? Because if he remains as he is for much longer, he won't be able to sit up ever. It's been way too long as it is."

Grace wraps her arms over her head.

"Listen," Amy says, "you're going to have to find something within you that can do this. It'll take a solid month of misery, and if all goes well, each day will get better and better. Be a drill sergeant now, and later you can love him."

But I won't, Grace wants to say. I won't love him.

Grace becomes an unwilling nurse during a string of days that in themselves seem endless. A routine is established. Grace wakes early to prepare Gene's breakfast before he makes his way into the kitchen and eats it standing up. Hard-boiled eggs and toast pieces serve him well. Her mother knows to keep the children upstairs until seven-thirty, when Grace spirits Gene back into his room or to the sofa in the sitting room. Mindful of his pain and boredom, she tries to carve the day into three separate sections: mornings, during which she sometimes reads the newspaper to him or lets him lie by himself in the sitting room; afternoons, which are devoted to physical therapy (for the first several days until she could convince Gene to cooperate, Grace had to call in her mother to hold his feet down, episodes that made her mother cry after she left the room); and evenings, which he spends back in the sitting room with a plate of finger food beside him. Often, Grace joins him. They remain silent while she knits or sews, or he asks her questions. She can hardly comprehend that the room in which she unwillingly sits with her damaged husband is the same place in which she came to love Aidan Berne. Such utter happiness then, and now such despair.

Grace's duties as her husband's nurse and her sense of having lost whatever freedom she once had cause her to be exhausted nearly every evening. When she climbs up to her bedroom (her bedroom now, not Merle's; Grace has at least earned that), she clings to the banister. Her mother's comments that she needs to take better care of herself, that she is letting herself go, that sometimes her clothes aren't even clean, haven't helped. More and more, Marjorie remains on the third floor with the children, descending only to cook lunch and dinner. It has not escaped Grace's notice that her mother is a prisoner, too.

Winter hints at spring, not by temperature, but by the quality of the light. The stolen minutes Grace sits huddled in her
winter coat on the back steps give her hope. Is she really any
worse off than the dispossessed women of Hunts Beach, or
than the women who had to nurse injured loved ones back
from the war and transform them into husbands?

"We thought if we dug a trench wide enough, we could stop
the fire in its tracks," Gene explains, and Grace nods. "We
were stupid. None of us had ever had any experience with
fire. We were just following orders from the fire department.
The idea was to keep the blaze from reaching town." He
opens his eye. "Can you prop me up again?"

Grace lifts his right side so that he is straight up against
the back of the sofa but at a forty-five-degree angle with pillows behind his shoulders and back. They have to achieve
ninety degrees for him to sit in a chair, beyond that if he is
to get up and out of a chair. The progress is slow and often
there are setbacks.

"We'd been digging all day and into the night when we
felt an east wind, so we stopped for a break. We thought
we were saved. We didn't leave our post though because we'd
been told to stay put. Can you put that extra pillow there behind
my neck?"

Grace stands and maneuvers the pillow until he nods.

"We were pretty sure a truck would be coming for us
with food and coffee if not a lift back to our homes. And one
by one, we began to sit on rocks or against tree stumps, and I
remember that I dozed off. I woke to shouting."

As Grace had, with Claire's cries.

"When I stood, the fire had crested Merserve Hill and was roaring its way down to us. Balls of fire tumbled down the hill, hitting trees, missing others, and the wind behind the fire was ferocious. I remember thinking that fire was really pink and red, not orange. Within minutes we could feel the heat and see animals running around us for safety. Two of the men ran with the animals, the others stayed with me. Then I felt Jack dragging on my sleeve and shouting at me to go with him, to get out. I shook my head. I had another idea. I could see that behind the wall of fire the earth was black—the fire traveled that fast. Tim and Jack dug holes in the ground knowing they couldn't outrun the blaze. When it got too close to bear, I saw a space about the length of a truck and ran through it as fast as I could. My mistake was not having something to cover my head. I felt intense heat and knew my sleeve and hair had caught fire. I panicked and stumbled and tried to put out the flames by slapping them. I fell onto my left side, the ground so hot I couldn't bear the pain. And then I fainted."

"I'm so sorry," Grace says. No other words will do.

The crocuses emerge, purple and white, and are soon joined by the bright yellow of daffodils and forsythia. As she explores the gardens, Grace's spirits are buoyed by the greening lawn, the buds on the fruit trees, and the stalks of tulips breaking the soil. After the winter months, the soil will produce a bounty of surprises with flowers blooming every day or every week, small gifts for Grace. She will see the buds, but won't know their color until days later. She wonders if the

lilacs are deep purple or lavender or white. She has no idea
what shapes and hues the roses will have. Soon she'll be able
to bring in bouquets to freshen the house's stale smell—an
odor worse than stale that she suspects emanates from Gene,
no matter how much she launders his sheets and clothes.

Gene has remembered the name of the insurance company
and even the salesman's name. Grace calls and explains
their situation, which is near destitute. But when the claims
adjuster comes to the house and looks around, he's reluctant
to discuss benefits. Grace points out that the house is not
theirs, they have no money for food or clothes, that Gene
can't work, and the enormous tank of fuel oil is empty.
Should they have a series of cold days, she doesn't know
what they would do. In addition, she says in a strong, clear
voice, her husband who was burned in the fire needs medical
attention they can't pay for. When the salesman has the nerve
to suggest that she sell some of the obviously expensive pieces
of furniture, she raises her voice. Does the adjuster have the
paperwork? Yes, he does. Did Gene Holland ever miss a payment? No, he did not. Fine, says Grace, they need the money
to build a house, to which they are entitled, and they need
additional sums in order to be able to eat and clothe themselves. She is firm, she will not be moved. But it's only when
Grace brings the adjuster in to see Gene during a moment
when he isn't wearing his eye patch that the adjuster writes
her a check for seventy-five dollars to bridge the gap until
another man from the insurance company arrives with a
much larger check.

———

One morning, after Grace has made her bed, she stares at the
smooth covers, the sheets taut beneath them. She kneels on
all fours and pounds her fists into the coverlet. She bangs and
slaps until her hands hurt. She stops and looks at her fingers.
She tries hard to remember what she felt when she and Gene
were courting—there is no other word to describe the deco-
rous study dates and walks into the hills, where occasionally
they lay down together. She can't now recall a single word
of love. One of them must have said something. On the day
they married?

Gene grows oddly querulous, as if he, too, were filled with
barely concealed rage. One might imagine his anger a result
of having met such an odious fate, but Grace suspects his rage
has something to do with hers. Gene is as much a prisoner as
anyone in the house, more so because of his disabilities. His
only outlet is his wife, who cannot take on the burden of his
constant pain, his helplessness. One day, when she starts the
physical therapy, telling him to raise his head, he refuses.

"No," he says.

"What do you mean, no?" Grace asks.

"I'm not going to do it."

"Just today or forever?"

"Forever."

"If you stop now, you'll undo all the good that therapy has
done you. A year from now, you won't be able to accomplish
the simplest thing."

"Maybe not, but you can do it for me, can't you?" he
points out.

"You want me to wipe your ass for the rest of your life?"

Grace snaps away from Gene, at least as horrified as he by her own revolting question, her cynicism, her anger. But she won't tell him she is sorry. She leaves the room with the realization that her statements to him will get uglier and uglier, that they could so easily spiral out of control. And who would get hurt? The children. Pretty soon, they'll be able to hear what goes on in the library, the sitting room, the kitchen. She puts her forehead to the wall. She doesn't want that for Claire and Tom, for them to have to hunch their shoulders at a raised voice, to have to pretend not to hear an obscenity, to want to absent themselves from their parents, which in time will mean not wanting to be in the house. She has done a good job with the children so far, especially with her mother's help, but she doesn't know if she has the self-discipline to keep it up.

Grace thinks of hiring a day nurse, which would free at least eight hours to be with the kids. If she could manage it, she'd hire a live-in nurse so that she would see her husband in the way the children do—during lighthearted visits. And though she can afford to hire such people, Gene will want to know where the money has come from. Since they have received only seventy-five dollars from the claims adjuster, he will quickly figure out that she is selling items from the house to pay for the nurses. She doubts he knows about the jewelry, unless Merle often wore it in his presence. Still, he would needle Grace, and life would become even more impossible than it is. She might one day hit him, a thought that appalls her. Or simply let him fall to the floor. So easy to do. She has had to catch him when he lost his balance at least a dozen times since he arrived.

She takes a deep breath. She can't think these nightmare scenarios.

"Hello, this is Grace Holland. May I speak to Dr. Lighthart?"

"Grace, it's Amy."

"Hi, Amy. Actually, it might be better if I spoke to you."

"Okay."

"I need help." The statement strikes Grace as true on so many fronts that for a moment she nearly laughs.

"Yes?"

"I need to hire a nurse to come on a daily basis, to help with Gene. I'm having difficulties."

"I thought so. I know of an organization that does just that. Hang on, I've got the number here. But how are you?"

The truth, Grace thinks. "At my wit's end."

"His care is too much for you. I knew it would be."

"It's not just that. Things are . . . difficult. It's made taking care of him nearly impossible."

"How's your health?"

"My health? I don't even know."

"I tell you what. I'll call first thing in the morning and get someone out there straightaway. You'll be all right?"

"Yes. And, Amy? Send someone strong-willed. And big."

Grace watches as a large woman in a white cap and navy cape emerges from a car that with its dents and rust looks as though it's barely survived a military skirmish. There are no pleasantries, hardly enough time to tell Judith, the nurse, the nature of the difficulties she is having with Gene. Grace, trying to keep up with the nurse's long strides, makes it to Gene's door just before Judith does. "Wait here," Grace says, trying to stop the woman.

"No need to wait. He'll figure it out."

Grace steps away and lingers long enough to hear Judith announce herself and tell Gene that she's been sent to check him out. Not wanting to hear his reply, Grace walks away, but doesn't dare go farther than the sitting room in case the nurse needs her. From time to time, loud sounds emanate from the library-bedroom, but she stops herself from investigating. She doesn't want to know.

After a time, she climbs the stairs to Merle's closet and retrieves Aidan's letter from the hatbox. When she holds it, she begins to recall the music he once played, but stops short when she discovers that she can't remember certain phrases in their entirety. She presses the letter to her chest. Will time erase the notes that are more precious to her than jewels?

She sees vividly the day she met Aidan and can feel her physical reaction when he played the piano. She recalls being happy and how she naïvely thought that state would continue forever. She will buy a record player and fill the house with classical music. The children will appreciate it and remember when Aidan was here—and a time when their mother smiled often.

Grace, back in the sitting room, is startled by a door slamming. When she looks up, Judith is standing before her, wiping her hands on a towel.

"I won't be returning," she says.

Grace stands. "I'm sorry. What happened?"

"I worked him hard, I'll admit that. You probably heard the shouting. And for my troubles, I got a glob of spit down the front of my uniform."

Grace wants to apologize for her husband, to explain.

"You seem a nice person. But your husband— There's something wrong with him. And I mean more than his burns."

"I'm sorry this has happened to you."

"I don't mind telling you that I don't like leaving you alone with him."

"I'll be fine," Grace says, gathering herself. "He was just furious with me for getting a nurse behind his back."

The nurse peers at Grace. "Are you aware of how crazy that is? Most men in his situation want to get better."

"Men have pride."

"I've seen pride and stubbornness, yes I have. This is something different."

When Grace goes in to see Gene, she finds a subdued husband. "I don't need anything," he says in a quiet voice.

The next afternoon, Grace arrives home with a secondhand record player that the salesman in the music store turned on for her so that she could listen to a Mozart record. He didn't need to talk up the quality; Grace could hear it for herself. He helped her select music from Chopin and Brahms, from Beethoven and Bach. Nearly giddy with her purchases, she asks her mother to bring the kids downstairs. Grace plugs in the machine, puts a record on the spindle, and lets the music of Chopin fill the house, a grand salute to her mother and Claire and Tom as they make their way down the staircase. Grace beams at them. "I've bought a record player. We'll have music now."

"It's beautiful," her mother says, putting her hands to her cheeks. Claire hears the music as her cue to start dancing. Tom holds on to the coffee table and shakes his hips and dips his knees, trying to imitate his sister, which makes Grace and her mother laugh. Marjorie asks Grace to dance. The pair hold hands, and Grace remembers the silly joy of dancing for Aidan. Because neither she nor her mother really knows any steps to this sort of music, they make up their own movements, sometimes following rhythm, more often moving too fast for the stately composer. They meet in the center, smiling, and Grace twirls her mother around and spins her out, only to have her roll back again.

"WHAT IS GOING ON?"

Grace, her mother, and the children stop short as if they had been shot. A pianist, oblivious to the disruption, plays on.

"What's that?" Gene asks, pointing a finger at the machine.

Because the children are present, Grace holds her sarcasm in check. "I bought a record player," she says.

"You bought a record player knowing how I hate loud sounds, knowing that I have a constant headache, knowing that I need silence at all times?"

"Could you hear it?" Grace asks, not so innocently.

"Could I hear it?" He performs a truncated roll of his head to indicate what an idiotic question that is. Claire and Tom gravitate to their grandmother, who gently leads them into the kitchen.

"The children need music," Grace says in as calm a voice as she can manage.

"Did you have music when you were growing up?"

"There's a thing called progress," she says. "There's another thing called beauty. There's a third thing called fun. And believe it or not, there's such a thing in the world as a choice."

"Not in my house," he says. "Get rid of it."

Grace sticks her hands in the pockets of her dress. "You get rid of it," she says.

"You know very well I can't get into a car and drive it back to wherever it came from."

"Then break it for all I care."

Marjorie confides to Grace that she isn't feeling well.

"Is it your stomach?" the daughter asks, feeling her mother's forehead with the back of her hand.

"Not sure yet. I'm achy all over. And tired."

"Of course you're tired."

"I don't want to give it to the children."

"The children will be fine. Just go up and rest."

As she watches her mother climb the stairs, Grace is aware of Claire and Tom touching her clothes, as if now she must be activities director. She closes her eyes but can't think of a single game they used to play together. Has she lost the part of her brain that functioned on automatic? "Shall we go up to the nursery and see what's there?" she asks in an overly cheery voice.

Claire shakes her head. Grace kneels down to be at her level. "Say the word."

"No," says Claire.

"Why?"

"Boring."

"We could color," suggests Grace.

"Boring."

"We could cook."

"Boring."

"I know! How about we go upstairs and jump up and down on my bed?"

"Yes!" cries Claire as she heads for the stairs. Grace follows more slowly behind Tom since he insists now on doing everything "byself." When Tom and she enter the bedroom, Claire is already bouncing high, her hair leaving her head. She falls deliberately on her bum and pops right up again.

My little gymnast, Grace thinks. She takes off her shoes and climbs onto the bed. Mindful of the chandelier, she jumps in rhythm with Claire, trying not to tip over Tom, who can't keep his balance on the constantly moving surface. Grace feels gleeful at the thought of the subversive activity she's invented. Exhausted, she quits before Claire, but even Claire winds down.

"Yay for us!" Claire says, breathless.

The playing on the bed annoys Gene. Infuriates him.

"That's my mother's bed."

"We were only fooling around."

"What mother lets her kids jump on the bed?"

"I do. Did."

"If you ruin the springs, you won't have a bed left. God-damnit, Grace. What's got into you?"

Grace pauses, studies her husband's face. "What's gone out of me is a better question."

In quiet moments Grace understands that Gene went to the fire to perform his civic duty. He was all but killed in the blaze. He's suffered enough pain to last a hundred men a lifetime. He's so disfigured he doesn't want to leave the house. If he's true to his word and no longer participates in his physical therapy, he will become a bedridden invalid.

Who would want that kind of life?

If you love a man, Grace thinks, you might be willing to do anything for him. And if she loved Gene, she might touch him on his good side, say soothing or funny words. She would stay in his room every free minute that she had, perhaps even installing a cot so that she could sleep beside him. She would cajole him into more and more physical therapy and would praise him for every small accomplishment. She would kiss the good side of his face and, if he wanted her to, find a plastic surgeon who might be able to improve his appearance. She would sell all the jewelry so that he and she were set for life, able to be companions and, one day, lovers again. She would take him for walks outside in the spring. They would sit together under the cherry tree she knows is about to bloom, and they would hold hands and laugh.

She is thinking of Aidan.

Time passes so slowly that Grace hates to wake up. Every moment longer that she sleeps is a minute she won't have to fill. There are so many of them in a single day. When she was with Aidan, she was unaware of time. When she worked for Dr. Lighthart, she was so busy she was often surprised to look up and discover that it was already five-thirty in the afternoon. Now it seems as if it takes days to get to five-thirty, never mind eight o'clock, when she can reasonably go to bed.

Grace can't read anymore, can't even finish a magazine article at the kitchen table. Her concentration is shot. She no longer reads to Gene, who doesn't seem to miss it.

She wonders what can be inside his head.

When she thinks it might be time to reintroduce the children to their father, she speaks to Claire and Tom for a long time and then enters Gene's room with them. Before they have even reached the bed, Gene confronts his daughter. "What the heck did you do to your hair?"

"Mommy did," Claire answers in a tremulous voice.

"I loved your long curls," Gene wails. "You were so beautiful."

Claire begins to cry.

An hour later, Grace charges into Gene's bedroom. "Can you just answer me one question?"

He tilts his head on the pillow, his face uncertain.

"Why did you marry me?" she asks.

"You got pregnant, remember?" he says defensively.

"Yes. But before. You were romantic, you courted me."

"Did I? I don't think we should discuss the past."

"But I want to know."

"You were there."

"But I wasn't inside your head."

"I could lie to you."

"But don't."

He props himself up with his right elbow. "You reminded me of my love," he says.

Grace at first doesn't understand. "I reminded you of . . . your love?"

And so he gives it to her, the answer she thinks she wants, the answer she'll wish she had never asked for. "You reminded me of the woman I loved when I was in the war."

He waits to see how Grace will take this announcement, but she's motionless.

"She was French," Gene adds. "She looked a lot like you. I couldn't persuade her to come back to the States with me. I used to write to my mother, and once I sent a picture of the two of us together. I told my mother I would marry the woman." He pauses. "It's why she didn't like you."

The explanation smacks Grace in the face as if she had walked into a glass door. She leaves the library, climbs the stairs to her bedroom, and lies on the bed facedown.

Amy comes to visit, bringing new supplies. After her time with Gene, she addresses Grace, who is waiting outside his room.

"I heard the visiting nurse was a fiasco," Amy says.

"What did she say specifically?"

"Only that your husband was completely uncooperative. What happened to the physical therapy? He's as limp as a fish."

"He won't do it."

"It's your job to make him do it."

"There's only so much I can do," responds Grace.

"You look like hell. What's happened?"

Grace shrugs.

"I'm going to go in there and give him what for," says Amy.

"Good luck with that."

When Amy drives away, Grace walks down the driveway, reaches her hand into the postbox, and takes out the mail. She sees, between the electric bill and a final check from Dr. Light-hart, a cream-colored envelope. The return address is a hotel in New York City.

Dear Grace,

You thought I was asleep, but I wasn't. I heard you leave the bed, and it took all my strength not to snatch you back. Stay, I called in my mind. But it wasn't you who was leaving that house, it was I, and it's likely I never did a more difficult thing.

You, with me, all the time.

A.

Grace leans against the mailbox and closes her eyes. A letter. A tangible letter. He still thinks of her. She is with him all the time.

Two letters now to parse and treasure and remember word for word. Two letters to touch, to trace the words. Two signs that what she experienced with Aidan Berne was real. She wants to savor the moment.

But before she has even climbed the driveway, she understands the agonizing thing she must do.

In her room, she sits at Merle's dressing table with paper and pen. She writes in care of his hotel address and adds, "Please Forward."

Dear Aidan,

If only you had caught my hand. Another hour would have been worth the risk. I think of you every day.

My husband, Gene, has arrived home. He was badly burned in the fire and remained in a coma for nearly three months. He has only begun his road to recovery. We are an injured family in many ways, but we are a family. I must keep my children safe and tend to my husband.

I wish you only the best of luck everywhere you go.

Grace

The finality of the letter makes her ache. She wraps her arms around herself and tries to imagine Aidan's reaction as he reads it. Will he crumple up the paper and throw it into a wastebasket? Who would want to keep such a note?

She knows she has to mail the letter immediately; otherwise, she'll tear it up. After carrying two recalcitrant children out to the Buick, she backs down the driveway and navigates the short distance to the post office. She marches to the mailbox like a soldier under orders. She holds the letter for a long time until finally she pushes it through the slot.

"Mommy, your eyelashes are blinking," Claire says when Grace slides back into the driver's seat.

"Just something in my eye," she answers, clearing her throat and peering into the rearview mirror.

It's possible Aidan might never get her letter. No one is obliged to forward it.

"Who wants to go to the playground?" she asks.

Grace can't make herself get out of bed the next morning. If she lies still for long enough, she thinks, she might be able to fall asleep again and what a luxury that would be. She forgets her children. She forgets her husband. She stares at the medallion on the ceiling, hoping it will hypnotize her.

When she rouses herself, she slips into her robe and heads to the kitchen to start the coffee. Claire, with a mix of hurt and pride on her face, sits before an overloaded bowl of Rice Krispies and milk, a cup of which has spilled onto the table and then to the linoleum. Tom, sitting on the floor with dry Krispies all around him, is eating only those inside his wet diaper because they're easier to pick up and put into his mouth.

Claire might have dropped the milk bottle, shattering it on the floor.

Grace will set an alarm clock and be in the kitchen at six-thirty every morning.

Gene cries out in the night. Grace sits upright and listens intently. There are no words, merely a harrowing cry into the void of his nightmares. He told her he might do this. She lies back and puts a pillow over her head.

For three nights he does this.

———

Grace moves herself and the children to the third floor, where they sleep together in the nursery, Grace on a cot she drags into the room.

The house that Aidan once called grand, the house that Grace came to appreciate, turns the way that milk does. The house that once held music becomes silent and menacing. No matter how hard she pushes back the curtains, it seems she can't get enough light inside. She tells herself that the smell and the lack of light are only in her head, that a house is a house and except for mild decay doesn't change. But the decay in this house has been fast and frightening. She keeps the windows open, the breeze moving the curtains, so that she can breathe.

Marjorie appears at breakfast better dressed than usual. "Grace, I need to speak to you in private," she whispers above the children's heads.

By the time the children have finished their breakfasts and have gone outside to play, Grace has already worked it out. "You're thinking of leaving," she says to her mother.

"I can't spend my life upstairs taking care of children, even children I love," Marjorie declares. "I was willing and happy to do it in the beginning, but now . . ."

"You feel stuck up there."

"I need to get out, see my friends."

"I understand, I do. But where will you go?" Grace asks, leaning against the counter.

"I'll stay with Gladys and Evelyn for now, until I can find a place to live. I want to be on my own again. Of course, I'll

visit every chance I get, but I need to be able to breathe," she
answers. "I feel selfish and terrible leaving you in the lurch
like this."

"Don't say that. You've helped me so much. I can take
care of the children and make the meals. I used to do it all
the time. Gene is becoming more and more independent,
and with each passing day, he seems to be getting stronger.
And now the kids can play outside." She looks down. She's
wrapped a dish towel around her hand and wrist the way
Amy might bandage an injury.

"You're making this too easy on me."

"I can't make it easy enough."

Marjorie embraces Grace. She catches her mother's scent
in her clothes, a natural perfume that has always comforted
her. "When are you going?" Grace asks as they pull away.

"This afternoon."

Grace is both surprised and dismayed but refuses to
show it. "This is a terrible situation, Mother, but it's one that
involves Gene and me. No one wants to live in the midst of
so much unhappiness."

"I kept the children happy."

"And so will I," Grace promises.

With the children napping, Grace steps into her mother's
room. It's been weeks since she's been in here. She notes her
mother's sewing basket, a short stack of books on the bedside
table, a glass ashtray filled with licorice drops.

Grace sits on the patchwork quilt. "I want to leave him,"
she tells her absent mother.

"How can you?"

"I can't bear it. It's not his disability—it's his hatred. Of me, of his situation. It's become intolerable."

"You have to stay," her mother says calmly.

"Why?"

"You're married."

Grace remembers a woman in pin curls and glasses who watched a boisterous sea and told her to hold on to her husband.

"You made your bed," her mother adds.

"I didn't make this bed," Grace says.

It feels like years since Grace experienced the mild weather of June sunshine, the miraculous array of flowers, a wonderment of birds nestled inside the hedge and making a racket. She picks a bouquet of peonies and lilacs and brings them inside to arrange in a vase to put on the kitchen table. On an impulse, she carries the vase into Gene's room and sets it on the desk.

"What's that?" he asks from the bed.

"Spring flowers. I thought they might brighten up the room."

"Get them out of here."

Grace is taken aback. Who doesn't want flowers?

"I get hay fever, remember?"

No, Grace does not remember. She removes the vase and carries it back to the kitchen.

The flowers are glorious.

One desultory afternoon in the kitchen when Claire and Tom fight over a toy fireman and Gene shouts from his room to keep it down, Grace puts her head in her hands. Tom, for the first time that Grace can remember, looks afraid, his lip quivering. She wants to go to her children, to soothe them, but she can't. She climbs to the third floor alone and falls onto her cot. She turns onto her side and puts herself into a fetal position and cries and remembers that the only other time she did this was when she lost the baby. She's amazed that she can weep, that the well isn't dry. Most of the time she's numb, refusing to think about her future. But now she sees the reality she's kept at bay: she and the children will be prisoners here for years.

She sits up. She's left the children alone downstairs. When she reaches the kitchen, Claire and Tom lie facedown on the linoleum, holding hands, still awake but not speaking. Grace asks questions, but neither will answer her. They are angry—of course they are—what mother abandons her children? Tom turns his head as if he would smile at Grace, but Claire, lovely little dictator that she is, whispers, "Shush!" and Tom puts his forehead to the floor. Grace tries to remember when she last washed it.

That night, in the children's bedroom, now her own, Grace opens all the stuck windows and inserts the screens she found in the closet. As she lies on her cot in her summer nightgown, she refrains from pulling up the sheet and instead allows the soft air to cover her. She feels it move over her face and arms and legs, and it's as if she's floating above the earth, aloft in the night, gently buffeted by sweet summer breezes. Her children are near her, asleep in their pj's. She refuses all thoughts, simply savors the sensation. This is peaceful. I can feel this. I can enjoy this. She drifts, and then she drifts. This is wonderful, she thinks as she begins to dream.

A man stands over her. She wakes as if seized but instinctively doesn't yell out because her children are in the room. She covers herself with the sheet and searches for Claire and Tom. Undisturbed, they are sleeping shapes in the dark. The man whispers to her. "Come out into the hall. I need to talk to you."

"Gene?"

"Just come."

Grace yanks the sheet from the cot and wraps herself in it. She makes her way to the door and follows her husband into the corridor. Why isn't it lit?

"How did you get up here?" she asks, breathless.

"It wasn't easy."

"What's the matter?"

"I just wanted us to talk."

"Now? In the middle of the night?"

The kiss is wet, his breath rank. She turns her face, but not in time. His tongue reaches deep inside her mouth. His right arm props him up, his hand next to her ear. She wrenches her head to one side.

"Come on, Grace, give your hubby a kiss." He swoops again and catches her eye this time. He doesn't have another hand with which to overpower her. Does he really imagine that she will somehow help him to have sex with her?

"Just a little kiss," he persists. He grabs the back of her hair to hold her head to the wall. "We can start over again," he coos, "wipe away the past."

"Gene, stop. You'll fall."

"But you'll catch me, won't you, Dove?"

The old nickname, the one she hasn't heard in over a year, fails to move her. She slides out of his grasp and away from him. "Gene, you have to go downstairs. The children are right through this wall."

"You should be good to me. I'm your husband."

"Let me take you downstairs. We can lie in your bed. The children won't hear," she explains. "You don't want the children to hear us, do you?"

"You'll help me?"

"Of course I'll help you."

"You love me, don't you?" he asks, sounding oddly like a child.

She switches the light on. "Let's just concentrate on getting you down the stairs. You shouldn't have come this far."

"I had to rest on my mother's bed," he says, squinting in the electric light.

What time is it? she wonders. How long did it take him to get to the third floor? They make the turn on the landing and descend. Trying not to hurry him, she walks with him to his bedroom.

"Here," she says, "let's get you settled, and then I'll come around and slide in with you."

"And you'll let me kiss you then?" he asks, catching her hand.

"I will," she answers, slipping her fingers through his.

A man has sexual needs. She is his wife. She uncovers the bed and lies next to Gene. He has lowered his pajamas to expose his rigid penis. "Just touch it," he says.

There will be no discussion, no loving words. She takes

hold of him, makes an open fist and slides it back and forth. He moans. In less than a minute, he jerks and his sperm spills out over her palm and wrist and sheet. He makes the same involuntary motions she sometimes feels inside her when he has finished. She wipes her palm and arm on her side of the bed and stares at her husband.

He is spent, nearly unconscious. Any woman's hand would have done. She hates that she had to touch him, that the sexual urge turned a frightful and nasty man into a wheedling beggar. She hates that he can ask her for this.

No, she was wrong. It wasn't that any woman's hand would have done—it has to be her hand. His demand and her hand.

He doesn't touch her. He doesn't call her Dove. He gives no indication that she is even in the same room with him.

She slides out of bed and walks to the stairs. Once there, she takes them two at a time to the third floor. Inside the room, she reaches high on the door for the bolt. She slams it home and leans against the wall. She presses her hand against her breast and can feel her heart hammering. She slides down the wall and sits with her back against it until morning.

Grace is careful to deliver Gene's breakfast before he can get up and come into the kitchen. He wakes in a fog. She doesn't give him a chance to mention the night before.

Back in the kitchen, Grace collapses onto a chair, paralyzed with indecision. Her thoughts swirl like ribbons inside her head. Trying to catch one to examine seems like a game too difficult for her. If only she could think logically.

Claire in her pj's stands at the threshold to the kitchen. "What. Is. Going. On?" she demands in a loud voice, hands on her hips.

Aping her father.

"Where's our breakfast?" she scolds. She turns her hands into little fists and pops them back on her hips. Behind her, Tom studies his fingers, trying to make fists, too. Giving up, he slaps the sides of his diaper.

Claire misses nothing.

At lunchtime, Grace finds Gene propped up against the sofa in the sitting room. She sets his meal, pieces of chicken breast, potato chips, and a pickle, on a side table that he can easily reach.

"I could drag you through divorce court," Gene says, as if he had absorbed her thoughts in his sleep. "It would destroy you." He nearly laughs. "Can you imagine what your mother would think? Her friends?" he adds, looking smug.

"Please," she says.

The word might mean "please don't do that" or it might mean "please divorce me." She decides to let Gene figure it out for himself.

An early summer day, and it will be hot. Already Grace can feel, at eight o'clock in the morning, as she passes from the shade of one tree to another, the surprise of the heat wafting up from the grass. She blows up a wading pool she recently purchased and then stands with the hose in her hand, filling it. Nearby, Tom and Claire, in their new bathing suits, hop about in anticipation. Grace has made the decision to keep the children with her at all times. She wouldn't put it past Gene to snatch one of them and use Claire or Tom as a hostage. Merely the idea of it sickens her.

How did Gene make it to the third floor? He can stand and walk, but he can't sit up straight. He must have two-stepped to the top of the house, keeping his left leg and side straight. Is that how he descended? She remembers it seemed to take forever.

The water up to the edge of the pool, Claire steps in, takes a breath, and then sits. She makes a wide swishing motion to keep Tom out.

"Claire," Grace says, "remember what you and I talked about? About being nice to Tom and letting him share? The pool is for the two of you. If you can't do that, I'll have to take you out."

Claire pouts but allows Tom to step into the pool. He falls in doing so and splashes Claire with his tumble. "Mom, Tom splashed me!" Claire whines.

"He couldn't help himself. Just be glad you're older and have more control."

The kids will jump in and out of the water all morning. By the time lunch is ready, the pool will be filled with grass and dirt and buckets and toys, and at least half the water will be gone. For a moment, however, Grace is content to sit in a lawn chair and watch the children. She doesn't have on a bathing suit. She knows that Gene will come to the kitchen window and look out.

When she arrives home late one morning, after having taken the children to the playground, Gene, in black silk pajamas, blocks the door. "Where have you been?" he asks. "I needed you."

"Claire, take your brother to the backyard," Grace says. "I'll call you for lunch."

Claire needs no instructions.

"Let me in," Grace demands quietly. Gene steps aside. "We went to the playground," she says, facing her husband.

"In hose, pumps, and a fancy dress?"

"This isn't fancy," she says, looking down at the navy sleeveless dress she has on. "I thought I might need to stop at the store on the way home."

"But you didn't."

"No, I was hungry. I wanted to make some lunch first. Never a good idea to go to a grocery store when you're hungry."

His hand rests on the wall. He's barefoot, but he's wearing his eye patch. A small concession for the children.

"What did you need?" Grace asks.

"I needed help getting dressed."

"You've learned how to dress yourself."

"It's hard. I just wanted some help, is that too much to ask?"

"I can't help you now," she says, turning.

He grabs a fistful of dress at the back of her shoulder. She can tell by his weight that he's using her to balance himself. Deliberately making her help him.

"Gene, I need you to let go of the dress," she says evenly.

"Why should I?"

"Don't be silly. I need my dress to make lunch. Please let go."

With her back to him, Grace relaxes her shoulders. She remembers that the dress has five large white buttons. She undoes them with fast fingers. With a slippery movement, she leaves the dress behind and walks into the kitchen in her slip. She shuts the door behind her.

She sits heavily in a kitchen chair.

After lunch, she'll find her dress on the floor. Or perhaps he'll have tossed it into the wastebasket. Or maybe he'll keep it and lay the dress out next to him on the bed in a ghoulish show of marital harmony.

What if she just walked to the stone wall and shouted for help? Would anyone come?

Gene doesn't speak to her when she brings the evening meal. His face is expressionless, as if she were a nurse he didn't particularly like. She asks him if he needs anything.

He pretends for a second not to have heard her. "Oh," he says. "Need anything? From you? Let me see. No."

She stands at the sink in her bathrobe eating a piece of toast when she spots, through the window, her husband lying on the waist-high stone wall that today is a backdrop for purple columbine, blue irises, and pink phlox. He has a pillowcase covering the bad side of his face.

She understands that he has every right to want to bathe in the sun. It's been months since he's spent any amount of time outside, and were the man not actually Gene, she would go out to him and ask if he would like a glass of water. She might buy him a sturdy chaise longue into which he could maneuver his body. She might, laughing, splash him lightly with water from the pool. But because it's Gene, Grace understands that he is lying on the stone wall to keep her and the children out of the backyard. He knows that Grace won't voluntarily enter a place he is in.

The temperature hits ninety degrees, and the breeze is from the southwest, making it a hot wind. The house fills with humidity, which the children experience as boredom. To stop their crankiness, Grace promises them ice cream cones, which activates them enough to settle themselves in the back of the Buick. But when Grace is ready to back down the driveway, she finds that the car won't start. She tries again. It's not the starter, because she can hear the whir. It's the engine that's failing to turn over. She tries again, reasoning that humidity might be the cause. She tries again, and the engine catches, but then almost immediately dies. Is she out of fuel? She gets out of the car and walks around to remove the gas cap and check. In the high sun, she sees a reflection of liquid. No, plenty of gas. What then? She tries again, but knows that if she keeps the starter going, the battery will die.

"Kids," she says, "how about we go inside and make Popsicles?"

She anticipates an outcry and gets one. "We want ice cream," Claire whines, beginning a chant.

"Well, look," Grace says, swinging around to confront Claire. "The car won't start. Period. I have to have someone come fix it. You can either sit here in the hot car whining about how you don't have an ice cream cone, or you can come inside with Tom and me, I can put on the fan, and we can make Popsicles."

With a pout that could put her in the movies, Claire opens the back door and slides out.

While the children are making Popsicles, Grace watches a man hitch the Buick to a truck and take it slowly down the driveway.

Not having a car means that Grace cannot get groceries with the children in tow. It means not being able to take the kids to the playground or to visit her mother. It means that she is an actual prisoner now, not just a psychological one. But then she wonders: Wasn't she always a prisoner of sorts? At Hunts Beach, they had a car, but Grace couldn't drive it. Gene had to take her to a grocery store every Thursday night. But then again, she had neighbors in Hunts Beach, Rosie for one. She had Gardiner's, where she could pick up the fixings for dinner. And her mother was within walking distance.

Pull yourself together, she tells herself, a week is nothing.

By the fifth day without a car, the pantry holds only canned ravioli, a box of macaroni, a dozen Campbell's soups, a jar of jelly, and half a box of cornflakes. Grace calls her mother and asks her to bring milk.

Her mother, chauffeured by Gladys, brings with her a carton full of fresh vegetables and fruits and hamburger and milk and bread and cookies she baked herself. Grace receives it as if she were a desperate refugee. She puts on the kettle and the two older women, both in sleeveless dresses, their arms white, the skin loose and damp, sit at the table. Claire climbs up onto her grandmother's lap, and Tom wanders over to Gladys with a curious look. Gladys produces from her purse two sets of keys and dangles them in front of the boy, who takes them and sits at her feet to play with them.

"Bad luck not having the car," Gladys says to Grace.

"Especially now that the town pool is open," her mother adds.

Grace pictures the deliciousness of falling into the water, feetfirst, and having it close over her head.

"But," Gladys points out, "having two children who can't swim at a pool might be more work than staying at home."

"Worth it to get out," Grace says, pouring iced tea into glasses. She unwraps her mother's plate of cookies.

This is help, Grace thinks. This is the help that might have come to her rescue at the stone wall. Right here in her kitchen. With the children underfoot, she might even now be able to convey to Gladys and her mother her fears for her own and the children's safety. Gladys would think her overwrought; her mother would reassure her that once the car came back, she'd be herself again. Both would say as they left that it was only a matter of time.

Time until what? she'd want to ask.

On the seventh day, Grace calls the auto repair company. "Hello, this is Mrs. Holland. I've been wondering if you were able to fix my car."

"Yep, we fixed it good."

"What was wrong with it?" Grace asks, curious.

"There was a heck of a lot of water in your gas tank."

"Water?" As if in slow motion, Grace falls onto the chair by the telephone table and bends her head to keep herself from fainting. Sweat breaks out on her palms and face, and she thinks she might vomit.

She sees it with absolute clarity. A man. A garden hose. A Buick.

"You still there?" the repairman asks.

"Yes," she says. "I'm here. Can you drop it off and I can pay you what I owe you?"

"But . . . well . . . your husband didn't tell you? We sold it."

Grace stands and spins with disbelief. "You sold it?" she asks incredulously. "But it was mine! That was my car!"

"You're a mister and missus, aren't you?" the mechanic asks.

"Well, yes."

"What's yours is his, I guess. I called this number to tell you it was ready and he answered and he told us to get rid of it. We did. It's gone now."

Grace swallows. Her disbelief turns hard.

Grace walks down the driveway, across the street, through the cut grass and pebbles, and screams into the roar of the surf.

That night, after the children have brushed their teeth, the reality of her situation penetrates. If she is not a prisoner behind bars, she is one in a house she now can't abide. Every night she will have to sleep in the nursery with her children and the door bolted. The ugliness she has seen in Gene will intensify. Whatever was good in her—as a mother, as a person—will begin to shrivel in confinement.

Grace reads to the children, watches them fall asleep, and then lies on her own cot. She guesses it safe enough to leave the screens open as she did before, but she knows not to let down her guard, not to give in to the pleasure of the gentle breezes that so seduced her on the night she woke with Gene standing over her. She tries to remain in an alert state. She listens to every sound in the house, but all she can hear are the waves crashing on the rocks across the street.

In her dream, she's a child again, and her mother is knocking on the door. No, it's her birthday, and her mother's banging on the door so that she won't miss her birthday party. Grace sits upright and knows that the person on the other side of the door is Gene. He bangs hard, and the children wake. He keeps up the pounding. Claire jumps out of bed and races to Grace's cot. Tom, standing, tries to climb out of the crib. Gene shouts, "Grace! Grace! I need you!" A fist on the door again, over and over and over. Grace lifts her children, one to a side on the narrow cot, and holds them tight so that they won't fall out. Tom crawls on top of her. Claire whispers, "Is that Daddy? Why is he doing this?"

"I don't know."

"Mommy, please make it stop!"

"Shhhh," Grace says.

Gene begins to wail, a sound that starts softly and then rises in ghastly volume. The cry is so haunting that she presses

Tom to her chest, Claire to her side, and covers her daughter's remaining ear with her hand.

Yes, maybe Gene is owed a piteous wail. But not here, and not now. Maybe he wants his life to go back to the way it used to be, but it can't ever. Grace knows it's a ploy to get her to open the door.

She has seen his anger, his bitterness, his deception. She believes him capable of anything. He might hurt the children if he thought it would crush Grace. He would certainly hit Grace, she knows that now. If she opens the door, he won't again believe in her calm voice suggesting they descend the stairs to go to his room where they might this time have sex.

The wailing continues. She wishes she could cover her own ears. Claire makes scurrying motions as if she would bore deeper into her mother. "Make it go away!" she begs.

"It will go away," Grace says, trying to calm her daughter. "I'll protect you, no matter what. Just try to go to sleep."

"I can't go to sleep. Make him stop!"

"Shhh," Grace whispers, but inside she's trembling.

Before she is even out the door, he grabs her by her upper arm. His grip is strong. He puts his weight against the top post of the banister, pulling her along with him. She knows that if he loses his balance, she'll fall to the floor, too.

"I want answers," he demands.

"Keep your voice down. The children are scared to death."

"It was the only way I could get you to come out."

"Don't you care about them at all?"

His face is red, and his hair is dirty. His yellow pajamas have stains on them. He doesn't look like a man who has been lying calmly in a bed.

"I asked about the razor blade, and you didn't answer me," he says.

She doesn't answer him now, either.

"I asked you about the piano, and you brushed me off. A piano doesn't just float through the air and take itself down a flight of stairs."

"And a gas tank doesn't just suddenly fill itself with water!" she exclaims with fury, knowing instantly it's a mistake to mention the car.

"How did you buy it?" he asks, shaking her arm.

"I worked for it," she answers, bracing herself with her feet apart.

He seems surprised, but he doesn't lessen his grip. "You worked? I don't believe you. Where?"

"In a doctor's office."

"That injun?" he asks, his eyes narrowing.

"Yes, that man."

"I see now. The razor blade was his."

"No. It isn't. I don't know whose blade it was. Are you really imagining I would get a job and bring the boss home to live with me? I worry for you, Gene."

"You've been lying to me all along," he insists. "How could you not tell your own husband that you once had a job?"

"How could you not tell your wife-to-be that you were marrying her because she looked like your true love?" she counters.

"That's ancient history," he says.

"Not to me," she says. "It's a fresh cut to me."

"You want to discuss that now?"

Beyond Gene's back, Grace sees the door open and Claire put her head outside. Grace shakes her head back and forth in an exaggerated manner and says a loud, "No!"—the message not for Gene but for her daughter.

"I have marital rights," Gene states, but Grace is unable to respond. She wills Claire back into the room. Go inside and shut the door, she begs in her mind.

"You can't ignore that," he adds.

With growing horror, Grace sees that Claire is all the way out of the bedroom and moving toward them.

"Let go of Mommy!" the girl cries as she pushes out her hands.

The fall is so brief, so light, that she doesn't have time to be afraid. The weightlessness is shocking, the house soundless. Did Claire cry out? Possibly she did. Grace can't hear Gene. Did he fall, too?

She touches a middle step with her foot, another step with her hip and thigh, and then shoots into the far corner of the landing. She lies still. Messages of pain begin to reach her brain. She grabs the banister and tries to pull herself up. She can't stand, but she can turn her body enough to see that there's no sign of Claire. She hears the distinct rhythm of two-stepping below her. Gene, descending.

By the time Grace crawls up the stairs and into the bedroom, she finds Claire on her cot lying faceup with her own blanket over her. Tom is huddled into her side, sucking his thumb and sleeping deeply. Pain hits her. Left wrist, right ankle, and a searing all along her right hip and thigh. She crawls to the space next to the cot and lies down on the floor. She doesn't have to move right this minute. She needn't disturb her children just yet.

Claire, subdued, doesn't mention the night before, even when Grace is icing her ankle in the kitchen. When Grace looked at herself in the bathroom, a purple bruise spread from her hip to her thigh. Her left wrist is swollen and will need ice as soon as Grace is done with her foot.

How to explain to a child that a push against one person can knock the next person down? What must seem like magic to Claire has to be explained to her. She guesses Claire feels responsible for her mother's fall. Grace can't let her daughter go another hour with confused feelings.

"Claire," she says, smiling, "I need to talk to you."

Her daughter shyly walks to her. Grace smooths her hair and lifts her chin so that they can look into each other's eyes.

"I won't pretend that last night wasn't scary," Grace says. "It was. But your daddy wasn't going to hurt me."

"Yes he was! I saw."

"He had hold of my arm because he wanted me to pay attention to what he was saying. I understand why you came out of the bedroom—you were curious, and you were afraid for me. Those are good instincts. And what you did wasn't wrong at all. You pushed into Daddy so that he would let go of me. And that's exactly what happened. He let go of me. But because I lost my balance, I fell down the stairs. Your daddy didn't push me. It was just an accident. Do you understand?"

Claire responds by moving closer to Grace, laying her head down on her lap and flopping her arms over her mother's thighs.

With her children in the backyard, and her foot taped, Grace stands at the kitchen counter with a pencil and a pad of paper. She knows from long experience that sometimes a list is the only way from one side to the other.

She waits two days until the throbbing in her foot has subsided and she can put weight on it. She dresses the children in matching summer suits and informs them that they are going on a bus ride into town. Claire, who seems to have forgotten the incident in the nighttime, follows Grace from dresser to closet to dresser as she gets ready, asking questions about the bus. Do we ride up high? Will we have to sit with other people? Can you buy candy on the bus?

Because Tom and Claire fight for space at the window, Grace makes them kneel on the seat and share the view. A headache that started with the fall onto the landing seems, with successive days, to have lodged deeper into her brain. She wants to lie down and sleep for a week, but the urgency of her mission in addition to the need to keep the children from falling off the seat keeps her alert. They pass empty land where houses have not yet been rebuilt but where wildflowers and tall grasses provide a kind of lush landscape. The soot from the fire has been an effective fertilizer. Both children are silenced when they reach the city: so much to look at in so short a time. Tom leaves sweaty handprints on the window.

From the bus stop, Grace takes each child by hand and crosses a number of streets in search of Jensen, Jeweler to the World. Jensen greets Grace with a quizzical look. Claire seems dazzled by all the watches and rings and bracelets and necklaces in the cases. Grace's purse is heavy with the bounty from Merle's clothing, and when she tips the contents onto the top of the glass case, she feels more like a thief than she ever has. Jensen is at first skeptical and stares at Grace as if she might be a fence. She tries to keep her own personal guilt from showing on her face.

"My family and I have to move to Boston in order to find work," she tells Jensen. "We have no house to sell; we have only this jewelry that my disabled husband inherited from his mother. You remember when I was in here before."

"Yes, of course," he says. He stares at the jewelry for so long that Grace thinks he might ask to see the will. When he glances up, his face is lit.

"Let's write out an inventory first," he says.

Grace glances at the children. Claire is holding Tom up so that he can see the diamond rings.

Grace checks the inventory against the items on the counter. Jensen walks to the front door and flips the sign from OPEN to CLOSED. When he returns, he begins to assign a number to each item, numbers he shares with Grace. There are fifty-seven pieces. Jensen uses his adding machine to arrive at a total. He rips off the slip of paper and lays it on the glass counter so that Grace can see the sum.

$45,655.

If Jensen is cheating her, Grace doesn't care.

"I'll have to sell these first before I can pay you," he says.

"I need some of the money now."

"The best I could do today would be a check for five thousand dollars. I'll send you the rest as I sell the pieces."

Grace studies the man and makes a critical decision. "I trust you," she says. "I'll take a check for seven thousand dollars now, and in a week or two, I'll send you my address. I would, however, like a receipt for the lot."

Across a counter sparkling with precious gems, Jensen and Grace shake hands.

"Claire, how about we spoil our lunches with ice cream cones?"

"Yes, yes, yes," crows Claire, knowing she must use her words.

Tom, sensing something great in the air, claps his hands and smacks his mouth.

At the bank, the children, sated, are content to sit in the chairs provided for customers. Grace asks to speak to the manager and explains to him, when he arrives from a back room, what exactly it is that she will need.

The weight of her purse lessened from having transformed jewelry into paper money, Grace walks the kids to the used-car lot. Ralph Eastman, in stained seersucker jacket, rushes out to greet them.

"I know you," he says, pointing a finger at Grace. "The Little Sister. Does the Little Sister want to buy another car? What happened to the old one?"

"The Buick is just fine," she says, "and I've come to pay you the balance of what is owed to you."

"Well, honey, you just made my day. Don't have too many customers like you. These your little ones?"

Claire has turned suddenly shy and won't look at the salesman. Good taste, Grace thinks.

"I'd like to buy a car for my mother," Grace announces. "I've been happy with the one you sold me, and now she wants one of her own. Something small. Not as expensive as mine. A sedan."

Ralph pretends to think. "I've got a 'forty-six Ford that might be just the ticket."

"How much?"

"For you, seven hundred."

She can probably talk him down to six. "You can bring it around."

Eastman steps out of a black Ford and calls Grace a Sweetheart. After a quick test-drive, during which he refers to Grace as Sweetie, Good Girl, and Nice Mommy, Grace buys the car for six hundred dollars. The Ford smells like spilt beer and dirty ashtrays, which Claire and Tom complain about. Good, thinks Grace. If Claire is complaining, she's back to being herself.

Her right foot throbbing, Grace drives the children home, but parks a block from the green Victorian that Gene Holland owns. When Claire questions her, Grace answers that driveway cleaners are coming in the morning and that they've asked her to give them some room to do the job. She prays that Gene is not up and around. Claire, perhaps wanting to distract her father, might blurt out, "Mommy bought a new car!"

But Grace thinks Claire will not blurt out anything to her father. More likely than not, her daughter will walk into another room.

That afternoon, while the children sleep in Merle's bed, Grace uses the telephone on the dressing table. She speaks softly so that she won't wake Claire and Tom. She reaches the clinic and asks for Dr. Lighthart.

"Grace," he says with some surprise.

"Hi. I need to talk to you."

"Shoot."

"Could you come to my house?"

"I can be there in twenty minutes."

"Don't drive up to the house. Go just past the house, and I'll meet you at the bottom of the driveway."

The sleek Packard pulls to the curb, and Grace gets in.

"What happened?" John Lighthart asks as he turns toward her, one arm resting on the steering wheel. He is in his white coat, and she notices a tiny bloodstain on his sleeve.

"I need to hire a nurse to take care of Gene, and I can't go back to the agency. I was hoping you knew of someone."

"Days? Full-time?"

"Live-in."

"Well, I'm glad," he says. "Now you're being sensible."

"No, I'm not," she says, looking directly into his eyes. She trusts him. "I'm leaving Gene."

"Does he know?" the doctor asks.

"No." She pauses. "Will you help me?"

"You know I will," he says, adjusting his position. "But are you sure you know what you're doing?"

"No, but I have to try."

"You're taking the children?" he asks.

"Yes."

He gazes down the street, thinking. "There was a young woman who came to us looking for work. I couldn't hire her, though I wanted to. I know she's done live-in care before."

Grace notes the kindness mixed with strength in his eyes, in his mouth. She has only minutes left until the children wake, if they haven't already.

"I'll call her when I get back," the doctor says.

"I need her tomorrow morning."

John raises an eyebrow. "That's awfully soon."

"I have to leave before I lose my courage."

"It's live-in, room and board and so forth?"

"And eighty dollars a week," Grace adds.

"That's high," the doctor says.

"It's for supplies and groceries, too. I'm also hiring a housekeeper."

"Well, it's not an offer she's likely to refuse. Her name is Sarah Brody."

"Please tell her to come to the kitchen door at seven o'clock in the morning."

He studies her face. He touches her hand. "When you worked at the clinic, for a while there, I conveniently forgot that you were married. I thought of you as single."

"At times, so did I."

"Just remember how strong you are," he says.

———

After Grace has put the children to bed, she walks into the room that used to be her mother's. The books and the licorice drops are still there. Maybe Sarah will go exploring and find the drops and eat them.

"Mother, I'm about to do a terrible thing," Grace says, again addressing her absent parent.

Grace has two letters to write.

Dear Gene,

> *This is to tell you that I've gone on a long trip with the children, and I'm not sure when I'll be back. By now you have met Sarah, and I trust you'll mend more quickly in her care. She's extremely capable and well recommended. I have also hired a housekeeper named Peggy.*

> *If you think about the last several days, I'm certain you will agree that there's been an unhealthy atmosphere between us and that it was beginning to affect the children. I will bring them back to you soon for a visit, and I will never deny your right to see them if it can be managed.*

> *I've arranged for Sarah's and Peggy's salaries and the bills to be paid by my bank, so you needn't worry about anything.*

> *I think that if the fire hadn't happened, we'd have continued as the little family that we were. In time, I believe, we would have come to care about each other in a way that was companionable. But the fire did happen, and that changed everything.*

> *I hope you'll be happier and that your injuries will heal.*
> *Grace.*

Dear Mother,

By the time you get this, I'll be on a journey with the children. I could call this a little vacation, but I won't. Truth is, I'm leaving Gene and taking the children with me. He's become intolerable, frightening all of us. I have reason to believe that we all might be in danger. I know you'll think this melodramatic on my part, but you'll just have to trust me. I've hired an experienced live-in nurse to take care of him. I'm hopeful that without me in the house, and the poisonous relationship that has developed between us, he'll make more progress and be happier. I've hired a housekeeper, too.

As soon as I've reached a destination—I don't know exactly where I'm going right now—I'll call or write you with a phone number and an address so that we can be in touch. I can never thank you enough for taking such good care of the children while I was trying to find my way. And for taking such good care of me, I might add.

Don't worry about me, Mother. I've discovered, ever since the fire, or maybe more recently, that I have inner resources I can count on.

The check is for you to make a down payment on a house. I can pay for all of it. In my next letter, I'll explain everything.

With all my love,
Grace

It takes her three tries to get the letter into the envelope.

———

Grace lies on the nursery cot. In the morning, she'll change all the linen. She's already rid Merle's room of her personal items and photographs.

Ought she drive south to try to find Aidan? If she didn't have children, she would. She would hunt him down and surprise him and hope that he reciprocated her feelings. A soloist performing with an orchestra, however, might take her weeks to find. And when she did, she and the children would be a burden no matter how fond he was of them. But the urge to drive south is a powerful one.

To drive west is shortly to encounter John Lighthart at the clinic. She would like to work and keep his friendship. But she can't work and care for her children at the same time, and she doesn't want to relinquish Claire and Tom to a nanny. She herself must raise them and keep them safe. Of less importance, but still critical, is the fact that the clinic isn't far enough away from Merle's house that word of Grace's whereabouts might not somehow get back to Gene. Might Grace be arrested for kidnapping? It seems absurd to her, but she believes Gene capable of anything.

To drive east is to drive into the ocean.

She will have to leave with no destination then. She won't focus on a place to settle, but rather on the mechanics of freeing herself.

Sarah arrives at seven in the morning in her uniform. The woman has dark blond hair, blue eyes, and an air of confidence. Grace has made a large breakfast for her and the children. When the kids aren't listening, she asks Sarah to

give Gene the envelope with Grace's letter inside sometime
after lunch. Grace tells Claire that they are all going on a
little vacation, and that Sarah, a nurse, will take good care
of Daddy. Claire warms to the idea of a vacation and asks,
"Will there be new toys?"

"Yes," says Grace.

While her children chat with Sarah in the kitchen, Grace
moves to the library and stares at the paneled walnut door.
In this room, she and Aidan once made love. She has never
adjusted to the fact that it has become her husband's room,
its resonance no longer that of passion, but rather that of
sadness and emotional turmoil. Reaching for the brass doorknob, she hesitates before turning it. Only her fingertips
touch the metal. Inside, Gene is lying painless and asleep, or
he is waiting for his own day to begin. Does he feel remorse
of any kind? Grace thought, in a moment of empathy and
generosity, that she would go into his room, sit in a chair,
and try to talk to him about the terror he was creating in the
night for the children. She wasn't going to mention herself,
because that was the point, wasn't it? To punish her, to have
power over her.

She removes her fingers from the knob in case she inad-
vertently turns it.

As if by mere touch she had instructed the door to swing
open, Gene stands at the threshold, startling Grace so much
that she grabs on to the back of a chair. His jaw is set, he has
on clean navy silk pajamas, and he's wearing his eye patch.
"Where are you going?" he asks.

Grace shakes her head, stunned by her terrible luck.

"You were about to come into my room, weren't you?"

She puts a hand to her chest and remembers that she has on a good dress. Not a special one, but a good one. She has fake pearls at her ears.

She's struck dumb.

"You're going somewhere?" An entirely different question from his first one.

Her vision narrows to a black dot, but then returns.

"What's going on?" he asks, beginning to suspect something.

"I was coming to wake you," she says, her voice thin. "There's someone I want you to meet. Wait here."

Fighting for air, she enters the kitchen, where Sarah is sitting with the children. "Sarah, I'd like to speak with you for a moment. Claire, you stay here and watch your brother. You're a big girl now."

When Sarah stands, Grace notes that her back is straight and her legs are strong. The nurse looks like a woman who, while polite, can handle a challenge. There's no time to explain anything further to her, just a moment for an introduction that has only a small chance of being successful.

"Gene, I'd like you to meet Sarah Brody. She's an extremely qualified nurse and is going to help with your care. Sarah, this is my husband, Gene."

There's a long moment of silence. Sarah smiles. Gene cocks his head, considering.

Does Gene understand? Does he know that he's about to exchange one life for another, and that the other is potentially a better one?

His scrutiny of Sarah continues. Then he looks at Grace as if he knew her plans. Before he can say another word, however, Sarah moves in front of Grace, and with a deft turning motion of her hands, she coaxes Gene back into his room.

Sarah is more welcome than a vase of flowers. Than a wife.

Grace lifts Tom and tells Claire to come with her. Collecting one of the suitcases, she hustles her children down the driveway and along the block to the Ford. "Wait here, don't move," she says to Claire.

Grace, crouching, runs and limps as best she can to the top of the drive and collects the second suitcase.

With legs shaking and stomach hollow, Grace drives slowly along the coast road as if tempting the hand of God to hook on to the car and haul it back to Merle Holland's house. She remembers the old baby carriage lost in the fire, the one with the navy enameled chassis and the white leather trim, and for a moment she pictures pushing Claire and Tom out of town with steely determination. When she comes to a stop sign, she rolls down her window, sticks out her arm, and bends it at the elbow. She's headed north.

Epilogue

1950

Grace

"What are you doing on the ground?" Rosie asks.

"I'm trying to take a picture of the stars." Grace peers through the lens of the camera Rosie and Tim gave her for Christmas. "They're so clear tonight."

Rosie lays a towel on the seat of a teak deck chair and sits.

"I can see them with my eyes, but not at all with the lens," Grace adds.

"The camera isn't perfect."

"It *is* perfect. You've seen the photographs of the kids."

"I have," says Rosie, "but aren't the stars awfully far away?"

"I don't get it. The camera is a lens. My eye is a lens. The sun is the same distance from each, and I can take a picture of the sun. Well, sort of. The stars are the same distance from each, but I can't find a single twinkling dot in the camera."

"Not enough light," Rosie says, putting a cigarette to her lips. "Now get up. You'll catch your death."

Grace props her body on her arm and then stands. "My mother used to say that when I was a kid."

Rosie lays another towel on another deck chair meant for Grace.

"Thanks," Grace says, fitting the camera back into its

case. "Have you seen how curious Claire is about this? Yesterday, I let her hold the camera and look through the lens and
push the shutter. I can't wait to get the roll of film developed
so that she can see her pictures. I'm excited about the idea of
teaching her the rudiments of photography."

"Don't leave the camera lying around Ian. First thing
he'd do is take it apart."

"And then he'd put it back together again. He's going to
be an engineer one day."

"They're both asleep?"

"Yes, yours?" Grace asks.

"I left the whole bedtime thing to Tim," Rosie says and
laughs. "It'll be good for him. He hasn't done it in ages.
And if I have to read *The Poky Little Puppy* one more time,
I'll scream."

When Grace arrived in Tim and Rosie's driveway in Nova
Scotia during the summer of 1948, she bent her head to the
steering wheel while Rosie and Tim, stunned and elated by
her presence, took Tom and Claire out of the Ford. Grace
had driven straight through, and she was more exhausted
than she'd ever been. She hadn't dared to stop for fear that
she'd lose her nerve.

She was malnourished and dehydrated, and for two weeks
she lay in a guest room bed, sickened by remorse and guilt
and also a kind of moral anxiety. One day, after much careful attention from Rosie, Tim and she appeared at Grace's
bedroom door. Tim sat in a chair and called a halt to the
remorse. He told Grace she had a new life before her as well
as happy children. Then Rosie took Grace outside, where

they sat together on the rocks by the sea and talked. In that hour, Grace could feel her body repairing itself. Rosie swore it was the sea air that cleared her head.

Grace's first act of independence was to design a house for herself and the children. It was constructed on the land beside Tim and Rosie's. Grace's is a simple cape with three bedrooms upstairs, painted white and unadorned: white trim, no shutters. Inside, she has a washing machine, a dryer, a bathtub, a shower, and a record player, luxuries she decided she couldn't live without. Both Grace's and Rosie's houses lie on land owned by Rosie's mother.

Grace's mother visits twice annually, Christmas and summer. Because the journey, by train and bus, takes three days, Marjorie makes a vacation out of it, staying overnight in hotels that appeal to her. Now there's a plan in motion to launch a ferry from Bar Harbor to Yarmouth, Nova Scotia, which will cut the time in half.

The deck chairs are perched on an invisible dividing line between Grace's house and Rosie's so that they can hear the children. The first warm evening of the season envelops them after a winter Grace can describe only as gray. She thinks Gray ought to be a season of its own—running from early January to late April. "Happy Gray," she could write to someone on a note card.

"Iced teas," Tim calls from the porch.

"That was fast," says Rosie when Tim reaches them.

"I just tell them to jump in bed."

"And they do that for you?"

Tim smiles. "I confess I took advantage of the novelty of

the situation. I skipped the bath and told them a short story. Then I lifted them high in the air and plopped them into their beds."

"That wasn't the deal!" Rosie cries. "Now I'll have to bathe them in the morning. They were filthy."

"Nothing that'll kill them. Anyway, I came out here because I have an idea for you."

Grace raises her glass. "First iced tea of the season," she says to both.

"Drink it slowly," warns Tim. "It's really a watered-down Dark and Stormy."

"What's the occasion?" Rosie asks, sniffing her drink.

"I was thinking that you need a break."

"A break?" Rosie asks as if she doesn't know the meaning of the word.

"A break, a trip. You and Grace could go to Halifax for the weekend."

"Both of us?" asks Grace. "Who would watch the kids?"

"We'll let the mothers fight over them."

Rosie takes a long sip. "I have to say . . . I could really use a break. It's been a hell of a long winter. How about you, Grace?"

Rosie and Tim go to Halifax once a year, but Grace hasn't been yet. Apart from her semiannual journeys to Gene's house, she hasn't been much farther than the next town over, where a market and shops line a small main street.

Halifax. A city. Just her and Rosie.

"Yes," she says.

—————

The first trip Grace made to Gene's house with the children, this time stopping to eat and sleep, she couldn't catch any air as she mounted the steps to the front door: She dreaded what she might find behind it. Sarah, the nurse, who was no longer wearing a white uniform, ushered Grace and the children into a room that smelled floral despite the absence of flowers. Gene was sitting upright in a chair and had been fitted with a glass eye. The skin on the left side of his face no longer looked raw, but instead scarred, which was somehow better. He wore a cap and had cut his hair short so that his head no longer looked as lopsided as it had. The most astonishing change, however, was the moment he bent forward in the chair and stood. In a freshly ironed shirt and pressed trousers, he held Tom's hand and walked with him and Claire into the kitchen, where Grace guessed a snack awaited.

"He's improved so much!" Grace couldn't help blurting out.

"He works hard at it," the nurse replied.

"Does he?"

Grace suspected it was all Sarah's doing. "How are your funds?" she asked. "Do you need anything?"

The nurse blushed. "We don't need anything. Gene has his inheritance now."

We.

Inheritance.

Grace didn't betray the fact that she hadn't known about an inheritance. She thought, as she observed Sarah, that possibly she and Gene had fallen into a mutually satisfying relationship: Gene had a "wife"; Sarah's financial future was set. Or was Grace selling the nurse short, and she truly loved the man? A man who had not spoken to Grace when she entered, or even acknowledged her existence.

Grace understood then that she was dead to Gene, and a great weight was lifted from her.

Grace is content. Sometimes happy. Rarely troubled or anxious except when the children are sick. She knows the money from Merle's jewelry will run out in time, but she hopes that she can get Claire into school in the fall, thus allowing Grace to look for a job to supplement that income. She'll still have Tom during the school hours, though it's possible she could find a babysitter to allow her to work for some of them. At first she thought she might try to be a receptionist at a doctor's office, but after Christmas and the camera, she began to dream of becoming a photographer for the local newspaper. She's noticed that they often use stock photos, some of them years old, when they print their stories. She doesn't know what such a job would pay, but she doesn't need much. Food and clothing, a babysitter, gas for the car, heating and electricity, and, of course, film for the camera. Both the house and the car are paid for. Even if she could earn thirty dollars a week, she might be able to make it. For some assignments, she could take the children with her.

Grace tries to decide what to pack for her trip. She may as well take her best dresses since she knows Halifax will be more sophisticated than the village in which they now live.

Because the temperatures will be changeable, she decides to wear her lined raincoat, a dull khaki. She livens that up with a red leather bag and a pair of red pumps. She refuses to wear rubbers to the city. She puts her spectator pumps in the suitcase along with a navy purse in case she ruins the red shoes. How odd to pack for only one person.

When she's finished, she sets the suitcase by the front door. They'll be leaving early in the morning to take advantage of the three-day "break."

The kettle she left on the stove begins to whistle. She carries her tea to her favorite spot, a wooden chair next to the kitchen table that she's arranged so she can see her lawn and garden. Signaling the beginning of spring, the daffodils are up, and she can make out the cracking of the soil where mounds of tulips will be next. The grass is still gray-brown with sporadic patches of green, and in the corner of the yard are dark red shoots of rhubarb. The thought of the red shoots gives her an idea. She'll photograph the garden each day, one photo per day, and date the pictures. Birth, life, decay, death: a complete record. At the very least, the series, though costly, will please her next winter.

When the yellow and white bus arrives, Tim gives Rosie a quick kiss while Grace hands the driver her suitcase. Grace has brought the lunches because the trip will take five hours.

Rosie has on a chic cornflower blue spring coat with pumps to match.

"Your coat is terrific," Grace remarks. "Wherever did you get it?"

"Would you believe my mother made it for me?"

"Yes, I would."

"I saw a picture in a magazine. She not only made the coat, she created the pattern for it just from the picture." Rosie has on fake emerald earrings, which draw attention to her red hair. Grace feels dowdy in her raincoat.

Rosie reapplies her lipstick after Tim's kiss.

"Maybe I'll buy a spiffy coat in Halifax," suggests Grace, knowing that she won't, that she wants to save her money. "Window-shopping will be fun."

"I have a list of all the best department stores. Well, all two of them. But there are smaller shops on Barrington Street we can try."

"It feels strange not to have the kids," Grace muses.

"Feels good to me."

"Think they'll be all right?"

"As long as they're still alive when we get back, I'll be fine."

"You've stayed at the Lord Nelson," Grace says.

"I have. You'll love it. They do a delicious tea. But I've arranged for us to have dinner tonight at the Prince George."

Lord Nelson. Prince George. A delicious tea. How far this seems from Hunts Beach, about which John Lighthart was correct. Land on the coast, according to her mother, is selling for high prices now. Some of the tin shacks remain, while the houses that were rebuilt by the government are tiny capes, none with fireplaces. How long will those last?

"First we'll get our nails done," Rosie announces.

"Our nails done? Just as I'll be digging in the garden?"

"Now, listen, Grace, for three days we are not mothers

or garden diggers or housekeepers. We are ladies on the town."

As soon as they arrive at the hotel, Grace highlights her ears with rhinestone earrings and applies red lipstick to match her shoes and handbag.

"Nice," says Rosie as she emerges from the bathroom.

After the appointment with the manicurist, it seems they shop for hours, stopping only to have a tea. Rosie takes her shoes off and sticks them among a half dozen packages under the table. "Most of what I bought was for the children," she says, sighing.

"It's too bad that mint satin with that gorgeous waist was already spoken for. The shawl collar was perfect on you."

"But where would I have worn it?" Rosie asks, slipping a cigarette from its pack. "Want one?"

"Rosie, you're not playing the game. You're supposed to buy it because it's beautiful and someday you might have a chance to wear it," says Grace, who takes a lit cigarette and inhales deeply. "These are your rules, by the way. I didn't buy one thing for the children, and I'm feeling guilty."

"There's tomorrow."

"Teahouse scones are always better than the ones you can make at home," muses Grace, taking a good-size bite. The ham sandwiches they had on the bus barely constituted lunch.

"Put the cream and jam on them," Rosie advises. "They'll be even better."

"You're not eating?"

"Oh, I will, believe me. Just resting my dogs."

Grace's feet hurt, too, but it's a point of pride not to remove her shoes in a public place.

"Now see that man over there at the banquette?" comments Rosie in a low tone. "Don't look now. I think he's exceptionally handsome."

"You shouldn't be looking," Grace chastises lightly. "You're married."

"I'm not looking for me."

"You're looking for me?" Grace asks, surprised.

"You need a man," her friend says.

"I thought we agreed you wouldn't do that."

"The statute of limitations has run out."

"I don't want a man," Grace explains, "and that's the truth. And I really, really don't want to be married."

"Look," says Rosie, taking a bite of her scone, "you had a bad experience. Get over it."

"I am over it. I just don't want the complications."

"You're afraid because you think you'll get another raw deal."

"I'm not afraid. I like being a single mother. I don't pine for a man or a marriage. I like my own bed. I'm proud of the life I've made."

They walk through a park so green that Grace has difficulty believing in it. Their heels click on the pavement and stick in the gravel. Around them, tulips in provocative colors compete with the dresses of strolling women. They come across a boy in a red cap and bow tie, a dark man in a powder blue linen suit. Grace and Rosie have on dresses with wide full skirts and have to walk a few inches farther apart than they normally would. Grace admires the park—how can she not?—but she's developed an antipathy to nature in confinement. Banks of perfectly spaced tulips, hedgerows precisely clipped, conical mazes of rosebushes that haven't yet bloomed fail to delight her in the way they once did. She prefers her garden at home, the one cultivated so close to the sea that the wind whips every bush and flower to its will. She prefers her long and wild forsythia to the neatly pruned balls through which they meander.

The sun sets cold on them, and Grace wishes she'd brought something more substantial than her sweater. She's both frigid and ravenous when they step into the dining room, where a fire is lit; Halifax is a schizophrenic city this time of year. When seated, they order winter drinks—Manhattans—not yet ready for summer's gin and fizz.

Grace scans the room. The clothes on the diners are not as fashionably cut or as rich in material as those in Merle Holland's closet (are they still in her closet?), but they're a step up from Sunday best. She catches glimpses of yellow chiffon, a gold watch, and earrings so dazzling they might be real diamonds. She notes draped hands with long, painted fingernails. Grace's, too, are newly red to match her shoes, and sometimes, when her hand crosses her line of sight, she's startled by the shiny color. The nails make satisfying clicks on the smooth surface of the table.

"Date night," Rosie asserts as she sips her drink.

"Don't you think they're tourists like ourselves?"

"A little soon for tourists. The weather is too unpredict-able. People don't come until mid-June. Tim and I pretend when we come here that we're on a date, but you can't really. Most of the time we just end up talking about the kids, or drinking too much to make the evening feel festive."

"But you and Tim are so good together!"

"Oh, we are. But, you know, a marriage is a marriage."

"I'm surprised we haven't talked about the children," Grace says.

"Not till tomorrow. And maybe not even tomorrow."

Rosie offers a cigarette to Grace, who shakes her head. "It'll steal my appetite, and I plan to indulge tonight." She orders a shrimp cocktail, a bowl of vichyssoise, and a steak, medium-rare, which comes with scalloped potatoes, carrots, and peas. She and Rosie split a baked Alaska for dessert.

"We'd better walk a mile," groans Rosie. "My dress is about to bust its seams."

"Then we'd better walk fast," adds Grace, contemplating the night temperatures.

"We could ask the waiter to order us a taxi."

"Come on," says Grace, standing, "we're tougher than that."

They walk with heads bent into a cold wind off the water.

"Want to go dancing?" Rosie asks.

"Tomorrow maybe. It's been a long day. I was up at four. Couldn't sleep."

"Too excited?"

The wind picks up. Conversation comes in fits and starts and then is carried away on gusts.

Grace passes a granite building and stops. She puts a hand on a column. She bends, unable to straighten.

Rosie, fifty feet ahead of her, realizes Grace's absence and returns. "What's wrong?" she cries, running the last twenty feet.

Grace, unable to speak, not wanting to speak, shakes her head. She knows the moment Rosie understands because she says, "Oh my."

Grace stands, gathering herself. "I want to see," she says. "I want to hear."

Rosie checks her watch and then the poster. "It's half over. I'll see if we can get in."

Grace follows Rosie into an ornate lobby. Though her mind is spinning, she's aware of massive doors, parquet floors, and a ticket booth where Rosie is talking and gesturing.

"We can go in during intermission," Rosie says when she reaches Grace. "But," she adds, sounding hesitant, even wary, "are you sure you want to do this?"

"Yes."

Doors open, cigarettes are lit, a crowd rushes for the bar. Rosie leads Grace through an entry and hunts for seats together. The hall is grand with gold leaf carvings, red velvet booths, and a large crystal chandelier. Grace fixes on the impossibly long black piano being rolled onto the stage.

"Breathe," Rosie says when they are seated.

"I'm fine."

Rosie raises an eyebrow, removes a compact from her handbag, and reapplies her lipstick. Grace clutches her hands together to stop the shaking.

The lights dim. The conductor threads through the orchestra to great applause. Then the soloist, dressed in a black tuxedo, his hair thick and longer than she remembers, sits in front of the sleek machine and waits.

A hush of anticipation.

"Breathe," whispers Rosie.

Grace hears the haunting, piercing notes of a French horn and the beautiful reply of the piano. She has listened to the record dozens of times. She can't see Aidan's body or his hands, but she can just make out his face and shoulders.

When he begins to play, goose bumps slide down her arms. She feels the notes at the back of her neck, just as she did that first day she walked into Merle Holland's house. She knows the melodies by heart. Rosie reaches over and takes her hand.

Aidan launches into a difficult section she remembers well. Grace can pick out the repetitions of the first theme, the introductions of others. What strikes her now is how tumultuous the piece is, how often that tumult is followed by moments of quiet. It's the combination that creates the beauty.

"Your face," Rosie whispers.

Yes, her face must show her rapture, but the soloist, Grace reminds herself, is not hers. He belongs to the orchestra, to the audience, and to the elegance of the concert hall. This is his turret now, his sitting room, his library.

This is his life, moving from city to city, entering concert halls, and paralyzing audiences.

There are multiple sections to the concerto. She listens and sometimes holds her breath. She listens and closes her eyes. She listens and knows that the end is coming and that she is again powerless to stop it.

The audience is on its feet, clapping. Rosie and Grace join them. Aidan Berne takes three, four curtain calls, sweeping his arm to include the orchestra. When he leaves the stage the final time, the lights come up.

"You're crying," Rosie says.

"It was beautiful."

"It was amazing."

It's a few minutes before Rosie is able to lead Grace out of the concert hall. When they have moved away from the din of the crowd, she turns to Grace. "That's him, isn't it?"

Grace embraces Rosie.

"He's magnificent," Rosie whispers in her ear. "In every way possible. You lucky girl. You lucky, lucky girl." She draws away from Grace. "Come on."

Rosie takes Grace to the back of the concert hall, where already there's a crowd. Men and women have programs and pens in their hands. Grace will have one more glimpse of the man who was once her lover.

While they wait, the cold penetrates Grace's shoes and blows through her sweater. She shivers, a combination of the temperature and nerves. She can't manage the business of smoking, so she hugs her sweater close.

The murmuring grows louder, and Grace watches as the stage door opens. A man steps out, not Aidan, but he beckons to someone inside. Aidan emerges and stands on the stoop, an iron railing running around it and down a short set of concrete steps. The murmuring breaks up into individual pleas to sign programs. Grace knows the moment Aidan sees her because his face blanches, and then his color is restored. He descends the stairs and moves toward her, gently parting the crowd, and Grace knows, in the time it takes for him to reach her, that her life is about to change.

She can see it all. The astonished but happy gaze. The kiss, the night spent together. The promises and plans they'll make. He'll learn to fly, he'll say, so that he can see her more often. Grace will travel to attend some of his concerts, she'll say, and she'll wear a cloth coat. Aidan will come to her house, and her children will perhaps remember the man who made music and played with them. Aidan will buy a piano and install it at Grace's so that he can practice when he comes home and sleeps with her. She'll have a life she could never have imagined, a life different from anyone else's. They will be lovers whenever and wherever they can. They will never be separated, no matter how great the distance between them.

He reaches her and takes hold of her wrist. "Hello," he says.

Grace meets his eyes. "Aidan, this is my friend, Rosie."

"Hello, Rosie," he says with a smile.

Rosie grins. "Your concert was wonderful."

Aidan, not letting go of Grace, invites the two of them to dinner. Before Grace can explain that they've already eaten, Rosie begs off. "I've had a headache since this afternoon. Blissfully, it went away during your concert, but now it's back. I think I'd better go lie down."

Grace turns to Rosie. "I might be late," she whispers.

"I certainly hope so."

It occurs to Grace, as she watches Rosie walk away, that

she could be wrong, that what she imagined moments ago might not come to pass. She and Aidan will have dinner and talk, and he will see her back to the hotel and promise to let her know when he is next invited to play in Halifax, which will never happen.

But the grip on her wrist is fierce.

Acknowledgments

I would like to thank my editor, Jordan Pavlin, and my agent, Jennifer Rudolph Walsh, both of whom were brilliant, wise, and encouraging while I was writing this book.